BLACK MAIL

A Black's Bandits Novel

LYNN RAYE HARRIS

The Hostile Operations Team® and Lynn Raye Harris® are
trademarks of H.O.T. Publishing, LLC.

Printed in the United States of America

First Printing, 2022

For rights inquires, visit www.LynnRayeHarris.com

ISBN: 978-1-941002-71-1

Chapter One

"WHAT DO YOU MEAN YOU GOT FIRED? THEY CAN'T FIRE you! You're the best they've got!"

Cassie couldn't help but smile at the vehemence in her best friend's voice. "I didn't get *fired* from the job. I got fired from the project."

Kari snorted on the other end of the phone. "Fine, but they're making a mistake."

Cassie shifted her tote as she fumbled for her car keys. The bag fell down her arm and into the crook of her elbow. The weight of it sent her phone flying. "Dammit," she growled as she dropped to the parking garage floor to find her keys and pick up her phone.

She found the keys in the bottom of her bag, but she had to lie on her side to reach for the phone, which had predictably slid under her car. It was just that kind of a day.

"Cassie? Cassie? Are you there?" Kari sounded far off.

Thank God Cassie had put the call on speaker.

"Yeah, just a sec. I dropped my phone." She reached

as far as she could, her fingers touching the edge of the phone. If she could just stretch a little further…

"What are you doing, Dixon?"

Cassie yelped and bumped her head at the unexpected voice sounding so near. She bit off a whole bunch of swear words as she peered up at the person standing over her. Amelia Crawford was the creative force behind Elite Events. She was also the boss who'd told Cassie she was off the project just moments ago.

"I dropped my phone," Cassie said. "It went beneath the car."

Amelia arched a perfectly manicured eyebrow. "You're never going to reach it. Your arm is too, uh…"

Fat, Cassie supplied in her head.

"Short," Amelia said, looking pleased with herself for thinking up a suitable word. Amelia was tall and thin and, though she never said it, seemed to view being fat as a failure.

"I can touch it," Cassie said, heat blossoming in her cheeks. "I just need to slide it this way."

Amelia rummaged in her bag and held out a neatly folded umbrella. "Here. Try this."

Cassie rolled to one side and took the umbrella. Leave it to Amelia to carry an umbrella when snow was in the forecast. "Uh, this is Louis Vuitton."

No way did Cassie want to use her boss's thousand dollar umbrella to scrape her phone across the pavement.

Amelia waved a hand. "It's a fake. I never use the real one."

"Oh. Great."

Kari had gone silent, but Cassie was pretty sure she hadn't hung up. Cassie managed to sweep the phone toward her and grab it. "Give me a sec, Kari," she mumbled.

"I got all the time in the world, babe."

Cassie huffed as she levered herself upright. Amelia didn't offer a hand, but Cassie didn't expect her to. When she got to her feet, she gave Amelia the umbrella. "Thank you so much. I'd still be trying to reach it."

Amelia tucked the umbrella into her bag and shrugged. "No problem. Look, I know you had a lot of great ideas for the Kelly Cosmetics convention, but my hands are truly tied. Debra Kelly insists she doesn't want you in the building."

"I know, and I'm sorry," Cassie said. Thankfully, Kari did not snort on the other end of the phone.

"That doesn't mean you can't help from home, though. You have such great ideas, Cass. You should use them for your job, not to make YouTube videos that insult our clients."

Cassie didn't point out that Kelly Cosmetics hadn't been a client when she'd reviewed their contouring palette and concealer a couple of months ago. That video had only gotten a couple thousand views—until a little over two weeks ago when Kelly Cosmetics had announced an IPO of their stock. Someone had unearthed it, and the views had soared. She was at half a million and still climbing.

Which hadn't been a good thing today when Debra Kelly had put two and two together in a planning meeting with Elite Events. She'd kept staring at Cassie and then she'd leaned over to whisper something to her assistant. A polished young man named Odin of all things. He did not look like an Odin to Cassie. More like an Oliver. Ollie for short.

But *not* the Norse god of war. No way.

"I didn't mean for her to ever see it," Cassie said. "I just review makeup and clothes for fun. It's a hobby."

A hobby she loved. She got to be someone else when she made her videos for YouTube and TikTok. She wasn't shy, chubby Cassie Dixon. She was cool, suave, confident Cassandra, the hostess of Cassandra's Closet. Cassandra had her shit together. Cassie did not.

"Yes, well, she *did* see it. Took all my persuasive powers to keep her from taking her business elsewhere."

Cassie didn't point out that it was rather late in the convention planning phase for Debra Kelly to fire Elite Events. Amelia didn't want to hear it anyway. Not when she had a point to make.

"I appreciate that," Cassie said.

Amelia's eyes narrowed. "I'll have Darcy send you the latest files. You can join us via Zoom tomorrow morning."

"Okay. Great. Thank you."

"You know, it would go a lot easier on you if you'd just take the video down. You could come back to the office, apologize to Debra, and we could put this whole thing behind us."

Cassie hesitated as she collected her thoughts. "I'm afraid that's not really an option. People have downloaded and shared. There are copies everywhere."

She didn't really know if there were any copies, but she wasn't going to be bullied into taking her video down when she'd done nothing wrong. It was *her* opinion about two products, nothing more. She hadn't been snarky or mean about it. She'd been honest. And it wasn't like she was freaking Estée Lauder herself. She might talk a couple hundred women into avoiding the makeup, but that would hardly put a dent in Kelly Cosmetics' bottom line.

"Well, I tried. Suit yourself," Amelia said as she sashayed away to her Mercedes S-class sedan.

Cassie unlocked the Hyundai Santa Fe that she'd bought used two years ago. It wasn't fancy, but it worked.

"Coast clear?" Kari asked.

Cassie got into the small SUV and shut the door. The call transferred to Bluetooth as she fired up the vehicle and blasted the heat. "Yes."

"Damn, girl, that woman is a witch. Why do you work for her?"

Cassie sighed and stared at nothing in the parking garage. "Because she offered me a job, Kari. Because I didn't want to go back to Bear Creek, no offense intended, and end up waiting tables or working at the Piggly Wiggly for the rest of my life."

She'd had a good job before she'd left town, but she'd left because her employer had decided to close up shop and retire.

"Not that there's anything wrong with either of those things," Kari said a touch firmly.

It was just like her bestie to point out there were many paths in life, and working an honest job in any industry was nothing to be ashamed of.

"No, of course not. But it's not what I want. I don't want to work side by side with Lottie Dixon somewhere and regret my life choices, you know?"

"No, I know that," Kari said. "I totally understand."

They both knew that Lottie—Cassie's mom—had made life hell growing up. If she wasn't picking on Cassie's weight or her shyness, she was bringing home random men and getting drunk in Coot's on Saturday night.

Lottie Dixon was everything Cassie was not. Beautiful, loud, a hell raiser who attracted men like honey attracted flies. Cassie stayed in touch with her mother, but not often. It was too much work, and too depressing. Not to mention that Lottie had never grown tired of her favorite catchphrase; *"You could be so pretty if you'd just lose weight, Cassie."*

"So you're going to work from home then," Kari said. "Did you tell Amelia about the emails?"

Cassie's skin heated. "No. I told you they're nothing. I get crank emails sometimes. And you should see some of the comments on my videos before I hide them. Lord, you'd think a fat, homely girl had never before transformed herself with makeup the way some of those dudes act personally affronted."

"You are not fat and you are not homely. You're perfect the way you are, so stop that, Cassie Dixon, or I will drive up there to DC and kick your ass."

Cassie laughed as she drove toward the exit. "You and which army?"

"I don't need an army. I just need me. And you make yourself look worse in those videos so the transformation shocks people. It's how you get views."

Cassie couldn't help but smile. "Fine, yes, I definitely do that. Camera angles are everything. I can make this double chin into a quadruple with the right angle."

"What about Brian Woodruff? Did you ever think about contacting him about the emails?"

Cassie's belly tightened. "No. I told you, it was only a few dates and we weren't compatible."

Kari huffed. "You never really explained that, you

know. One minute you're going out with a cop you met and telling me about your dates, and the next you don't want to talk about it."

Cassie sighed. "He was too much, okay? Too loud, too outgoing, too, I dunno, *much*. I like to stay home and have a quiet night in. He's the kind of guy who's the life of the party. He was never going to understand why I didn't want to go out all the time, or why I think sitting on the couch with a glass of wine and six seasons of a show I haven't seen on Netflix is a perfect evening."

Not to mention all he ever did was talk about himself. She'd thought it was fine at first, because they were getting to know each other, but it had never stopped. Gave her a definite bad vibe. If he didn't want to know anything about her in the beginning, what did that say for the future?

She'd already had one boyfriend who'd torn her self-esteem to shreds. She didn't need to head down that road again, especially when it'd taken her so long to work up to getting rid of the last one. And she didn't feel like explaining any of that to Kari just now.

Kari sighed. "Okay, fine… Crap, I gotta go. The bus just stopped in front of the house. The twins will be bursting through the door any minute looking for their after-school snacks."

"You love being a mom and you know it."

"I do. But these two are hellions sometimes."

Cassie heard the chatter of two eight-year-olds as they came through the door and pelted their mother with questions. She sometimes envied Kari for having met and married the love of her life so soon after graduation. It hadn't always been easy for Kari and Heath, but there was no doubt they were devoted to each other.

"Talk later," Cassie said.

"You let me know if you get anymore emails," Kari said past the clamoring voices of her twin daughters.

"I will."

"Just a second you two. I'm talking to your Aunt Cassie. Go sit at the island for a moment."

"Hi, Aunt Cassie," the twins sing-songed in unison.

Cassie laughed. "Tell them I said hi back."

"I will. Hey, I called Ty about those emails."

Cassie groaned. "I told you it was nothing."

"He's a former Marine, honey. Some sort of commando—and that's what he does now, only for a private firm. Since you don't want to call Brian, Ty can help if you get more threats, okay?"

"Okay," Cassie said, though she had absolutely no intention of asking Kari's cousin for help. No way did she want to see Tyler Scott again. She hadn't seen him since high school. She'd crushed on him for two solid years back then and he'd never looked at her.

Well, he'd looked at her once, when he'd saved her from some mean girls, but he'd never noticed her again. He'd only been nice to her because she was Kari's friend, but that's where it ended. She'd already had a crush on him, but that had sent it into the stratosphere. She was over it now, of course, but she still didn't want to see him. She'd never been anything but awkward around him, and she was pretty sure that hadn't changed in the past fourteen or so years.

"Let me know and I'll put him in touch."

"Will do," she lied. "Now go feed those little monsters of yours."

"On it. Love you."

"Love you more."

The call went silent. Cassie turned on the radio to fill the emptiness as she headed for the townhome in Falls Church that she called home. It was a rental, and it was expensive, but her growing YouTube income helped her afford it. Without that, she'd be sharing space in an apartment with someone else, the way she'd done for the first few months after she'd moved. She'd probably still be in that apartment if her roommate hadn't decided to move in with her boyfriend.

She probably should get a new roommate to help with expenses, but she preferred her privacy. Cassie had never liked having other people in her space. She was an introvert at heart and people exhausted her. She could function fine at her job, but she needed to go home and be alone at the end of the day. Other than Debra Kelly getting her fired from the Kelly Cosmetics Convention team, the idea of working on projects from home was heaven.

Her ultimate fantasy was for her channel to take off so she could afford to live on the proceeds from that alone. Then she wouldn't have to think about having a job where someone else called the shots.

Cassie pulled into the space in front of her town-home and turned off the car. She tucked her phone into her tote, shouldered it, found her house key, and exited the vehicle. It was a little after three, but it was a cloudy day in January and growing darker by the minute. It was cold, too. There'd been snow recently, and more was expected, though at least the roads were good and clear.

Cassie locked the car and dragged herself and her load of crap up the steps to the front door. A box was tucked to the side of the door, out of view until she reached the landing. Cassie grumbled as she picked it up. She didn't remember what she'd ordered, but she was always ordering something. She constantly tried products and clothes for her subscribers, so she got a lot of packages. Some of it was sponsored because her subscriber numbers had been steadily climbing. But the sponsorships had only begun recently, and she still bought a lot of products herself.

Cassie unlocked the door and went inside. She dumped everything on the kitchen counter and left it. First things first. She wanted to get out of these clothes and into her jammies. Then she was going to heat up a Lean Cuisine, go through the mail, and then edit one of the videos she'd made this week. She had to work ahead to upload fresh content every couple of days, so she always had videos waiting to be edited and loaded.

After she changed and twisted her long hair onto her head and secured it with a clip, she returned to the kitchen to select a Lean Cuisine. While it heated, she grabbed a knife and slid it beneath the tape on the box. She was only half paying attention to the box, wondering if it was the new eyeshadow palette and foundation she'd ordered, while scrolling through her notifications at the same time.

Once the box was open, the microwave dinged and she retrieved her meal. And though she shouldn't, she stood at the counter to eat while she flipped through the mail. Then she pulled back one of the flaps on the box —and screamed as she scrambled backward.

The box slid toward the edge of the counter and stopped. Cassie put her hand to her heart and gulped in air. The Lean Cuisine had gone flying and spaghetti sauce dripped down the front of her cabinets.

She crept forward again, her heart hammering,

wondering if she'd really seen what she thought she'd seen. Maybe she'd been distracted and she'd only thought it was a rat. Except there was a slight odor coming from the box, and it wasn't flowers.

Cassie grabbed a long knife from the drawer and leaned forward to move the flap aside so she could see what was nestled in the tissue paper inside that box.

Her heart skipped, and she pressed a hand to her mouth.

The rat was still there. And it was still dead.

Chapter Two

Ty's sleep schedule was still off after the trip to Austria to rescue Natasha and Daria, his boss's woman and her daughter. Well, the boss's daughter now —and his fiancée. Ian had proposed to Natasha on the flight back, and she'd said yes.

Ty hadn't liked Natasha much just a couple of weeks ago, but now he thought she was pretty fucking cool. He'd never seen anybody move the way she had when she'd taken out the person who'd threatened her daughter. She'd been poetry in motion—like a ballet dancer, but with martial arts moves that were lethal.

Ty scrubbed a hand over his face and blinked, wondering what had woken him. Mystery solved when his phone buzzed on the nightstand. He reached for it and peered at the screen.

It was his cousin. He thought about sending the call to voice mail, but she wouldn't give up if he did.

He stabbed the screen. "Kari."

"Are you in bed?" she asked, sounding affronted and perky at the same time.

He pushed up on an elbow and yawned. "Some of us have to work, Care Bear."

"You annoying shit. Don't call me that."

Ty chuckled. He loved that he could still get under her skin. She was thirty, he was thirty-two, and she was the closest thing he had to a sister. Considering their mothers were sisters who'd married the Scott brothers, they were closer genetically than most cousins. Thankfully, Kari had gotten the good Scott brother for a dad.

"What do you want? Cassie Dixon again?"

"Yes, asswipe." She was silent for a moment. When she spoke again, he could hear the wavering of her voice. Like she was holding back tears. "Someone sent her a dead rat, Ty. A. Dead. Rat. In. A. Box."

Ty frowned and pushed upright until he was leaning against the headboard. "Did she call the police?"

"No. She says she doesn't want to waste their time."

"Tell her to call them, Kari. She needs to register a complaint, get this documented."

"I know, but she insists it's nothing sinister. She says it's that damn YouTube channel of hers and a disgruntled viewer. But how did they get her address, Ty? That's what scares me."

He didn't like it either, but he didn't want to upset Kari more than she already was. He'd already pissed her off when he'd failed to remember who Cassie Dixon was when Kari had started texting him about her a couple of weeks ago.

In his defense, it'd been a lot of years and Cassie was forgettable. He'd remembered when he thought harder about it, but Cassie had always been the quiet shadow to his cousin's bright light. She'd never said much the few times he remembered being around her.

She just stood there and kept her head down while Kari did all the talking. He'd figured she was shy and insecure because she was a bigger girl in shapeless clothes and kids picked on her. The more he'd thought about her, he'd eventually remembered putting a stop to an incident one day when his cousin hadn't been in school and a couple of mean girls had cornered her near her locker.

He'd strode up to them, big for his age, a star linebacker on the football team, and asked Cassie if she'd like to walk to class with him. She'd nodded, her eyes wide and scared. He'd walked her to class, then found the mean girls still hanging out by the lockers and told them if they ever picked on Cassie Dixon again, he'd make sure they got blacklisted from the inner circle of Bear Creek High School.

"What is this YouTube channel again?" he asked, too weary to resist. When Kari got a bee in her bonnet, as his mama always said, she wasn't going to stop until she got her way.

"I told you before it's *Cassandra's Closet*. You didn't look at it, did you?"

"No, sorry. I was on a mission. I didn't have time. But things have calmed down now, so I can take a look."

"I need you to do more than take a look. I need you to go and *talk* to her. Find out what's going on and get to the bottom of this."

He was too tired to argue. Besides, the only way he was going to ease Kari's mind was if he agreed to talk to Cassie. And he really did have the time now, so he was out of excuses.

"Fine. I'll talk to her. Send me the channel info again and give me her number. I'll call her."

"You have to go see her, Ty," Kari said. "She's just going to blow you off if you call, same as she does me."

Ty raked a hand through his hair and yawned. "Is she stupid or something? Because this is getting fucking complicated and I haven't even started."

"You know how she is," Kari said.

Except he didn't. He wisely kept his mouth shut though.

"She's shy and insecure. If you call her, she'll lie and say everything's fine just to make you go away. She'd rather hide out in her house and pretend everything is okay than admit this is a real issue."

She sounded like an idiot to him, but he knew how that would go if he said so. "All right. Give me her address then. I'll go this weekend."

"Tonight, Ty. Please."

"For fuck's sake, Kari. I just got home from overseas. And it's dark, which means that Cassie isn't going to open the door for me. Not after getting a dead rat from somebody."

"Text me when you get there and I'll call her. I'll make sure she opens the door."

"You're killing me, Care Bear. Killing me."

"But you love me!"

"I do, dumbass. Speaking of dumbasses, how's Heath?"

Kari snorted. "He's fine. Reading to the girls as we speak."

"Kiss them for me. Not Heath, just the girls."

"Ha, I'm kissing him too and telling him it's from you."

"Figured you would. This is important to you, huh?"

She knew he wasn't talking about Heath or the girls.

"Yes. Cassie had a difficult life growing up, and she's stubbornly independent. She doesn't like asking anyone for anything. Hell, I think she'd die of thirst before she'd ask for a glass of water if she thought someone was going to be inconvenienced by the request. I just… She's my best friend, Ty. She's amazing and sweet, and nobody ever gave her a chance growing up. But wait until you see her channel. She's going to blow you away. Take a look at it while you're getting dressed. Text me when you hit the road."

Ty couldn't help but snort a laugh. Whether he wanted to or not, he was about to ride out to assist a damsel in distress. If he didn't, his cousin would rain down hellfire from afar. He knew she could do it, too. She'd call his mother, and he'd never hear the end of it.

"You owe me, Kari. I expect you to defend me the next time I'm home and Mom and Aunt Karen start in on my marital status. And I expect your homemade banana pudding too."

Kari laughed. "I can do that. Texting you the deets now. Gotta go rescue Heath. Love you, Jarhead."

He loved that she knew Marines were called jarheads. She'd howled with glee when she'd found out that detail after he'd enlisted.

"Love you too, nut job."

Ty dragged himself from bed, showered, and yanked open the fridge to peer into it. He thought longingly of the home-cooked meals he'd been eating recently when Natasha had gone on a cooking spree, but Ian wasn't about to let him, Dax, and Rascal stay at his house now that they'd squashed the threat to Natasha and Daria. The boss wanted time alone with his family. Ty didn't blame him.

But that meant he had to fend for himself now. He dragged out jars of peanut butter and jelly, found some bread, and made a sandwich. He'd pick up something better on the way home later.

While he ate, he flicked on the television and surfed over to YouTube. Then he typed in *Cassandra's Closet* and waited.

He queued up one of the videos and watched as Cassie faced the camera. She didn't have any makeup on, and she looked... kind of awful, really. He didn't remember her looking like that in high school, but then he didn't remember all that much about her.

She couldn't possibly have found a less flattering angle to film herself. The lighting was harsh, her skin was blotchy, and her hair was scraped back from her head so tightly he couldn't tell how long it was. How the hell was she getting hate mail for looking so pitiful?

She talked about feeling ugly and unattractive while she began to swipe on makeup with brushes and sponges. Five minutes later, because she'd sped up the filming, she cut to black and then turned back to the camera with an exaggerated sweep of her lush body. Her long reddish-brown hair swirled over her shoulders, green eyes sparkling as she winked. Her face was perfect. She had gorgeous cheekbones, a small nose, eyelashes for days, and the most kissable lips he'd ever seen.

"Holy shit," he breathed.

Cassie Dixon was fucking gorgeous. Ty picked up the remote and rewound the video just so he could see her at the beginning again. Plain. Chubby. Not the kind of woman anyone would look at twice.

But then she transformed herself like she'd waved a magic wand.

Abracadabra—and poof! Plain Cassie was replaced with sultry Cassandra. Cassandra had beautiful green eyes, a gorgeous face, and a banging body. She wore a black sweater dress that clung to her full breasts and generous hips. It made a man get ideas. It made *him* get ideas.

"Don't let anyone define your image of yourself," she said, sounding confident and firm, two adjectives he would have never associated with his memory of her. "You're beautiful. You may not be a size two, and you may have a few rolls around the middle, but honey, you are AH-MAZING."

She lifted her hand and wiggled her fingers at the camera. "Links for the products I used are below. If you enjoyed this video, hit the thumbs up button and don't forget to click the notification bell so you don't miss any new videos from me. Thanks for going on this journey with me to find what works for big, beautiful girls like us. Until next time, beautiful babes. Keep being fabulous!"

Ty looked at the video description with her links. She had over forty-thousand subscribers, which wasn't insignificant, and her views were in the thousands. He scrolled to the comments, which were mostly positive. A few thought she wasn't the same person from beginning to end, but considering she'd applied the makeup on camera, he figured they were stupid.

There was a recent comment from someone whose handle was Big Guns that said, *"This is why men have trust issues. Go to bed with a model, wake up with a troll. You're a liar and you need to be stopped."*

Ty clicked the profile. It took him to a channel that had no content so he clicked back out again. Typical internet troll. He watched a couple more videos, found a few more recent comments from Big Guns that he screenshotted, then hopped into his truck and texted Kari he was on his way.

Cassie lived in Falls Church, Virginia, which was a long way from his rental in Maryland, especially in traffic. By the time he got there, it was almost eight p.m. He parked, texted Kari, and strode up the front walkway to Cassie's door.

It took a few minutes before the door jerked open. Kari had texted to tell him not to leave and then she presumably went back to arguing with Cassie until she got her friend to come to the door.

Cassie didn't pull the door all the way open, but she'd slid the chain off. Her hair was piled on her head in a messy bun, and she was wearing a baggy sweatshirt with a pair of pajama pants that had cats on them.

She wasn't wearing the makeup she'd been wearing in her video, but her green eyes were just as beautiful. She didn't look like the woman in the finished video, but she didn't look like the one in the beginning either.

Cassie Dixon was something in between the extremes, but it was her eyes that held his attention. She looked uncertain, vulnerable. Scared.

"You plan to let me in?"

"I-I-I…" She closed her eyes and drew in a deep breath.

And then she shut the door in his face.

Chapter Three

CASSIE STOOD ON HER SIDE OF THE DOOR AND SUCKED IN a deep breath. She was going to kill Kari the next time they were together. Kill. Her.

She'd just shut the door in Tyler Scott's face. Ty, who looked even more handsome than he had in high school. Why couldn't his big body have gone to fat? Why couldn't he have a paunch and maybe be balding?

He's thirty-two, dingbat.

Yes, well, men could start to bald at that age. And they could definitely get paunches.

There was a hard, sharp rap on her door. Her cheeks flared with heat. She pulled in another breath and steeled herself to open the door again. If she didn't, Kari would drive up here tomorrow, and Cassie couldn't do that to her best friend. Kari didn't need to leave Heath and the girls just to make sure that Cassie was okay.

Kari's heart was in the right place. Cassie's issues with people—especially tall, handsome people like Ty— were her problem. She'd told Kari she didn't need Ty's help, but here he was. Kari had ambushed her, calling to tell her Ty was outside and she needed to let him in.

She'd worked herself up to it, opened the door—and panicked.

Cassie glanced at her kitty cat pajama pants and the loose sweatshirt that said *Boss Girl* on it and groaned. Too late to change. She pasted on a smile she didn't feel and pulled the door open again.

Ty was still there. Still tall and imposing on her front stoop. It was dark and snow was coming down in light little flakes, landing on his broad shoulders and dark hair. His hands were shoved in the pockets of his jacket, and annoyance flared in his eyes. They were as piercing as she remembered. Light green, though they sometimes looked almost blue in pictures. His jaw was broad and hard, and one dark curl hung over his forehead.

Her insides were putty. He was even better looking than when she'd followed him around like a puppy back in high school. Well, followed him with her eyes, actually. She'd have never followed *him*. He'd have noticed. Everyone would have noticed, and the last thing she'd wanted was to be noticed.

Cassie did not attract attention if she could help it. At least not in person.

"Hi," she said brightly.

"You shut the door in my face."

"Yes. Sorry."

"And you look like you want to do it again." He nodded at the death grip she had on the door.

She uncurled her fingers from the edge. "Sorry. Um, do you want to come in?"

Please say no, please say no….

He tipped his head back to look up at the snow falling. "It's a little cold out here, so yeah."

Cassie's heart tripped in her chest as she stepped back and pulled the door wide. Ty walked past her, bringing a wash of cold air with him. She didn't mind it, though. She needed it to cool the heat beneath her skin.

She shut the door behind him and hesitated for a moment, then turned to face him. He was shrugging out of his jacket and draping it over his arm.

"Let me take that," she said, shifting into polite hostess mode. Because what else was she supposed to do?

He handed her the jacket, and she walked it over to the row of hooks in the hallway near the back door. She thought about heading to her bedroom and changing, trying to make herself more presentable, but there was no point. He'd already seen her in her baggy pajamas and no makeup. His impression was fixed—probably had been since high school—and she couldn't change it.

He was standing at her kitchen counter when she went back to the front of the house.

"Where's the box?" he asked.

"I, uh, threw it out."

"Where?"

"Um, out back. I actually just dropped the box outside the door, so it's still there."

While having a serious case of the heebie-jeebies, though she didn't add that part. Last thing she wanted was a dead rat in her house.

He nodded and headed for her back door. She didn't follow him. When he returned, he had the box. She took a step backward, and he frowned.

"I dumped the rat."

"Oh. Okay."

She still couldn't believe someone had put a rat at her front door. She hugged her arms around herself, feeling self-conscious because she wasn't wearing a bra. Oh hell, who was she kidding? She was self-conscious about *everything*.

Her teenage crush was standing in her house, looking more gorgeous than ever, and she was still disappointingly not perfect. She hadn't changed into a dynamic, outgoing, skinny girl who everyone loved to be around. She wasn't the heaviest she'd ever been, but what did that matter? She was still too fat for the likes of him.

Ty turned the box over and looked at every part of it. "It didn't come through the mail. Someone put it at your door. You piss off any neighbors lately?"

Cassie blinked. "I don't think so. I'm not loud and I don't have guests over, so there's nothing to get mad about. I park where I'm supposed to, and I roll my trash to the curb on the designated days."

"Kari said you've gotten threatening emails. Can you show them to me?"

"I, uh…"

He frowned. Hard. "Don't tell me you deleted them. Please don't tell me that."

Fresh heat flooded her. "I didn't delete them. I'm just, uh, overwhelmed a bit. I wasn't expecting you, and I'm not at my best right now."

His gaze slid past her to the laptop computer on the coffee table. "Are they on there?"

"Yes, but I also printed them." She went over and pressed the laptop closed. "I can get them for you. But really, it's nothing. Like I told Kari, people don't like it that a fat girl can make herself look pretty. Some people, I mean."

"You think that's all it is?"

She was glad he didn't trip over his tongue to tell her she wasn't fat. Lies about her weight didn't help. Kari said she wasn't fat because she knew that Cassie's mom had always used the word negatively. But they both knew she was plus-sized.

"Yes. I make people angry because I don't fit their idea of what constitutes beauty. They tell me I need to lose weight because I'm unhealthy, and that I'm a bitch for pushing the idea that fat can be sexy. They say I'm hurting people by not telling them to lose weight and eat a proper diet instead of putting on makeup and clothes that flatter their figures. People get very angry about that."

"Angry enough to put a dead rat on your front porch?"

"Maybe so." She nibbled her lip. "I'm not sure how they would have found where I live, though."

"You used your real name on your channel. It wouldn't take too much work to dig out where you live for someone who knows what they're doing. Got those emails for me?"

He sounded impatient, and it made her flinch. He thought she was an idiot and he didn't want to be here, but he was doing it for Kari. She envied Kari for that. Cassie didn't have any men in her life who'd drop everything to do her a favor. She never had.

Not that she needed a man to do so. She had Kari, who'd pit-bulled Ty into coming tonight. All because she was concerned for her friend.

"Yes. Hang on," Cassie said, determined to cooperate for no other reason than to ease Kari's mind. And maybe hers too since that rat had scared her more than she cared to admit to anyone.

Though if she hadn't wanted to admit it, why had she called Kari all upset in the first place? If she'd kept it to herself, Ty wouldn't be here.

But once she'd thrown the box onto the back porch, she'd been shaking and furious. She'd showered and scrubbed off all her makeup, then thrown on her baggy clothes and reached for her phone. She'd called Kari before she realized what she was doing.

Kari had known something was wrong and she'd forced Cassie to spill the story. Cassie should have known Kari was taking it far too well when she'd said she had to go because the girls needed her. No, she'd had to go so she could call Ty.

Cassie hurried upstairs and into the second bedroom she used as an office, closet, and filming studio. She grabbed the stack of emails from Glockman123 and carried them downstairs again. Ty took them from her with a muttered, "Thanks," and flopped onto a chair to read.

Cassie watched him bent over the paper, her stomach churning with anxiety and discomfort. She would feel so much better if she could get out of her schlubby sweats and into something better.

"I'm going to go, uh, change while you do that. Be back in a few minutes."

"Yeah, sure," he said without looking up.

Cassie went back upstairs and riffled through her closet. She finally settled on jeans and a green surplice top with flowing sleeves. She didn't have time for a full makeup job—nor was there any point—but she did put on a quick sweep of foundation, some eyeliner, and a touch of mascara before rolling on some pale pink lip gloss. Presentable, but not date night ready.

As if she'd ever be going on a date with Tyler Scott, Bear Creek High School's dreamiest athlete at one time. All the girls had crushed on Ty, and he'd certainly had his pick of them. He'd had a different date every weekend when he'd cruised into the diner where she'd bused tables. Bused, not waited, because she'd had a hard time talking to people back then.

Everyone but Kari Scott, who'd taken one look at her in kindergarten and proclaimed they were besties. Which they'd been ever since. Kari hadn't been one of the popular girls in school, but she could have been with a little effort. And if she'd ditched Cassie, which she never had.

Cassie shook out her hair, ran a brush and then her fingers through it, and let it fall over her shoulders in messy waves. Her hair was her best feature. Long, naturally wavy, and thick. It looked great up or down, curled or straightened. Her natural color was a shade browner, but she'd discovered that adding a little bit of a red wash into her hair made it stand out that much more.

"Here's to nothing," she muttered to her reflection.

Chapter Four

EVEN IF TY DIDN'T NOTICE, CASSIE FELT MARGINALLY better. Like she'd donned her armor and could now talk to him. She was Cassandra instead of Cassie.

She took a deep breath and glided down the stairs like a queen making an entrance. Ty was still reading, but he looked up when he heard her. Their eyes caught and held, and Cassie's breath felt like a stone in her chest.

He was looking at her, and she was looking at him, and sparks were flaring in her tummy. Or maybe that was hunger since she hadn't finished the Lean Cuisine.

"Have you called the police about any of this?" he asked, and the sparks died.

She finished descending the stairs and went over to the couch and sank gracefully onto it. Ty was still watching her. Waiting.

She looked down and fiddled with the pen and notebook she'd placed beside her laptop on the coffee table. Then she met his gaze again.

"No."

"Why not?"

She blew out an annoyed breath. "Because there are thousands of people on social media, and everyone gets harassed. I'm in online groups with other influencers, and everyone gets comments and email. It's not enough to bother the police with."

"Okay. But do these other influencers get dead rats in boxes?"

She dropped her gaze again. "Maybe not. That's a new thing, though. This is the first time I've ever gotten anything so disgusting—"

"But you've gotten other things?"

Cassie squirmed. "I-I don't know. Maybe."

"How can't you know?" He sounded doubtful. Like he questioned her sanity or something.

"I got some pizzas," she whispered.

"Pizzas."

Her head snapped up, her gaze meeting his. She didn't know why the way he said the word made her defenses flare, but it had. "Yes, pizzas. Large pizzas loaded with meat, delivered to my house five nights last week and five nights the previous week."

"And you didn't order them."

She shot to her feet. "No, I didn't! Or maybe you thought I did because I'm fat."

Jeez, Cass, stop saying that word. You tell your followers they're beautiful the way they are, which means you are too...

"I'm trying to get a handle on the facts, not piss you off. And I didn't say you were fat. You did. Remember that the next time you want to accuse me of it."

"Sorry."

He leaned back in the chair, studying her. "You're on edge. I get it. And while we went to high school together, we don't really know each other. You're tolerating me because Kari sent me, but you'd really like me to go away."

"It's not personal," she said, dropping her gaze.

"I know that too. I also know that you don't let your followers get down on themselves, so why are you doing it?"

Cassie couldn't help but stare. "You watched my channel?"

He nodded. "Kari told me I should. I only watched one video, but it was enough to know that you encourage people to be comfortable in their own skin. More than that, you make them think it's possible because *you* are. Is that a lie?"

Cassie could feel the heat in her cheeks. "Sometimes," she said truthfully, lifting her chin. "I've been on a long journey to learn to accept myself as I am. It's an ongoing battle. The channel keeps me positive, even when I don't quite feel that way."

"You purposely filmed yourself with bad lighting in the one I watched. Why?"

She was still stunned that he'd watched a video of hers. She wanted to ask which one, but she didn't want to seem needy. "It's a mercenary decision. People love transformations, so the worse you look at the beginning, the more payoff at the end. I'm not trying to fool anyone. It's still me. But it's also about lighting and angles. I try teach people that. We're all beautiful under the right circumstances."

He nodded. "It's a good message. You had a lot of grateful comments."

"And some ugly ones. I try to delete the worst ones and block the user from commenting on my channel if they have a history of being really bad, but I know I've missed some lately."

She hadn't been able to keep up when the video about Kelly Cosmetics went viral. And she didn't want to read some of those comments because they made her feel bad. She needed to, though. It was best to get rid of them ASAP.

"I saw some of those. You can delete and block?"

"Yes." She sat back down, slowly, and clasped her hands over her knees as she faced him. "When you hide someone from the channel, all their comments disappear from public view. They can still watch the videos, but they can't comment or message you anymore. If you unblock them, everything comes back."

"Have you blocked anyone?"

"A couple of people. I try not to unless they're really ugly. Or just trying to sell things to my followers, which also happens."

"I'd like to see the users and comments."

"I can screen-cap them and send. There aren't many."

"That'll work. You also need to block someone named Big Guns, if you haven't yet. He's started commenting recently."

Cassie frowned. "I must have missed him. Things have gotten a little crazy lately."

"Kelly Cosmetics."

"Yes." She sighed. "It happens to everyone, you know. The comments, I mean. If you're providing good content, you get more views. More views equals more trolls, and sometimes you miss things."

"So why do it?"

He seemed genuinely curious. She shrugged. "More

views also equals more money. More money equals more freedom."

He frowned as he lifted the emails in his hand. "Could a rival do this kind of thing?"

"They could, I suppose. Their time would be better spent making content, but if they thought they could scare off a rival, maybe it'd be worth it. So long as they didn't get caught."

"I'm going to see if I can track down the person behind the email address, so I'll need you to forward me the actual emails."

She wasn't comfortable looking at those emails again, but she understood why he'd need them. "Okay."

"I might not find anything, but it's worth a try. If they're smart, they're using a VPN. That'll make it more difficult, but not impossible."

She knew what a VPN was. A virtual private network obscured your IP address by sending you through different sites to make it look like you were online in, say, Toronto, when you were really in DC.

He flipped through the pages again. "Sounds like a man, but that doesn't mean anything. Could be a woman. You get anything besides pizzas?"

"A rat," she said. "That's bad enough."

"Definitely. The emails aren't nice though. He says you lie about how you look, and that you set up false expectations that give men hope, when in reality you should be grateful they give you any attention at all."

Her face burned. "I know what they say. He also says I should be taught a lesson by someone with a big dick, but that nobody would fuck me anyway. He says I need to be beaten to make me humble, and that I need to learn respect. I should shut down my channel and stop lying and misleading people. He says if I don't shut it down, he'll make sure I do."

Ty raked a hand through his hair and shook his head. "You need to get the police involved, Cassie. At least make a statement and get the complaint on file. This guy is trying to black mail you into taking action by using threats against you. That's not nothing."

She dropped her gaze and clenched her hands tighter until her knuckles whitened. She'd known this moment was coming. She'd known since the minute she'd opened that box tonight. "If you think I should."

"I do think you should. Don't let this guy harass you. If the pizzas and rat are related, then he's escalating." He took out his phone. "Kari gave me your number. I'm texting you my email address right now. Add me to your contacts, and promise to call me if anything else happens. And forward those emails to me."

Her phone dinged and she picked it up and added him like he said. "Okay, I will."

He snorted as he stood. "You're just saying that about calling me, but I fucking mean it, Cassie. This is what I do, and I will protect you from this asshole to the best of my ability. Still need you to report it, though."

"I'll go tomorrow."

"Promise?"

She must have hesitated too long because he closed the distance between them to glare down at her. Her heart thumped.

He was intimidating. Handsome. Good lord, the man had muscles that went on for days. His T-shirt was stretched over his arms and chest like a second skin. Her gaze settled on the tiny scar that curved from his nostril to his lip. It had been more noticeable in high school, but it had faded over the years.

"What time do you get off work?"

Her mind scrambled to make the turn he'd taken. "Um, I'm working from home these days."

"Fine. I'll be here at noon to pick you up."

"Wh-what?"

He went over to retrieve his jacket. Shrugged into it. "Noon. Tomorrow. You and me. Lunch. Stand me up, and I'll tell Kari. She'll hound you into an early grave."

She nearly laughed because he was right, but she was too shocked to do so. He was taking her to lunch?

"I'll be here."

"Good. Lock the door behind me, Cassie. Call me if you need anything. Don't accept any deliveries after dark, and don't let anyone in. I'm taking these emails," he added, holding up the stack. "I'll give them back tomorrow."

Cassie watched him walk down the stairs, panic rising inside her. She loved being alone, and now she didn't want to be. She wanted him to stay.

He turned and shot her a look. "Lock the door, Cass. I'm not leaving until you do."

She did as she was told, though her belly churned with fresh unease as her gaze swept her living room. He was gone, and she was utterly alone.

And for once she didn't like it.

Chapter Five

Ty managed to get some sleep again before getting up early and hitting the gym at Black Defense International. After he worked out, he dressed and took the elevator to the fifth floor. It was only a few days into January, and he wasn't sure who he'd find back at work after the mission and recovery.

Ian was in his office. He looked up as Ty walked in and flopped into the chair across from his desk.

"What's up, man?"

Ty shrugged. "How are Natasha and Daria?"

Ian grinned. His entire face relaxed as he thought of the women in his life. "Doing good. Natasha is cooking up a storm—"

"Oh Jesus, don't tell me that," Ty groaned. "I had to stop at a fast food joint last night. Hamburgers and fries aren't nearly as good as Natasha's homemade meatloaf or pasta."

Ian laughed. "She made chicken noodle soup yesterday. Big pot. Comfort food."

"I hate you," Ty said. "What about Daria? She recovering okay?"

Ian sobered. "Yeah. Some nightmares, but she's resilient. Tasha told her that Lissette went to heaven."

"Shit."

"She had to. She said that telling the kid her nanny was in the other place wouldn't help. She's right."

He could understand that. Daria was a great kid, and smart as heck, but she was going to have to process what'd happened in Austria.

"I told you my cousin was bugging me about some girl we went to school with, right?"

"Yep. Did you go see her?"

"I did." He thought of Cassie Dixon opening the door in her baggy sweats last night, and then shutting it in his face. Then he thought about the green shirt and jeans she'd changed into, her amazingly lush body, and the way her hair had framed her pretty face. Her eyes had been mossy, deep, and he'd wanted to keep looking at them until the unexpected swirling in his belly went away.

It never did.

"And?"

Ty pulled the wad of folded emails from his back pocket and shoved them at Ian. "Threatening emails, and someone left a dead rat in a box on her porch last night. They've also been sending unsolicited pizzas. Ten of them so far."

"Why?"

Ty blew out a breath. "She has a YouTube channel. She also does makeup videos on TikTok. Her angle is that you don't have to be a size two to be beautiful."

He'd binged Cassie's videos last night. He'd only

been mildly shocked when his cock got hard and wouldn't stop throbbing. The only thing that'd helped was jerking off. Which he'd done while watching Cassie giggle and talk to her viewers about clothes and makeup.

Made him feel like a perv, but damn, the girl was fine as hell. Sure, she was a bit thick in places—but he liked the way it looked on her. He tried to imagine her as a skinny girl, but it wasn't right. Cassie Dixon had thick thighs, amazing tits, and her belly wasn't flat. And for the first time that he could remember, those things made him harder than stone.

Had she looked like that in high school? He didn't think so. He thought she'd worn baggy clothes and no makeup back then. She'd hidden her figure, not shown it.

Ian flipped through the emails. "Jesus. Have you given these to Dax?"

"Not yet. I wanted to get your permission first."

Ian gazed at him in surprise. "You have to ask? After everything we've been through?"

Ty shrugged. "I still feel new sometimes. Like I just left the Marines, and I don't want to fuck this up."

"You've been with BDI for two years. I trust you, Ty. You know that. Get Dax on this, and do what you have to in order to help this girl."

"I plan on it. She doesn't want my help, though. And she doesn't want to report it to the police either."

"But she's going to."

Ty nodded. "She's going to. I'm taking her down there after lunch and making her write a statement."

"Good."

"I intend to be involved, but I think it's good for the

police to have a record. This guy may not be the one behind the pizzas and rat, but if he is, I think he's going to escalate. The last couple of emails are uglier in tone."

Ian frowned as he skimmed the emails. "I think so too. Seems angry as hell, doesn't he?"

"Yep. He also sounds like he lives in his mommy's basement and hangs out online all day. I'm not so sure, though. Pizzas are easy to get delivered. Takes no thought really, and any online troll could do it. But a rat? That took planning. It was a white rat, like a pet, but partly frozen. It wasn't cold enough to freeze in the box, so the guy likely picked it up at a pet shop, pre-frozen for snake food. There was no blood or gore. Just the dead rat in tissue paper. He could have paid someone to buy a rat, box it up, and deliver it, but it's more likely he did it himself."

"Agreed. Does she need protection at work?"

"She's working from home for now. An event planning firm. Elite Events in Crystal City. YouTube and TikTok are her hobby. There's something else related to her work though. It might be the source of the harassment, though I think it's a fairly remote possibility."

Still, nothing was certain in this world. That's why he looked at all the angles.

"What's that?"

"Her channel does reviews of clothes and makeup. She reviewed makeup by Kelly Cosmetics about two months ago, and it wasn't favorable. Not nasty, but not favorable to the product. The video went viral after Kelly announced an IPO of their stock. There's no way one video by a small YouTuber can make a difference to that process, but Kelly Cosmetics had retained Elite Events to plan their spring convention in the city before the video went viral. Yesterday, Debra Kelly had Cassie removed from the planning team when she recognized her from the video."

Ian looked thoughtful. "How many subscribers does Cassie have?"

"It's been climbing since the video went viral. It was almost fifty-thousand this morning when I checked."

"That's pretty good, but it's still not big enough to worry about. Why harass one woman for an opinion video? All they'd have to do is bury the video with a bunch of positive videos of their own. Sending ugly emails, pizzas, and dead rats is risky if they get caught."

"That's true, but it's possible someone on Kelly's team is more old school. Harass Cassie until she takes down the video or stops posting. There have been several emails and comments demanding she remove the video. They don't seem to be from the same guy, but it could be a coordinated attack."

"A two-pronged approach," Ian said thoughtfully. "Attack her personally and attack the video, scare her enough to make her disappear for a while. YouTube requires new content or your videos sink in the algorithms. If she stops posting, her channel will most likely go into a free fall since she hasn't amassed a ton of followers yet. The video will still get views, but anyone checking her profile won't stick around for more. And they won't take her seriously about anything she says."

"Which would be a win for Kelly Cosmetics, if they really care about one bad review."

"Have you watched the video?"

Ty nodded. "It's fourteen minutes long, and she reviews foundation and something called a contouring palette." He had an idea what those were now that he'd watched several of Cassie's videos, but he wasn't about to admit it. "She said the foundation broke her out and the contouring cream made her look like she'd rolled in dirt no matter how much she blended it. She said it was overpriced and nobody should buy it. She wasn't mean about it, but she was opinionated."

"Not the worst thing anyone's ever said about a product," Ian said with a shrug. He handed Ty the printed copies of Cassie's emails. "Forward the emails to Dax and see what he can find."

Ty stood. "On it, boss."

"Before you go, Daria wants us to have you, Dax, and Rascal over for dinner one night this week. You guys spoiled her and she misses you."

God, he loved that kid. Home cooking for the win. "I should be able to make it. Just let me know."

"Will do. Bring Cassie along if you want. Tasha cooks enough for an army anyway."

Chapter Six

CASSIE DIDN'T SLEEP WELL, BUT SHE WAS UP AND DRESSED
by nine so she could make Amelia's Zoom meeting. She
had a page full of notes for things she was supposed to
get to work on, but it was almost noon and Ty had said
he was taking her to lunch.

She picked up her phone, intending to text him and
tell him she didn't have time, but the doorbell rang. She
went over to peer out the peephole. A delivery driver
was walking toward a FedEx truck, so she slid open the
locks and opened the door. She called out her thanks, he
waved, and she bent to pick up the package.

It was brown, longer than it was wide, and it had
her name on it. She didn't recognize the return address,
but that wasn't uncommon since she ordered a lot of
stuff. She stood uncertainly, her belly churning, then
angrily went back inside and put the package on the
counter. It had come via FedEx, but that didn't mean
anything.

She hated that she was apprehensive about opening
it. Hated that someone had made her fear opening her

own damned packages. She grabbed a knife and reached for it, then hesitated.

Maybe she should wait for Ty. She'd open it while he was here, that way he could deal with anything unpleasant. She prayed it wasn't unpleasant, but she was still feeling skittish after last night.

She glanced at the time, then decided to run upstairs and change. She'd worn a nice top for Zoom, but she'd had on her pajama pants. She was *not* wearing those to lunch. She chose a cute, flippy black skirt with black tights and boots, and a wine-colored shirt made of soft jersey that draped beautifully over her full chest. By the time she touched up her makeup and gave her hair a quick brush, it was nearly noon.

She returned downstairs and tidied up her workspace at the kitchen table. She did all her video editing and other work at the table or on the couch at night, but she did her filming upstairs in the bedroom she'd turned into a closet and studio.

Cassie glanced at the package sitting on the counter, but she still couldn't bring herself to open it. Which made her angry. How the hell was she going to work on her videos if she couldn't open packages to get her products?

Her phone dinged with a text. It was Ty announcing his arrival.

She peered out the peephole and then opened the door as he strode up the walk. Her breath caught just a little at the sight of him. It'd been dark last night, but it was brighter today, even with the gray clouds that threatened more snow.

And Ty was still big, still handsome, and still so very unattainable for a girl like her. He wore a dark jacket and his hair curled against his collar. He had on faded jeans and heavy hiking boots. He walked up the stairs and stopped.

"You ready?"

She thought about the package. It could wait until they returned—but what if it was another rat, or something equally nasty?

"Actually, I got a package delivery a few minutes ago. I was afraid to open it."

She stepped back and he followed her inside, but not before knocking his boots on the threshold. "Do you want me to take them off?" he asked.

He hadn't asked last night, but the ground hadn't been wet from melting snow. "No, it's okay. I can mop. The rugs wash."

Because she'd spent money on the kind that could be thrown in the washer when they got dirty. Might as well use them the way they were intended to be used. He was still careful to wipe his boots though, which she appreciated.

Cassie folded her arms and nodded at the package. "There's a return address but no sender. I wasn't sure."

"Did you Google the address?"

Oh jeez…

"No. I didn't think about it. I just got out of a meeting, and I had to get dressed for lunch, and—"

He held up a hand, effectively cutting her off. "It's okay. I got it."

He took a knife from his jeans pocket and flipped it open. She'd planned to open it herself with him there, but now that he'd taken charge, she was content to let him do it. He cut into the package and put the knife away. Cassie nibbled her lip, staying out of range just in case, and waited.

He folded one flap back. She saw him stiffen slightly and her stomach took a dive to her toes. But then he turned toward her, box in hand, a slight grin on his face.

"I think this is, uh, personal," he said, handing it to her.

Cassie took the package carefully, studying him as she did so. He seemed… amused. She drew in a breath and folded back the flap.

"Oh my stars," she breathed.

"Well, that's what the card promises," he said mildly.

Cassie's cheeks were on fire. Her entire body went hot and cold and hot again. The giant dildo—purple, translucent, with a nub that promised to stimulate her clit while she, uh, used the other part to bring herself to orgasm—lay in the packaging, smelling slightly rubbery and looking like it was meant for a horse.

"It's not mine," she said in a rush.

"It has your name on it."

She dropped the giant dildo on the table. And yes, the card inside did promise she'd be seeing stars when she used the big dong on herself.

"I didn't order it, Ty. I swear I didn't."

She dropped into a chair and put a hand to her head, blinking rapidly to stop the silly tears that threatened. She was thirty years old, for goodness' sake. A giant dildo was much better than a rat.

He had his hands in his jeans pockets. His jacket was open in the front. He frowned down at her. "You're an adult, Cassie. If you want to order a dildo, it's none of my business."

She sucked in a breath. Her heart pounded and her

skin was on fire. But she told herself she would be cool. Calm. "I know that, you big idiot. I did *not* order it! Somebody else did."

Her phone rang. It was work. "I have to take this," she muttered. "Hello, this is Cassie."

"Cassie, you better get in here and pick up this stuff that just got delivered," her coworker hissed. "Amelia is fit to be tied. What were you thinking?"

Cassie's belly churned. "What stuff? What are you talking about?"

"Holy shit, girl. You messed up big time with this. Were you drinking when you went on a spending spree?"

"Pamela, I swear I have no idea what you're talking about."

"It has the company name on the box, so we opened it, figuring it was the swag samples. But the invoice is in your name—and it's all, uh, personal."

Dread pooled in Cassie's gut. "How personal?"

"There's a sex doll," Pamela whispered. "A couple of dildos, some edible glitter, handcuffs, anal beads, a whip... Jeez, I thought your channel was tame."

"Put it in the box and send it back. It's not mine."

"Amelia says you have to come get it ASAP. She doesn't want it here. You can send it back yourself, but you better pick it up before Amelia has a kitten."

Cassie closed her eyes. Her heart was pounding and her eyes stung with tears. "Okay, yes, I'll be there. Please hide it somewhere, okay? There's been a mistake."

"I'll stuff it under your desk. You better hurry, though. Odin is coming by in an hour to pick up some stuff for Debra. You don't want him to see you. Amelia doesn't want him to see you."

Then why the hell couldn't Amelia shove the box into a closet and let Cassie get it later? But she didn't say that.

"Fine. I'll be there as soon as I can."

The call went dead and she met Ty's gaze. He didn't look too thrilled.

"Apparently there was another order," she said as coolly as she could. She felt like she was looking down at herself from a mile above. This was happening to someone else. Not to her. She was quiet, reserved. She didn't bother anyone. The only thing she did was try to make people feel good by showing them how to flatter their figures and faces. Why was that bad? How was that deserving of harassment?

"What kind of order?"

She gestured at the dildo. Tears filled her eyes. "Adult stuff. At my work. Someone sent a sex doll. Dildos. Other stuff. I have to go get it before my boss fires me."

"Jesus, Cassie."

"It wasn't me," she said fiercely. "Why would I order that stuff at work? Even if you think this one is mine"— she flung her arm in the general direction of the giant purple dong—"it's *not*. I would never buy something so... *so* idiotically meant for someone with no cervix. I'd get something reasonable, something approximating a real male—and not purple!"

Ty came over and hunkered down in front of her. His gaze was on a level with hers, and when she dropped her head, he put a finger under her chin and lifted it so she had to look at him again.

His eyes were greenish-blue, ringed in a darker color, and utterly mesmerizing. He hadn't shaved. He was scruffy, but in the best way. In the *oh my goodness, I want that beard scraping my inner thighs* way.

Not the right time, Cassie. Not with dildos and sex dolls getting delivered right and left.

"I'm sorry, Cassie. For not believing you at first. I thought you were embarrassed by it, and I wanted you to know it's okay to buy these things. I need you to be truthful with me whenever you get something, okay? If you ordered it, no matter how embarrassing, I need to know. It's important to distinguish between your stuff and the stuff someone's harassing you with."

She nodded. "I don't order embarrassing stuff. I order many things for the channel, but not sex toys. And I don't order them for myself either."

She didn't tell him that she already had a vibrator. It wasn't huge or deformed. It wasn't even shaped like a penis. It was just a nice, plain vibrator that she used sometimes when she needed a little relief. Like a lot of single—and maybe even married—women did.

"Someone is trying to humiliate you."

"They're doing a very fine job of it," she said, squeezing her hands in her lap. "I'm humiliated. I have to walk into work and get that box in front of all my coworkers, and I have to do it before Odin shows up."

"Odin? The Norse god of war?"

She snorted. "Hardly. A snivelly little turd who works for Debra Kelly."

He stood and held out his hand. She hesitated, then put hers inside it. He helped her up and she tried not to feel dizzy at the press of his skin to hers. It was just a hand, after all.

"Let's go get the box, then," Ty said, smiling. "Before the god of war sees you."

Chapter Seven

CASSIE DIDN'T SPEAK TO HIM ON THE WAY TO ELITE Events. She kept her head turned and seemed more fascinated by what was happening on the sidewalk and streets than she was with him.

Ty glanced at her from time to time but she never looked away from the window. She clenched her phone in one hand, but she didn't look at it. He didn't know if she was still embarrassed by the adult toys, or if she was just shy and didn't know what to say to him.

With Cassie, it could be either. Or at least with the Cassie he was remembering more and more from high school. Always a silent shadow with his cousin. Head down, trying not to attract attention. Unless it'd been just her and Kari, and then she'd been animated. He'd gotten a flash of a memory of one summer when he'd gone over to Kari's house and she'd been in the back-yard by the pool with Cassie.

Cassie had been sitting on the edge in a turquoise one piece, legs swinging in the water. She'd been laughing, head thrown back, joyful. She'd been pretty in that moment. He remembered being surprised by it, which made him ashamed of himself now. Cassie *was* pretty. She'd always been pretty. She'd just hidden it by trying to make herself disappear.

When she'd looked up and seen him that day, she'd slipped into the pool and gone utterly silent. Like now.

"You okay?" he asked, suddenly wanting her to look at him. Wanting to see her face.

She turned. She looked wounded, and it made his gut clench. But she nodded before turning away again.

Ty let out a breath. "You know, if you don't like me, just say so. I'll still help you. But I'll stop wondering how I'm making you uncomfortable."

She swung around again, her eyes wider than before. "I never said I didn't like you."

He shot her a look. "You never said much of anything, actually."

"Sorry." She shrugged. "I don't know what to say. It's the introvert curse."

"You know what to say in your videos."

"That's different. I'm alone when I make those. I'm not really talking to anyone."

"You have almost fifty thousand subscribers. That's a lot of people."

"It is, but they aren't in the room with me. I know it doesn't make sense, but it's easy for me because it's just me. Put me on a stage and tell me to talk to that many people, and I'd run screaming."

"Am I making you uncomfortable?" Because he wanted to know. He liked when she looked at him. When she spoke to him. He wanted her to keep doing so. He wanted to know more about her.

"No."

"Are you sure?"

She sighed. "I know high school was a long time ago, and I don't give a crap about those people anymore, but you were one of the popular guys. Being around you kinda brings it all back in a way."

Shit. "Was I ever mean to you? If so, I'm sorry."

"You weren't. Kari wouldn't have put up with it. But there were some who were."

He squeezed the wheel, wishing he could go back in time and kick some ass. "I'm sorry anyone was ever mean to you. Teenagers can be pricks, that's for sure."

"It was a long time ago, and I don't really think about it. Seeing you jarred some of it loose again. That's all."

He understood. It's why he didn't go back to Bear Creek very often if he could help it. He had his own things that got jarred loose. Things he'd rather not go through again.

"We aren't the same people anymore. I've had a helluva lot of life between my days as a football star and now. That kid might as well live on the moon, he's so far from who I am these days."

She was studying him in a way he didn't think she had since he'd walked into her house yesterday. "I understand that feeling very well. I don't want to be that same kid ever again."

"Me neither."

She laughed softly. It was the first time he'd heard her laugh—other than on her channel—and he liked it. "Kari wanted me to go to the ten-year reunion with her, but I wouldn't do it. The day after, she sent me a link to a video clip of Laura Charles. She was the reunion chair, and she made a tearful speech about how she wished she could go back to high school because life was so much easier then. Not for me, it wasn't."

Ty shook his head. He couldn't imagine wanting to go back. "I remember Laura. Cheerleader, right?"

"Of course. Tiny, perky, the center of attention. I guess life changed pretty dramatically after high school. Life was easy when you were popular. Not so much when you weren't. Or when your momma was the spectacle mine always was."

"I don't think I know your mother."

"Lottie Dixon. Life of the trailer park. Occasional resident of Bear Creek's jail cells when she was drunk and disorderly in public—or having screaming fights with her man *du jour* that resulted in threats being made or weapons being drawn. She's calmer these days, but still a hell raiser."

"I think I missed the spectacle."

She snorted. "You're one of the few then. You don't recall the time Lottie mooned the sheriff at a football game while hollering at everyone to kiss her lily-white ass?"

"Holy shit, that was your mother?"

Cassie folded her arms over her chest. "One and the same. It was delightful growing up with a woman who viewed public displays of her ass as her God-given right."

He was a little shocked at realizing who her mother was, but it made Cassie make sense now that he thought about it. "Yeah, damn, I guess that would have been difficult."

"It might not have been so bad if I hadn't been painfully shy. Though maybe I was shy because of how lacking in shame my mother was. Thankfully, your aunt and uncle didn't view my mother as a reason to keep Kari from being friends with me—though she was never allowed to spend the night with me. I always had to go to her house instead. Which I loved because it was actually a house and it didn't bounce whenever anyone walked through the living room."

"I don't think I knew any of that back then."

"Why would you? You were a senior when we were sophomores. You had your mind on football and girls, not on Kari's weird friend with the crazy mother."

"Honestly, and this doesn't make me proud to say, I didn't pay enough attention to you back then to have any opinion about you. When I noticed you at all, you were the quiet one with Kari."

She nodded. "That was me. You saved me from some mean girls once though. I appreciated it."

"Yeah, I kinda remember that."

"It meant everything to me back then. I didn't thank you because I couldn't speak, but I was grateful. I know you did it because I was Kari's friend, but it helped. They didn't bother me for the rest of the year."

"You're welcome." He heard what she didn't say. "They bothered you after I was gone, though?"

"A little. Kari defended me." She sighed. "I really wish I'd had the courage to defend myself. But I didn't."

"You had a normal reaction to bullying."

"I know. Funny enough, some of those girls are bigger than I am now. Having babies changed their metabolisms. Karma catches up to people sometimes."

The GPS announced they were approaching their destination. Ty turned the truck into a parking lot and pulled up to the guard shack. He rolled the window down, and Cassie leaned over so she could be seen.

"Hi," she said, holding out a badge she'd pulled from her purse. "I'm on my way to pick up some things from the office."

The guard nodded and pressed a button that lifted the arm barring their entry. Ty drove into the garage and up to the level Cassie indicated. When he shut the truck off, she looked at him.

"You don't have to go in with me."

"Actually, I do," he told her. "I'm not letting you carry that shit out by yourself."

"I can handle it. It can't be that much stuff."

He didn't tell her she might be wrong about that. "Still, I'm going."

She gave him a once-over, then shrugged. "You'll definitely create a stir, so why not?"

"A stir?" he asked when they stood on the concrete in front of his truck.

"Oh come on, Ty. You have to know you're attractive. The women I work with will drool all over themselves at"—she waved a hand to encompass his body—"all the muscles and plaid masculinity you've got going on."

"Plaid masculinity?" She was amusing him now.

"Lumberjack is probably more accurate. You've got that plaid shirt unbuttoned over a T-shirt, the scruff of a beard, and you look like you chopped a cord of wood before breakfast."

He snorted as they walked toward the elevators. "I live in an apartment. No wood chopping, I'm afraid."

"Too bad," she declared as they stepped into the elevator. She punched the button to take them to the eighth floor and then leaned back against the steel wall to study him.

He liked that she was looking at him now. That she wasn't avoiding him. He had a sudden picture of stepping into her, pressing her back against the elevator wall, and feeling her soft curves against his body. Then he'd thread his fingers in hers and lift her hands to press them against the wall. When he had her there, he'd press his mouth to her neck and listen to her intake of breath as he skimmed his lips up her soft skin before taking her mouth in a hot, wet kiss.

"Uh-oh," she said teasingly. "You look like you're suddenly wishing you were anywhere but here. Not that I blame you."

He shook himself back to reality. "Not at all."

"Right." She looked like she didn't believe a word he said.

He had a sudden urge to shake her up just a little. "Actually, I was wishing I could see if your lips are as soft as they look."

She blinked. Her cheeks flushed pink. Then her eyes flashed. "Don't you dare," she said, her voice quavering with sudden emotion. "Don't you dare say such a thing to me when we both know you don't mean it."

"How do you know what I mean?" he growled at her. "Are you inside my head?"

She turned away, breaking eye contact. Her arms were folded tightly over her chest. "I don't like being teased about something like that, okay?"

Frustration was beginning to hammer at him. "Again, who said I didn't mean what I fucking said, Cassie?"

The elevators glided to a stop on the eighth floor and the doors opened into a hallway. He stalked out and waited for her to join him. When the doors whisked closed again, he stopped her with a hand on her shoulder before she could walk toward the frosted glass doors that said Elite Events across them.

She spun to face him, her eyes wide and vulnerable. And hurt?

Something in him snapped. He pushed her back against the wall, a hand on her hip while the other tipped her chin up and forced her to look at him.

"I think you're fucking sexy, Cassie Dixon. I don't know what kind of crazy ass shit you've got going on in your head, but there's not anything about your body I don't like. It's true I didn't notice you in high school. I'm noticing you now. I haven't gotten you out of my head for a single minute since I saw you again yesterday." He leaned into her just a little and inhaled her sweet, floral scent. "Maybe this is too much to say, but I'm going to say it anyway. I'd love to strip you out of that cute skirt and spend a few hours exploring that lush body of yours. So you think about that the next time you want to tell me I'm making shit up, okay?"

Chapter Eight

CASSIE COULDN'T FIND HER BREATH TO SPEAK. NOT only that, but what would she say if she could? Tyler Scott, her crush, her dream when she'd been a shy teenager, had his big hand on her hip, his other big hand beneath her chin, and he'd just told her he wanted to take her to bed.

For hours.

Her first reaction was disbelief. Her second was hurt, because why would he keep saying shit like that? Her third was *oh my God, what if he's not kidding?*

His eyes flashed green fire at her. His expression was deadly serious. And he'd nudged his hips into hers just enough that she could feel he was harder in some places than others.

He'd called her body lush. *Lush.*

Like she was something beautiful to be explored, not like she needed to hide her flaws and think about turning the lights out if they got naked together. She was working on her self-esteem and on accepting her body, but she still had moments when she let fear win the battle.

She was instantly wet. It'd been a long time since she'd been with anyone, and her very serviceable vibrator was looking pretty pitiful when compared to what she could feel pressing into her abdomen. Ty was big all over, so it was no surprise—and yet it was, because she'd caused it.

Her.

The elevator whooshed open and Ty took a step back, letting her go. She swallowed as she stared at him.

"Hey, Cassie."

Cassie turned her head to find Janet, one of her coworkers, emerging from the elevator with a tray of coffees from the shop downstairs. Janet was tall, thin, and pretty. Her gaze slewed to Ty and she blinked visibly.

"Hi. I'm Janet."

Ty nodded. "Pleased to meet you. Cassie?"

Cassie shook herself. "Let me help you with the coffees."

"I've got it," Ty said, taking the tray from Janet's hands.

They started toward the frosted doors of Elite. Janet looked over her shoulder at Ty and then back at Cassie. "That was some adult product order you got today. But I think I see why," she whispered loudly. "Didn't know you had a boyfriend."

Cassie knew she should deny Ty was with her, but before she could say a word the doors opened and a client walked out. Then they were inside the office and she didn't want to say it. Not with the way all the women turned toward her and Ty, studying him appreciatively while giving her disbelieving looks. He handed the coffees to Janet, who winked at him before she carried them toward one of the conference rooms. Cassie turned the opposite direction and went toward her cubicle.

Pamela looked up. Her eyes bugged out when she got a look at Ty.

"Where's the crap?" Cassie asked, annoyed at the way everyone looked at her and Ty like it was a mistake.

"Under your desk. Barely." She shook her head. "Honestly, Cass, that was a hell of a mistake to have it delivered here."

"I didn't order any of this stuff," she said, peering under the desk.

"Maybe not," Ty said from behind her. "But let's not be hasty, babe. We might find a few things to try out later."

Cassie glanced at him. He grinned mischievously. She knew hot embarrassment was rising to her cheeks, but there wasn't much she could do about it. Not to mention, it was kinda fun to let her coworkers think Ty was sexing her up. That'd keep them talking for a week. Or more.

"We'll see, honey," she said, barely getting the words out.

Ty snorted. "Get out of the way, sweet cheeks. I'll get the box."

Cassie stepped back and glanced at Pamela, who was looking at her like she'd never really seen her before. Cassie shrugged. It felt good to let Ty be her pretend boyfriend, even if she kinda wanted to kill him for suggesting they were going to use the toys.

Ty tugged the box from under her desk and pulled open the flaps. "Wow," he said.

Cassie peered around his broad torso. "Good heavens… is that a vajankle?"

Ty's head whipped around. "How do you know what a vajankle is?"

"How do you?"

"Because I'm a dude."

Cassie rolled her eyes. "I saw it in a meme. It's pretty disgusting, really."

"Not if you like feet."

Cassie held up a finger. "Not another word. I don't want you to say something that makes me think less of you."

He laughed. "I don't, for the record. Not like that."

"Odin will be here in fifteen minutes, Cassie," Pamela warned. "You need to be gone."

"Leaving now. Is there anything else I need to know about?"

Pamela nodded toward her desk. "You got some mail. I didn't open it."

Cassie snatched the pile of envelopes from the tray on her desk. They were heavy, like they had catalogs in them. She dreaded to think.

"We're leaving. You got that box, babe? Or do you need help?"

He hefted it to his shoulder and balanced it there. She swore she heard a dozen sighs drift across the room. "Nope, I got it. Let's get home and try out the handcuffs."

Cassie's face flamed, but she walked through the office with her head held high, Ty trailing after her like her own personal fantasy man come true. Amelia ducked out of the conference room and halted like she'd crashed into a brick wall. She let her gaze slide over Ty before bringing it to rest on Cassie. Her eyes went cold when she did.

"I don't mind you getting a package here and there," she said. "But that is really too much, Cassie. Please don't let it happen again."

"It's not my stuff, Amelia. Someone's trying to humiliate me."

Amelia sniffed. "Nevertheless."

Anger flared.

"I'll do my best not to let someone I don't even know send me packages at work," she said with a touch of sarcasm. Because she was sick as shit of everyone assuming she'd do something so stupid and embarrassing as to order a vajankle at work. She was a woman, for heaven's sake. Vajankles were male fetishes. They even had life-like pussy openings for a man to stick his junk in. It was *not* a female toy.

"You don't have to be rude," Amelia said imperiously.

"I'm sorry. I'm not trying to be. But I don't know how I'm going to stop anyone from sending me crazy crap. I suggest you inform the mail room not to accept packages for me. I'll pick them up at the post office if necessary."

Amelia nodded stiffly. "That will work."

The frosted doors opened and Odin sailed in. Ten minutes early. He stopped short when he saw her, his face twisting in a frown. "What is *she* doing here?" he demanded. "She needs to go. Now."

Cassie started to say she was leaving, but Ty stepped in front of her like a bear guarding his cave. "Her name is Cassie. You'll speak respectfully about her and to her, or not at all. Understand me?"

Odin was tall, but he wasn't broad. Ty dwarfed him. And Ty wasn't looking particularly friendly at the moment.

"I, uh—" Odin began. "Yes. I mean—"

"We were just leaving," Cassie said, cutting off his stammering reply. "Y'all have a great day now."

She sailed through the doors and down the hall to the elevator. Ty was right behind her when she stabbed the button. Her heart hammered and her pulse raced. There was sweat popping up on her skin, and she felt hot and sticky instead of cute now. She damned sure didn't feel attractive. The fun of pretending Ty was her boyfriend was over.

"Nobody has the right to speak to you like that, Cassie," Ty said when they stepped into the elevator. He still had that damned box on his shoulder. It was big, and there was so much more inside than she'd yet seen.

Tears sprang to her eyes. Stupid tears. After a lifetime of living with Lottie Dixon showing her ass to the world and generally being a drama queen, one would think that a box of adult toys was a mere blip on the radar.

But it wasn't. It was a personal attack, just like when she'd been a kid and people had made fun of her for her weight, or her thrift store clothing (before it was cool to shop at thrift stores), or her mother's antics. It felt the same, and she didn't like it. Didn't like that some asshole could send her back to those days as if they'd never ended.

"Hey." Ty looked concerned as he studied her. "I'm sorry if I crossed a line by insinuating I was your boyfriend. Or when I threatened the Norse god of war. I didn't like the way he treated you."

She dropped her gaze and studied her feet. "I know. And thank you."

"So what's wrong then?"

"I just…" She blew out a breath and willed back tears. "I don't know who's doing this to me or why. It makes me feel like I did when I was a kid. I don't like it. That's all."

He shifted the box on his shoulder and looped an arm around her. Pulled her in close to his rock hard chest. She didn't want to resist him, so she didn't. It felt good to stand close to him. Like nothing could ever get past him to hurt her.

"I'm going to find him, Cassie," he said softly. "And when I do, he's going to wish he'd never heard your name."

Chapter Nine

HE DIDN'T LIKE SEEING CASSIE CRY. NOT THAT SHE WAS, but she was on the verge of it.

Ty ushered her to his truck, shoved the box of toys into the backseat, and opened the passenger door for her. She got inside quietly and belted in. She didn't look at him.

He closed the door softly and went around to his side. "What do you want for lunch?" he asked, deciding that was a safe topic for the moment.

She shot him a glance. "You still want to go to lunch?"

"Hell, yeah. You see these muscles? They have to eat."

She didn't even crack a smile. "I don't care what we eat. I'm not even sure I'm all that hungry."

"You have to eat, Cassie."

She made a noise that sounded like derision. "Clearly, I don't. I could miss a few meals."

He could feel his temper rising. "First, that's not how it works. If you want to lose weight—and I'm not saying

I think you have to—you have to eat regular meals, not starve it off. And second, you need to stop saying shit like that about yourself. You don't say it on your channel, and you wouldn't say it about any of your viewers. At least treat yourself as well as you want them to treat themselves."

She let out a sigh, her body seeming to deflate a little as she did so. "You're right. I'm just feeling a bit overwhelmed." She glanced into the backseat. "Somebody spent a lot of money to humiliate me at work. Why? And how did they find my work address anyway? I don't talk about where I work on my channel."

"Did you ever mention what your job was?"

"Maybe. I don't know."

"That's enough, Cassie. For someone who's determined. If they could find your home address, they could figure out where you worked. All they'd have to do is call every event planning firm in town until a receptionist agreed to put them through to Cassandra Dixon. Then they'd know, wouldn't they?"

"It makes perfect sense, but I didn't think of it that way."

"It's my job to think about things like that."

She nibbled her lip. He turned his gaze back to the road before he got hard again. He still didn't know why he'd pushed her into the wall and told her what he wanted to do to her, but it was too late to call the horse back to the barn. The information was out there. And now he couldn't stop thinking about how jiggly and perfect her tits were.

"Is that what you did in the Marines?"

"Not exactly. Look, I need to apologize for what happened after we got out of the elevator. Not because I didn't mean it," he added, "but because I didn't have your permission to touch you."

"Dear God, are you real?" she asked after a long moment.

He shot her a look. "Of course. And part two of that response is… what do you mean? Has someone touched you without permission?"

"Pretty much the definition of modern dating for women, Ty. If you go out with enough men, you'll meet at least one who feels he's entitled to whatever he wants because he bought dinner. Not that I have personal experience, but I know plenty of women who do."

"It's not how I operate. I lost my temper earlier."

She didn't look at him. "It's okay. I, um, liked that you were so passionate."

He didn't know what to say to that, other than he could show her more if she wanted him to. Which wasn't the best idea, probably. He pointed at a Korean restaurant up ahead. "How about that one?"

"I don't think I've ever had Korean food," she said, peering at the sign. "But sure. I'm game."

"Really? Do you have any feelings about fermented cabbage?"

"Uh, not that I'm aware. Should I?"

He couldn't help but grin. "I'm about to show you the wonders of kimchi then. Fair warning though—you won't want to breathe on anyone for a few hours or so."

She smiled this time. "Sounds interesting."

"It is. Come on."

He pulled into the parking lot and found a spot. He met her on the sidewalk since she didn't wait for him to open the door for her. They went inside, let the hostess seat them, and ordered drinks while they looked at the menu. Ty explained what the dishes were as Cassie looked them over and tried to pronounce a few.

"It all looks good—but I'm overwhelmed."

"I get that. How about trying the bulgogi then? It's probably the most popular dish, and you can have chicken, beef, or pork. It's not especially strong flavored, but it's good. There's sesame oil, soy, garlic, and sugar in the marinade."

She was watching him with a half-smile on her face. "You really know a lot about Korean food."

He grinned at her. "I like food. Can't cook though, so I eat out a lot. And I've been to Korea a few times for the job."

"Really? Korea?"

"Definitely. There's a lot happening in South Korea, plus it's close to China—and then there's that whole North Korea thing. Shit happens, believe me."

The waitress brought their drinks, took their order, and then returned with the *banchan,* or side dishes, piled high with kimchi and other fermented or marinated foods. Cassie looked at it all in wonder.

"This is part of the meal?"

Ty picked up his chopsticks and took a small slice of omelet. "Yep. Great, right?"

Cassie picked up a fork instead. "I never learned how to use chopsticks. I probably should."

"Takes practice, but you can learn to be proficient."

She tried a little of everything, scrunched her face up at some of it, but didn't cough or gag or act like the food was terrible. She liked kimchi. Wasn't so sure about the fermented fish cake. Liked the cucumber kimchi and the cold noodles with vegetables, the pickled radish, the eggs and the gelatin. By the time the main course came, she'd had a bit of everything.

Ty enjoyed watching her try Korean food for the first time. A person's willingness to try things that were strange to them, as well as their reaction to the food, could tell you a lot. What he learned about Cassie was that she was open-minded, curious, and willing to experiment. Bold in her own way, which she'd never be able to see about herself. But she was.

"So what did you do in the Marines?" she asked after she'd had a bite of her bulgogi—which she proclaimed unbelievably delicious.

He couldn't tell her what he'd really done, so he settled for a vague account. "I was in intel. Intelligence gathering," he explained. "It was our job to get the lay of the land for Marine Expeditionary Forces."

Force Recon was the reconnaissance arm of the Marines, but they also went on raids in support of the mission. They were the ones who provided commanders with the intel necessary for the larger force to succeed.

He'd loved the job—until he hadn't. Until things went catastrophically wrong. Half his team died on a mission. They'd walked into an ambush, and he'd never stopped thinking that if he hadn't ignored his gut that day, it wouldn't have happened. They'd still be alive, and he'd probably still be in the Corps.

"Was it dangerous?" she asked, watching him with those big green eyes he wanted to drown in.

"Sometimes," he said, taking a sip of his water because he needed something to soothe the sudden dryness in his throat.

"Kari is very proud of you, you know," she said,

taking a bite of bulgogi, oblivious to the tension twisting inside him.

He pushed it down and nodded. "She's the best. She's always been supportive."

"She likes calling you a jarhead."

He laughed. "She does. I don't mind."

"I looked up why Marines are called jarheads. There are a few theories. One, it's a World War II thing. Something about a high leather collar on the uniform. Two, it might be the haircut, which is flat on the top and square, though I notice you don't seem to have kept that style."

"Nope. Too much maintenance. I like getting a haircut when I feel like it."

"Three," she said, ticking her fingers. "It could also refer to a mule. Apparently they were once called jarheads because they're stubborn. And there were a few other theories as well. I gave up after that."

He laughed. "Why did you look it up in the first place?"

Her gaze dropped to her bowl. She shrugged. "I wanted to know what it meant. I like learning things."

"Fair enough." He studied her as she ate her next bite. She was very deliberate about it. She savored her food, and he liked that. "So why the YouTube channel?" he asked.

"I, uh…" She sighed. "I was in a relationship for a while. It didn't work out. I was kind of depressed when we broke up, so I started watching YouTube. I was trying to learn new makeup tricks, trying to make myself feel better. That's when I realized I was pretty good at makeup and clothes for bigger girls. I knew some things that others didn't. So I kind of went a little crazy learning how starting a channel was done. The equipment needed to film, the editing, everything. I started with a ring light, a tripod, and my phone, but now I use a digital camera mounted on a tripod for most things."

He wanted to ask about the relationship, but he thought that might be too much so he stuck to the channel. "You like making videos."

She nodded. "I feel like myself when I'm filming something. Or the best version of myself I wish I could always be. I'm not shy or scared, and I don't feel like everyone's staring and making fun of me. I know some are, but it doesn't feel real because it's not face to face." She frowned. "Or at least it didn't until I got that rat. Now I wonder who hates me so much they'd bring me a dead rat."

"Could it be the ex?"

She shook her head. "No. We broke up over a year ago, right before I moved up here. He contacted me a couple of months ago to tell me he was getting married, but that's the only time I've heard from him since we split. Kari used to run into him sometimes, and she'd tell me about it."

"A Bear Creek guy then." He'd have to ask Kari about it later.

"Yes."

He wanted to ask why it didn't work out between them, but that was more of a personal interest than a professional one. Which meant he needed to leave it alone.

"Do I know him?"

"I don't think so. His family moved to town my junior year, and you were gone by then. Dylan Webb is his name."

"No, I don't know him. Was it serious between you?"

Her gaze dropped. "I thought so at the time. He was, uh, my first. We were together almost five years. Turns out I wanted to get out of Bear Creek and he didn't."

He was glad it wasn't someone he knew who'd been her first. Doing the math told him that she'd been a virgin until she was twenty-four. A lot of stupid guys back home, apparently.

"I'm sorry it didn't work out."

"I'm not," she said with a glint of steel in her eyes. "Dylan wasn't good for me. I stayed with him for too long because I thought he was the only man who'd ever be interested in me. Kari tried to tell me, but I didn't believe her."

Ty hated that for her. So much. "Then I'm glad you figured that out."

"Me too." She took a sip of her water. "It took a while, though. Kari never liked him much, but she knew better than to try and get between us. I'm embarrassed about it now, quite honestly. And, like I said, I was depressed for a bit when it ended. I moved up here, but every day I wanted to run back home. I didn't, though."

"No, you found YouTube instead."

She smiled. "Thank God I stuck it out. I'm much happier now than I was then."

"You said it was the rat that made the harassment seem real, but not the emails. Why didn't those bother you?"

"I wouldn't say they didn't bother me, but it's kind of like getting spam, you know? You don't acknowledge it or click on anything, and they go away."

"Then why did you print everything?"

"It seemed like the smart thing to do. Just in case. I moved the originals to a folder. I almost deleted them, but I didn't. I really want to, though."

"I'm glad you didn't. When you know how to look for it, there are things in the header that aren't on the printed page. After lunch, we should head over to the police station and file a report."

Her face went a little pale. "Is that necessary? I mean it's not like I know who it is. And it's one rat. Maybe it's a child's prank gone wrong. If I get something else like it, then I could report it."

"It's necessary now, Cassie. Besides, are you forgetting the sex toys? That's not a child's prank."

She looked troubled. "No, I know. But can't you help me instead? The police have enough to do."

"I'm going to help you, but you still need to report it. I'm a private contractor, and I can only do so much. You need a record of the harassment in case we need to get a restraining order against someone."

She was toying with her food now. "Okay. I understand."

He frowned. "Is there some reason you don't want to go to the police?"

Her brows drew together and he wondered what she was about to say. But then she shook her head. "No, of course not."

"Good. Now finish your bulgogi and let's go file that report."

Chapter Ten

CASSIE HAD ENJOYED LUNCH, DESPITE THE BOX OF TOYS and the stack of mail waiting in Ty's truck. She'd put it aside to deal with later, but then reality crashed down on her when he'd said they needed to go to the police. She hadn't forgotten that he wanted her to.

She just hadn't expected him to drive her over there himself.

She knew he was right, but she'd been avoiding it. She hadn't told Kari, but she'd called the police after the pizzas kept coming. They'd told her there was nothing they could do, and it was probably a mix up at the store. Someone taking an address down wrong.

It wasn't, but she'd gotten the hint. The police didn't want to be bothered about little shit like online harassment when there were bigger problems in the world. Maybe a rat would make a difference, but she wasn't holding her breath. It was *one* rat.

Ty parked at the station, and she waited for him to come around and help her out of the truck. When she was standing on the sidewalk looking up at the building, her stomach swirling with butterflies, Ty touched her shoulder to get her attention.

She jumped higher than she should have, and he frowned. "Why are you uncomfortable, Cassie?"

"It's nothing. I just… I have bad memories of police stations. My mom was always in and out of the sheriff's office for one thing or another. Scarred me for life, I think."

He looked sympathetic. "I'll be with you. Just tell the truth about what happened, write out a statement, and you'll be done."

She tugged in a breath and nodded. It *was* her mother and her history with the police that bothered her, but it was something else, too.

Brian Woodruff. He worked at this station, and she'd broken up with him after seven dates. It wasn't that he'd done anything wrong. It was just that she hadn't enjoyed their dates very much the more they'd gone out, and she hadn't wanted to repeat past mistakes.

They'd met when he'd worked an event that Amelia had set up. Off duty cops often worked the events because the pay for a few hours was so good. It was a nice addition to the bottom line.

Brian had shown interest in her, and she'd been flattered. He'd asked her out, it'd gone well, and she'd agreed to go again. But somewhere along the way, she'd realized that Brian's favorite subject was Brian.

She'd told Kari that Brian was too outgoing for her, and it was true, but it was also the way he'd treated her as if she was nothing more than a sounding board for his life. He'd ask about her day, but he'd soon steer the conversation to what he'd done, and it never went back again.

She'd envisioned her life with Dylan, and she'd known history was on the verge of repeating itself. She hadn't told Kari because she hadn't wanted her to worry.

The night she'd told Brian maybe they should see other people, he'd looked at her like she'd grown another head. Like he couldn't believe she didn't want to discuss more of his fabulousness. He'd been polite enough, but they hadn't spoken since. She still felt guilty, but really, he needed someone who thought the sun rose and set out of his ass every day.

And now she was walking into his station to report that someone had sent her a dead rat, ten pizzas, and a box of sex toys. It was humiliating to say the least. If she was lucky, he wouldn't be working.

Ty led the way inside. They walked up to the desk sergeant, and Cassie told him what she wanted. He asked her to wait a minute and made a call.

A minute later, two officers emerged from the rear of the station and headed for where Cassie and Ty had taken a seat. Cassie stiffened as her gaze met Brian's. Of course he'd be on duty today. Just her luck.

He wasn't as tall or broad as Ty, but he was still a big man. Muscular. His hair was cropped in a buzz cut, and his arms bulged when he folded them over his chest.

The man with him looked a lot more friendly. "I'm Officer Jones. This is Officer Woodruff. You wish to report harassment, ma'am?"

"Yes," Cassie said, her voice little more than a whisper. "I've been getting threatening emails, and someone put a rat in a box on my doorstep."

Officer Jones nodded. "All right. If you'll come with me, we'll go to an interview room and take your report."

Cassie reached over and took Ty's hand, wrapping it tightly in hers. He didn't pull away or look at her questioningly, bless him.

"Can I bring my friend?"

"If you're more comfortable."

"I am. Thank you."

Brian gave Ty a once-over but didn't say a word as they followed him and Officer Jones to the interview room. Once there, Cassie explained—with some prodding from Ty—about the emails, the pizzas, the rat, and the adult toys.

The officers didn't blink, or smirk, and she was thankful for that. Even Brian sat there looking serious and made notes. He glanced at Ty from time to time but didn't ask any questions.

When it was over, Officer Jones asked if there was anything else. Anything she'd forgotten. She shook her head, and it was over.

Officer Jones gave her a card with his number. They walked her and Ty to the secure door with bars on the windows that led to the waiting area, and then Jones and Brian turned and walked away.

Once she was on the sidewalk with Ty again, she felt like she could breathe.

"You okay?" Ty asked.

She looked up into eyes that held concern. It made her more than a little melty inside. And guilty since she hadn't told him about Brian.

"I'm okay. They aren't going to do anything about any of it though."

"No, not really. They have bigger things to worry about. But if something else happens, if we discover who's behind the harassment, it'll help to have a police report when you need to have a lawyer go after them."

"Thank you, Ty. That was uncomfortable, and I wouldn't have done it on my own."

He smiled. "I know. Kari told me you wouldn't. But now it's done, and you've got a case number as well as a phone number to call if you need anything else."

She'd tucked Officer Jones's card into her purse. She was thankful that Brian hadn't offered his. "I'd rather call you."

"That's what I want you to do, too. I told you I'm going to help you. That hasn't changed."

She really was glad. Just last night she hadn't wanted him involved, and now she didn't know what she'd do without him.

He shot her a grin as they got into his truck. "You ready to get home and go through your toy collection? See what kind of kinky shit you got?"

"Not really. But I guess I need to repack it if I'm going to send it all back, right?"

"Right."

He started the truck and backed out of the parking spot, whistling softly.

It took her a minute before she turned to him. "Wait a second—are you whistling Rhianna's "S&M"?"

He winked. "That's the one."

Chapter Eleven

THE BOX CONTAINED A VARIETY OF DILDOS, ANAL BEADS, lubes, handcuffs, whips, a vajankle, a sex doll—female— and leather restraints. Ty looked at all of it laid out on Cassie's dining room table and shook his head.

"That must have cost a fortune. Someone spent a lot of money for that box."

There was an invoice, but the sender and total were obscured. A gift purchase, apparently. And non-refundable. Ty thought Dax could learn more about who'd sent it, but maybe not.

Cassie leaned against the kitchen counter, arms folded beneath her generous breasts, nibbling her lower lip, staring at everything. "I don't understand why anyone would go to those lengths just to make me look bad at work. Unless…"

"Unless what?"

She frowned at him. "This stuff was sent to work. The rat was sent here, along with the pizzas and the single dildo. What if they aren't related? Maybe Kelly Cosmetics is behind this one. Not the order," she added.

"I don't think they'd do that. But what if they had no problem doxxing where I worked to their fans? I haven't seen anything, but it doesn't mean it didn't happen."

He nodded. "Maybe. I'll get my team to check for anything with your personal information making its way around."

It'd be pretty stupid of them, but anything was possible, even with big companies. And the way that punk Odin had acted earlier when he'd seen Cassie—as if she'd been something nasty he'd discovered stuck to the sole of his designer shoe. Ty wouldn't put a stunt like this past a toady like Odin.

Time to get Dax looking up the man. That ought to be fun.

"What's Odin's real name?"

Cassie blinked. "You think it was him?"

"Not necessarily, but we need to look at him. Do you know his name?"

She rolled her eyes. "No. He's one of those dramatic first-name-only types. He's a flamboyant attention-seeker. I can't really see him doing something that he wouldn't get credit for, but who knows? Maybe getting credit from his boss is enough."

"Hard to say. I'll get it checked out."

She tilted her head to look at him. "Kari said you worked for a private firm. But is that true? Because it sounds like you work for the FBI or something."

He laughed. "Kari's right. We have resources. That's all. The boss knows people."

"Sounds like a good boss to have."

Ty couldn't help but nod. "He is. He saved me when he offered me a job after the Marines."

Why the hell had he said that? He never talked

about why he'd walked away from the Marines the first chance he'd gotten. Or how Ian Black had offered him a lifeline when he'd thought he'd lost his way. It was personal.

"Then I'm glad he offered you a job. Did you have to take time off to come help me today?"

He shook his head. "It doesn't quite work that way. This job isn't your typical 9-to-5, and we don't have regular hours."

She sighed. "That's the kind of job I want. Not a typical 9-to-5. And *not* a job where I go to an office and deal with a narcissist all day."

"How did you end up at Elite Events anyway?"

"I worked for an event planner in Bear Creek. She ended up closing, but she recommended me to Elite. Amelia hired me, and I moved up here a year ago. It hasn't all been bad. Amelia knows her business. So long as you get results, she's content to leave you alone. She can be a bit self-absorbed, though."

"But you'd leave if you could."

"I would. Amelia is high-strung, and she can be a pain in the butt sometimes. Plus, I feel like my channel has a real chance, and I want to do it full time. But I need more growth first." She frowned at the collection on the table. "I never expected anything like this. I guess I should have. Having your own channel puts you in front of people, and you don't know who those people are. Some people watch content on YouTube exclusively, and they get invested in it. In the people making it. And if you make them angry, they can turn on you."

"I don't think this is a crank delivery, Cassie. Too expensive, unless the sender is also a hacker who steals credit card numbers online. Possible, of course."

She reached for one of the toys and picked it up. It was a clitoral suction vibrator. Something inside him responded to the sight of her holding it. She turned it over in her hands before putting it down and picking up a life-like dong with a suction cup. It was thick, veined, and long. Seeing her hands wrapped around it made his throat dry.

"Good lord, who uses these things?" She didn't take her eyes off the toy.

He swallowed, imagining watching her use it on herself. Except he'd rather use his than watch her fuck a fake dick. "People who want to have a little adventure, I guess."

"Or don't have a real penis in their life," she said with a frown.

He almost laughed at her naïveté. "Not necessarily. What if someone wants to enjoy two dicks but only has one available? It's a way to have, uh, a ménage experience without the third person."

She looked a little shocked. "Oh. Right. Wow." She set the dildo down hurriedly. "I think I need to pack all this up and send it back."

"Why? It's paid for." He picked up a clitoral vibrator. The same one she'd been holding a moment ago. "Pick out the good stuff you want and drop the box at a thrift store collection site."

Her eyes widened. "I, um, didn't think of that. I'm not sure I want to keep anything, um, you know…"

Obviously, she wasn't comfortable discussing it with him. He got that. "Look, I need to get going soon. It's up to you, but I'd say you should keep some shit that you might want or think you might want. Some asshole spent a shit ton of money to send this stuff. You might as well enjoy some of it on them, right? Think about it tonight. Whatever you don't want, box it up and tape it shut. I'll drop it off at a collection site for you in the next few days so you don't have to worry about it." He nodded at the pile of mail she'd yet to open. "Do you want to open that with me here, or do it later?"

She picked up one of the envelopes. "I'll do it now."

He held out a hand. "Here. Let me open it." He took out his pocket knife and cut the envelope before handing it back.

Cassie pulled out a catalog. She turned it to him. "Adam and Eve. Figures. As if I don't have enough sex toys right now."

She pushed the stack at him and he sliced them all so she could pull out the contents. All of them were adult catalogs, some for fetishes like BDSM, and others for people who were overweight. Cassie tossed the last one down on the table like it'd personally insulted her before picking them all up and taking them to the recycle bin.

"You okay?" he asked.

Her eyes flashed anger. "Yes. Fine. Just pissed that someone thinks this is all it takes to make me, I dunno, *quit*. I won't quit. That's what they don't understand. I'm not quitting because what I do helps people—and it helps *me*. I feel better about who I am. Most of the time, anyway. I'm not giving that up."

"That's good." He went over and put his hands on her shoulders. He wasn't quite prepared for the zing of touching her. He wanted more, but this wasn't the time. "I had fun at lunch."

"I did too. Thanks for introducing me to Korean food."

"Don't hesitate to call or text me, Cassie. For anything."

"I won't."

"I mean it. Don't tell me you will and then you don't. I'll call Kari to tattle on you."

She laughed. "Fine. I'll text you something later just for the hell of it."

"I'll be back tomorrow afternoon for the box. Maybe we can get dinner."

She was so pretty when she smiled up at him like she was doing now. "I'd like that."

"Good." He hesitated—and then he thought, *why not?* He pressed his lips to her forehead before stepping away. It felt right, and she hadn't flinched or stiffened. He took that as a good sign. "Lock the door behind me. Don't open it for any deliveries. Let them leave it on the porch."

She walked him to the door and stood on the threshold while he went down the sidewalk. He turned at the bottom. "Inside, Red."

A furrow appeared between her eyes. "Red?"

"Your hair. It's not quite red, but in the right light, it is. I think it's beautiful."

She dropped her gaze shyly before looking at him again. "Thank you."

"You're welcome. Now get inside, Red, and don't open the door until tomorrow when it's light out."

"Aye, aye, Cap'n." She took a step back and started to close the door. She hesitated when it was partway closed. "Good night, Ty."

"'Night, Cassie."

The door closed. He listened for the locks. When he was satisfied, he got into his truck and reversed out of the parking space. He might be heading home alone, but he knew he'd be thinking about the way she'd been holding that dildo for the rest of the night.

Chapter Twelve

Cassie got to work filming one of her videos for release on Sunday. She had some new outfits to try on, so she set them up and got busy doing the changes and filming the jumps and other fun stuff she put in the videos.

Basically, she held up the clothes one by one, dropped them on the floor, and then jumped like she was jumping into the outfit. Then she had to painstakingly dress in the clothing and begin filming again at the exact point where she'd jumped.

The idea was to make it look like she'd jumped into the outfit. When done right with the editing, the transitions were seamless and the finished video was professional and eye-catching.

She tried to do new videos at least three times a week. More if she could. But if she could do even more, that would be better because more videos equaled more money. More money got her to her goals sooner. She also filmed a makeup transformation video for TikTok. Those were very popular, and they got eyes on her

YouTube channel, though the demographics for both platforms were a bit different.

She checked the comments, wary about what she might find. She'd gotten to where she didn't read the mean ones anymore. If she saw words like *fat* or *troll* or *butt ugly*, she skimmed right past it. But today's comments were the usual mix of excitement and disbelief, with a few disgruntled men complaining about how there was no way she was the same person from the beginning to the end. No matter how many times she filmed herself putting on the makeup from start to finish for YouTube, the TikTok comments were convinced she was two separate people.

The beauty of makeup-free skin, bad lighting, and unflattering camera angles. She really could make herself look awful. But then she looked like a model when she was done. That was her favorite part. You could be a size 14 or an 18 or a 22 and still look pretty. There was room for everyone in this world, and she was determined to prove it to all the women who'd always felt like she had.

Like she *did*, because she still felt that way more often than she liked. But, dammit, she was trying. She knew that being skinny wouldn't change her life or make all her problems go away, but that didn't mean she didn't have to fight her tendency to criticize herself. She always fought that, and she tried to be aware of where it sprang from.

She thought of Ty and how it'd felt to pretend like he was her boyfriend today. On the one hand, it had been fun. On the other, it had made her feel sort of sad because all it did was remind her of her desperate crush on him when they'd been kids. His only impression of her from back then was as a silent girl who stood next to Kari with her head down and her eyes on the floor.

But what about that moment in the hallway outside of Elite today? He'd backed her into the wall. Told her he wanted to strip her naked and spend hours in bed with her. And he'd been aroused when he'd said it. She'd felt the evidence of it.

She wanted to call Kari and discuss every single moment, but she wasn't going to talk about her lust for her bestie's cousin with said bestie. Nor was she going to mention the size of his package as it had pressed against her, or the way she'd gone absolutely liquid inside when he'd put the image in her head of using that realistic dong with the suction cup while she got to lick him like a delicious ice cream cone at the same time.

He'd told her to choose some things to keep. She wasn't going to do it, because *ewww*, but she couldn't seem to stop thinking about it. Finally, she logged off and went back downstairs to the dining room table where everything still lay. She wasn't naïve, but she also didn't peruse adult catalogs or order things from them. She'd gotten her vibrator from Amazon. That was enough, wasn't it?

Except, wow, a vibrator that mimicked softly sucking on her clit with little puffs of air? Maybe she needed that. Maybe whoever had sent her this box as a cruel joke had also done her a favor. Dylan hadn't liked giving oral sex, though he'd definitely liked receiving it.

Cassie swiped the little vibrator and set it aside. She wasn't interested in whips, no matter that Ty had been humming Rihanna's song earlier, but the handcuffs were interesting. Edible glitter didn't sound right, so that was a no. The vajankle was a *definite* no.

She went through the pile of stuff, her pace quickening as she forced herself to make snap decisions. It occurred to her that she was Marie Kondo-ing adult toys, except she was deciding what *might* bring her joy if she used it.

Once she went through everything, she piled the things she wasn't keeping into the box and taped it shut. Then she took everything she'd kept upstairs and set it on her dresser before getting ready for bed. She snagged the vibrator on the way back and put it on the bed as she climbed in between the sheets. And then, because she'd said she would, she texted Ty.

It's 10:30 and I'm going to bed.

A few moments later, a reply came. *Ty: You texted.*

Cassie: I said I would. Don't act so surprised.

Ty: I'm surprised.

Cassie: I'm pretty good at texting. Just ask Kari.

Ty: I'm glad you did. I was thinking about you.

Her heart thumped. *Good things, I hope.* Because what was she supposed to say to that?

Ty: Definitely good things. I was watching some of your videos.

Cassie: Why? You don't need makeup tips, do you?

He sent back a laughing-so-hard-I'm-crying emoji. *No, definitely not. I like listening to you talk. And I like how sexy you are when you're in your element.*

Cassie eyed the vibrator. Her heart hammered and she was starting to sweat just a little bit. *Careful, or I'll think you're flirting.*

Ty: I'm definitely flirting, Red. Did you go through the box?

Cassie gulped. Why not? *I did. I kept some things, like you said.*

Ty: Oh shit, now I really want to know what you kept.

Before she could change her mind, she snapped a pic of the clitoral vibrator lying on her duvet and sent it. She felt naughty, but that was part of the fun. It was definitely going to make using this thing later an experience to remember.

Or so she hoped.

Ty: Is that all?

Cassie: No. But I'm not showing you those. Not even sure I'll keep them very long. Hoping this one works out though.

Ty: You planning to try it tonight?

She stared at his words. What the hell was she doing? But also, why the hell not? She was an adult. So was he. There was no reason for him to pretend interest. There must be dozens of women he could have naughty texts with. Yet he was texting her. Asking her these questions.

Maybe it was time to stop questioning and start playing.

Cassie: Maybe. Not sure yet.

Ty: You could use it now. Tell me all about it.

She gulped. *Are you always like this?*

Ty: I'm a man. The thought of you pleasuring yourself makes me hot—and makes me want to be there with you, using my tongue instead of a vibrator.

Oh, her cheeks were on fire. And she was wet, too. So wet. She pressed her legs together, her pussy aching with the need to be touched. It'd been a long time since anyone had touched her.

In fact, Dylan was the only man who ever had. She wasn't someone who jumped into a sexual relationship overnight. She had hang-ups, and it took time to get used to the idea of being with a man. And yet she could imagine herself with Ty quite easily. Probably because of how long she'd worshipped him from afar when she'd been a shy teenager.

Which brought up a question she had to ask him.

Cassie: Please don't take this the wrong way, but why? It was only yesterday that you saw me again for the first time in over a decade.

She waited for the three dots to appear, but her phone rang instead. It was Ty. She answered, though she almost didn't. "Hi," she said, then rolled her eyes at how lame that sounded. But what else was she supposed to say? *Yo, dawg?*

"Cassie," he growled, his voice deep and sexy. "Do you want to know what I'm doing right now?"

"Um, yes?"

"It's dirty. You ready, or would you rather not?"

Her throat was dry. "I'm ready."

"I'm lying in bed. I'm naked beneath the sheets, and I'm getting hard. I'm about to push the covers back and take care of business. Because of you, Cassie. Because you're fucking sexy as hell and I'm hooked on the idea of exploring your curves."

Her heart hammered. Arousal swirled in her belly, her core. But doubt was there too, chipping away at her confidence. "I don't understand why. I really don't. You didn't pay any attention to me in high school. You didn't know I existed unless I was with Kari."

"Hate to break it to you, babe, but this isn't high school. That was a long time ago, and neither of us are the same people. We aren't strangers, because of Kari, and yet we are. No, I didn't notice you in high school, and I didn't remember who you were at first when Kari asked me to check on you. She was seriously pissed at me, by the way. I have no excuse, except that you never spoke to me and it was a long time ago. But the second I laid eyes on you again, I was intrigued. If I'd met you at a bar, I'd have asked for your number. If I'd met you at the grocery store, or a restaurant, or a coffee shop—wherever—I'd have asked for your number. I'd have asked you out, Cassie, and I'd have spent hours talking to you and getting to know you. And maybe I've leapfrogged over a whole lot of things I should have done before getting to this point, but our circumstances are a bit different than if we'd just met. Still, if I'm making you uncomfortable in any way, I'll dial it back to a normal level. But I definitely want to get to know you, and I definitely want to explore your sexy curves. I can wait until you're ready for it."

When she didn't say anything, because she was still trying to process everything he'd said and formulate a response that wasn't idiotic, he chuckled softly. "I guess I should also consider the idea you will never be ready, and this attraction isn't mutual, huh? Jesus, I'm making a mess of this. I'll let you go. Tomorrow, I'll take the box and drop it off for you. I won't say anything else about toys or how sexy you are, and we can forget this ever happened if that's what you want."

"I don't want that at all," she blurted, panic rising at every word coming out of his mouth. She gripped the phone and willed herself to tell him the truth. "I don't always know what to say, but I'm not upset at anything you said. I have a hard time accepting that you could be attracted to someone like me, but I'm working on it."

"Someone like you? Cassie, honey, where's that beautiful babe who tells women they're sexy the way they are and they need to own it? Because you are sexy the way you are, and you definitely need to own it."

She closed her eyes and tried to find Cassandra deep inside. Cassandra was comfortable in front of the camera, and she radiated confidence. And wasn't this situation sort of like filming? It was just her, alone, with her audience on the other end where she couldn't see.

"You're right," she said. "I'm not perfect and I know it, but who is? I just… I have a lot of baggage, Ty. My whole life, people have told me I was too fat or too quiet or too stupid. That I could be so pretty if I'd just lose weight, or if I'd smile more. The list goes on, and I won't bore you with it. But my channel is me working through those issues, and sometimes that hurt little girl inside has a hard time accepting that anyone can like the real her. Because I'm not really that woman on camera. She's me, but a better me. The real me still has doubts and fears, and she's afraid of getting hurt."

"I like you, Cassie. I'm attracted to you. I want to go out with you, and I want to know you better. Kari loves you, which tells me you're pretty terrific. I want to find it out for myself, okay?"

"Okay," she whispered.

"Okay. Good."

"You aren't making me uncomfortable, Ty," she added. "I just wasn't sure why you'd think of me that way."

"Now you know."

"Yes." She eyed the vibrator. Picked it up and slid the switch on. Air pulsed gently from the toy. Her confidence surged. She *was* sexy, dammit. "Do you still want to know how this thing works?"

He groaned. "I do, but I'm not sure I can take it."

She couldn't help but smile. "Do you want me to tell

you all about it later, or would you rather get a live report?"

"You don't have to do that, Cassie. I don't want you feeling like I expect it."

She put the phone on speaker and slid her panties off. "I want to," she said. "And I want to do it now."

He swore. "You realize I'm going to jerk off while you use that thing, right?"

"I hope so," she breathed. And then she slid the vibrator into place and pretended the suction on her clit was Ty…

Chapter Thirteen

Ty couldn't wait to see Cassie later, but first he had some things to do at BDI. He drove all the way to work with a hard-on because he kept thinking about the sounds Cassie had made last night when she'd started to use that vibrator.

He'd blown far too quickly, but it'd been worth it. Cassie had seemed surprised at the sensations, and then she'd gotten into it. He'd heard her panting breaths, her soft moans, and her gasps when she came. She wasn't loud, but he'd have never expected that from her anyway.

She was Cassie. Quiet, shy, and brave at the same time. He knew it'd taken a lot for her to get off with him listening in, but he'd fucking loved it.

He'd have loved it even better if he'd been the one causing her to make those sounds. He didn't know why he'd fallen into this utter fascination with her so quickly, but he had. He wanted to spend time with her, and he wanted to protect her. He also wanted to find whoever was threatening her and make them regret they'd ever thought it was a good idea.

Threatening Cassie Dixon was like threatening a kitten. It didn't make any fucking sense.

Ty's phone rang as he was pulling into the parking garage at BDI. Kari's name flashed on the screen of his truck. He had a moment where he wondered if something had happened to Cassie and she'd called Kari instead of him, but he was pretty sure she'd call him directly now. They'd talked for an hour after they'd both come last night, so he didn't think she was avoiding him out of embarrassment today.

"What's up, Care Bear?"

"Ugh, not today, Jarhead."

Ty snorted a laugh. "Fine, sweetest cousin in the world. What's up?"

"I just talked to Cassie."

His heart started a slow drop into his stomach. What if he was wrong about how she felt today? "And?"

"She said you're being very helpful. I appreciate it. That's all."

Thank God. "You're welcome."

"How does she seem to you? I haven't seen her in so long, and I'm not sure she's telling me everything. She pretends like she's happy. Good grief, this morning she was as giggly as a preteen. Trust me, I know what that sounds like." Kari scarcely drew breath before hurtling on. "But what if it's an act? She was taken off that project at work and sent home, plus she works so hard at her channel, and I wonder if she's really happy or just going through the motions. I—"

"Kari."

"What?"

"Are you going to let me talk?"

"Yes, sorry."

"Bearing in mind I don't know her as well as you do, I think she's fine. Worried about whoever is doing this shit to her, but she likes being at home. She told me she wanted to go full time with her channel, but she wasn't there yet. She'll probably use the time at home to work on growing her audience. In between Zoom meetings, she'll be making videos and editing them for the channel."

"Whoa. You know all that in two days?"

"Well, yeah. We had a conversation. I asked and she answered. It was kinda cool. You should try it sometime."

Kari groaned. "If I were there with you, I'd smack you."

"I know. Listen, Care, I'm at work now. I need to get inside. If you want to know what's up with your friend, ask her."

"I do ask, jerk! I'm just not sure she tells me everything."

Ty dragged in a breath and blew it out. "If it helps, she seems happy enough to me. She's focused and determined, and while she's angry about the threats, she's not hiding beneath the bed or anything. I'm doing what I can to track down whoever's threatening her, and she's doing what she can to grow her subscribers. I gave her instructions about answering the door and keeping everything locked, and she's got my number if anything scares her. I'll be heading over there later today to get rid of some things for her."

"The sex toys."

He couldn't hear the words without flashing back to last night. *Not the time, dude. Not the time.*

"Right. I said I'd drop them at a thrift store for her."

Kari snorted. "Man, I'd love to be a fly on the wall when they open that box."

"Wouldn't we all? Hey, tell me real quick about Dylan Webb. Any red flags there?"

"Oh, Jesus, that asshole? Cassie spent five years with him, and all he ever did was tear her down. Best thing she ever did was move away and leave him here. I haven't seen him in a while now. Heard he moved to Richmond with some chick he was going to marry."

"Who broke up with who?"

"It wasn't quite like that. Cassie got the job offer and wanted to move. Dylan wanted her to stay so she could wait on him hand and foot like she always did. I don't think he expected she'd really take the job if he pushed back hard enough, but she did. Best decision she made if you ask me, even though I miss having her around. I thought about him when this shit started with the emails and stuff, but he was never the subtle type. Plus, he moved on easily enough. Shacked up with somebody else a few days after Cassie left."

"Okay, just wondering," Ty said. "Gotta run, Care. Love you. Give my love to the girls. Tell Heath to behave."

Kari laughed. "I will. Love you too."

Ty went up to the fifth floor and found Dax, who looked up when he walked in. "Hey, man, I was hoping you'd stop by today."

Ty pulled a chair out and sat backward, arms resting on the chair back. "What'd you find?"

"Nothing you're going to like. Whoever sent the emails isn't stupid. He's used a VPN, obviously, and an encrypted email service. It's probably a burner email address, which means he didn't have to register for an account. There's no way to trace who sent these, unfortunately."

"Shit. And the YouTube comments?"

"Might be the same person. Also very careful and untraceable, but I ran the comments through a program with the emails and the syntax and usage are similar. It's not one-hundred percent, because nothing ever is, but you could be dealing with the same asshole for both. Probably are when you consider the two screen names."

"Yeah, Big Guns and Glockman123 seem like more than a coincidence. Not quite what I wanted to hear, but it's good to know it could be a single source and not multiple people making threats." Ty frowned. "Still don't know if it's the same person who's sending the packages and pizzas, though."

Dax frowned as he tapped his keyboard. "That's the problem with being popular online, Ty. It attracts the cranks and stalkers." He looked up. "I watched some of her TikTok feed. She's got some shitty comments over there too."

"Yeah, I saw some when I checked, but I was focused on YouTube and didn't spend a lot of time there."

"She's pretty amazing, really. Those transformations are incredible. She's engaging, she has a beautiful smile, and she's passionate about what she's doing. That kind of thing always attracts weirdos."

"Yeah." Ty raked a hand through his hair. He was proud of Cassie for coming out of her shell and creating something so awesome, but he was worried for her too.

It'd be a hell of a lot easier if she'd never made the first video. But that wasn't fair to her and her vision, was it? "Need to find out information about someone named Odin."

Dax arched a brow. "The Norse god of war?"

"A little prick who works for Debra Kelly of Kelly Cosmetics. He's her assistant or something, and he doesn't like Cassie much."

"I'm guessing you don't know his real name?"

"Nope. Cassie says he's never used anything but Odin with Elite Events."

"I'll find him," Dax said. "Won't be too hard. His employment records will have his legal name."

Ty told Dax about the box of sex toys and the catalogs Cassie had gotten at the office yesterday. Dax's eyebrows rose nearly to his hairline. "A vajankle? What the fuck?"

"Someone wanted to humiliate her at work. Could be that Kelly Cosmetics let her personal info about her job leak and one of their fans went a little berserk. But my money's on Odin. He wanted to humiliate her yesterday when he ran into her at Elite Events. Treated her like shit, but I set him right."

"Good. The fucker."

Ty blew out a breath. "And yet it could also be Big Guns Glockman, harassing her at home *and* work. Or someone we don't even know."

Dax was shaking his head. "Yeah, I know. I'm sorry I couldn't dial it in more precisely for you."

"You tried. I appreciate it."

"Hey, kids, what's going on?" Ian stood in the door, hands in pockets, looking far more relaxed and happier that he had in months. His eyes were blue today, Ty noted. He wasn't sure what color Ian's eyes really were. Or Natasha's, come to think of it.

"Talking about Cassie's stalker and the emails," Ty said.

"Find anything?"

Ty nodded at Dax. "He thinks it could be a single person making some of the comments and sending the threatening emails."

"Yeah," Dax said. "The comments only go so far because the user doesn't want to get banned, but the syntax and style are the same as the emails. Which are far more aggressive."

"I read them," Ian said with a frown. "Insecure prick who thinks he's superior to women. I hate fuckers like that."

"If I find him, I'm going to punch him in the balls so hard he'll have to look for them in his throat," Ty growled.

"Looking up someone named Odin, too," Dax said. "You think he could have sent the emails, Ty?"

Ty thought about it and shook his head. "Anything's possible, but I somehow don't think so. Unless he's hiding a lot of rage under his fluffy exterior, I don't think he looks at women as objects to be subjugated through sex. If he's behind the box of toys and the catalogs, that's more about humiliating her at work than it is about threatening her with sexual violence."

"Someone sent her a vajankle," Dax said.

Ian shuddered. "Fucking hell. That's just weird."

"It's somehow weirder in person than online," Ty said. "Looks like a human foot cut off at the ankle, but with a pussy opening where a leg should be. Like something Picasso drew because he was feeling particularly disturbed that day."

Ian snorted. "Good lord. There's some weird shit out there for sure. So, you guys want some homemade lasagna tonight? Natasha's in a cooking mood and Daria's helping. Daria specifically wanted you two to come over. Jace and Maddy will be there, along with Jared and Libby. The others can't make it tonight, but we'll do it again soon."

"Count me in," Dax replied.

"I've got to go to Cassie's later," Ty said. "Not sure when I'll be done."

"Bring her with you. Plenty of food. Besides, Natasha's started to worry about you guys and why you aren't married yet."

"Oh, Jesus," Dax said. "What is with the women around here? They get paired up and suddenly we're missing out on something."

Ian laughed. "Trust me when I tell you this, Dax—you *are* missing out. Not that I think you need to rush into anything. Took me over forty years on this planet to find the one for me. You've got time. But a pregnant woman is a nesting woman, and while Natasha isn't exactly typical in many ways, she's fond of you both and wants you to be happy."

Ty couldn't help but laugh. "She hated us not that long ago. Now she wants us paired up and happy."

Ian shrugged. "What can I say? She's pregnant and planning a wedding. It's on her mind."

"So if I bring Cassie, she might think there's hope for me?" Ty asked teasingly.

"Can't hurt."

LYNN RAYE HARRIS

"Cass is kinda shy. She might be overwhelmed by all of us in one spot."

"The woman behind *Cassandra's Closet* is shy?" Dax asked, eyes wide. "No way."

"She says filming is different," Ty said with a shrug. "I don't get it either."

"We'll behave," Ian replied, eyes twinkling. "Promise."

"Not sure I believe that," Ty said. "But I'll warn her. If she thinks she's ready for you nuts, we'll be there. I'll text if she doesn't want to, but save me some lasagna if I don't make it. I want to try it."

"Trust me," Ian said. "There'll be plenty. I'll bring you a doggie bag tomorrow if you can't."

Ty sniffed dramatically and put a hand over his heart. "This is why I love working here. My needs are important."

"More like I don't want to eat lasagna *and* soup for a week," Ian said with a grin. "But whatever makes you happy."

"Food makes him happy," Dax said. "Thought you knew that by now."

Ty got to his feet and flipped them both off as he walked backward toward the door. "I know when I'm not wanted. Later, gators."

"In a while, crocodile," Dax called.

Ty snorted. Yeah, he loved these guys. He just hoped he could convince Cassie to give them a chance tonight. Be a damned shame to miss an evening with his work family, especially sweet little Daria.

And lasagna. Couldn't forget that either…

Chapter Fourteen

CASSIE WOKE WITH A START THAT MORNING THEN immediately flushed red from her toes to her roots. The vibrator was on the bedside table, looking innocent. Her phone was there too, plugged in. She groped for it, wondering why the alarm hadn't gone off.

But she was awake fifteen minutes before she had to be, so she shut off the alarm before it could make a sound and lay there for a few minutes thinking about last night. About Ty.

She'd never had phone sex before. Dylan hadn't been the type. Brian had gotten a little flirty over the phone one evening, and she'd thought that was probably where he was headed, but she hadn't wanted to encourage him. She'd invented a reason to end the call, and he hadn't tried again.

But last night, once she'd determined that Ty really did find her attractive, she'd wanted to stay on the phone with him and keep the flirtation going. Even if it has resulted in her using a vibrator and moaning into his ear while he encouraged her to keep doing what she was doing.

She thought of his groans when he'd stroked himself to orgasm, and heat flared between her legs. If she grabbed that vibrator again, she could be finished in just a couple of minutes.

But she didn't. Instead, she got up and hit the shower, got dressed—entirely dressed since Ty would be there later—and prepared for the morning Zoom meeting with Amelia and the team. When she logged into her work email as the meeting was getting started, she had a bunch of unread ones. And they all said *Welcome to…*.

Cassie clicked the first one. It was a newsletter from an Overeaters Anonymous group, welcoming her to their online meetings. The next one thanked her for signing up for Irritable Bowel Syndrome news.

Cassie clicked email after email as fury lashed through her. There was a welcome letter from the Church of Satan, a newsletter about sinful fetishes—not that she knew what those were, but it's what the headline proclaimed. There was also an invitation to a pony play group weekend coming up—with prizes for the best horse costume—a welcome to a chubby chicks porn channel that thanked her for her interest in sharing nude videos of herself, a BDSM newsletter that promised she could find herself through spanking, and a newsletter from a website that was all about pretending to be a kitty cat for sexual pleasure.

She moved all the emails to the folder with the threats, then unsubscribed from every one. They might not all take, but at least she'd tried. She kept the emails because she knew it was evidence, but she was shaking with fury that she'd received them in the first place.

And she knew there would be more. Whoever had sent the sex toys was behind this. She had no doubt. If she found out it was Odious Odin, she'd wring his neck so hard his freaking head would snap off.

"Cassie, what do you have for us on the swag bag contents?" Amelia asked, slicing into her thoughts of revenge. "We need to get the ball rolling on ordering product."

Cassie fumbled with her notebook, utterly unprepared because she'd been so distracted. "Yes, I, uh, I have it right here—"

"Coming back to you in five," Amelia said, sounding exasperated. "Pamela, please update the team on registrations…"

Tears of frustration clogged Cassie's throat, but she didn't let them fall as she found the page of notes. She had to keep it together or she'd find herself without a job before she was ready to support herself on her channel earnings. Amelia wasn't going to put up with shoddy work, especially after Debra Kelly had demanded her removal in the first place. Add in the sex toys being delivered to the office, and she was on shaky ground at the moment.

The last thing she needed was to give Amelia more fuel for the fire. Amelia was a fair boss, all things considered, but fucking up at your job was not the way to her heart. By the time Amelia asked again, Cassie was prepared with facts, figures, and timelines.

"Excellent work," Amelia said when she was done. "I'll present everything to Debra and Odin, and we'll go from there."

The meeting ended a few moments later as Cassie's screen went blank. She let out her breath and went to pour a fresh cup of coffee. It would be hours yet before Ty arrived. So many hours.

———

WHEN THE DOORBELL rang at three, Cassie checked the peephole. It was Ty. She ripped the door open before she could freeze into a ball of indecision and insecurities, her heart hammering with excitement.

"Hey," she said.

Ty was frowning up at her from the bottom step. "You opened the door."

Cassie blinked. Then she rolled her eyes. "You texted me not two minutes ago and said you were walking up to the door. I looked out the peephole to confirm it was you."

One side of his mouth lifted. "Just testing you. How's it going, Red?"

Red. She liked that. "So far, so good. Nothing but those stupid emails I told you about."

"Ah yes, the subscriptions to kink newsletters. Anything good?"

"As if," she said. "Don't forget the emails from satanic churches and the ones dealing with medical conditions, too."

"Those as well. No packages or emails?"

She shook her head. "Not today. The mail ran, but UPS and FedEx have not. There's time." She sincerely hoped she didn't get anything else, but the day was young so far as deliveries went. She was still expecting some packages with clothes and makeup, which made her really glad that Ty was here and could slit the tape for her.

She'd checked the list of orders she had coming, so she would know if the packages weren't from those places, she had to be careful.

"Can I come in?"

"Oh, of course." She stepped back hurriedly, nearly tripping over that stupid box of sex toys as she did so. *Way to go, klutz.*

He was inside in a flash, gripping her arms to keep her upright. "Careful."

Heat sizzled through her. She wasn't sure if it was entirely due to embarrassment, or if it was the heat of his touch. "I forgot it was there. I moved it off the table this morning."

He slid his hands down her arms and let go. "You doing okay today?"

His eyes searched hers. Was he talking about last night or in general? She wasn't sure.

"I'm great. Thanks."

He took her hand and led her over to the couch then sat her down on it. Then he sank onto the chair that sat at a right angle to the couch. "I want you to know that I don't make a habit of engaging in phone sex. Last night was not typical for me."

Her heart thumped. "Thank you. I think." She tilted her head. "Are you saying you didn't like it?"

He reached for her hand and squeezed. "Not what I'm saying, Cassie. I just didn't want you to think it's the kind of thing I do whenever I start seeing someone."

Her heart thumped. "Um, okay." Were they seeing each other? She wanted to ask but couldn't find the guts.

"You aren't telling me what you're thinking," he said, a slight grin curving his mouth.

She focused on the small scar that trailed from the corner of his nose to right beneath his lip. He'd had it as long as she could remember. Something about getting hit with a baseball bat that had splintered. She remembered Kari telling her about it in hushed tones one time. Ty had been ten, and he'd had to get stitches.

"I was wondering if we were seeing each other now," she said, because she didn't want to mention the scar. What if he was self-conscious about it? She didn't think he was, but you never knew.

"Do you want to see each other?" His green-blue eyes were expressive in his handsome face. He still had the stubble, and she knew he didn't go clean shaven. It suited him anyway. Made him ruggedly handsome instead of just pretty.

"Do you?"

He laughed. "I thought I made that clear already. Yes, I want to see you, Cassie."

She couldn't help but smile. "Okay, yes, I want to see you too. I don't know that I'm very good at it though."

His smile didn't fade. He lifted their clenched hands to his mouth and kissed the back of hers. "Tonight's your chance then."

"My ch-chance?"

"The boss has invited us to dinner. At his house."

Her stomach flipped. "Dinner at your boss's house? That sounds important. I'm not sure I should go to something like that."

"It's not that kind of dinner. Ian is as laid back as they come. It's a long story, but he just got engaged, and his fiancée and her daughter are living with him.

Natasha loves to cook, and Daria—that's the daughter —loves me for some reason. She wants me there. A couple of coworkers will be there with their fiancées. It's a casual evening."

She was torn, but one look at his hopeful expression and she knew she couldn't refuse. "You showed up here less than forty-eight hours ago, and now we're seeing each other and you want me to go to your boss's house. I'll go, but I'm really nervous, Ty."

"Look at it like this. I'm your protector. It's what I do. You have to stick with me so I can do that. We'll drop that box off at the collection point, then we'll head to Ian's. It'll take a while in traffic. You'll love everyone, and they'll make you feel right at home. Ian and Natasha want me to bring you."

"I don't understand why."

"They know we're from the same hometown. We aren't strangers in the way most people who've just met are. We have history and a connection, even if we've never spent as much time together as we have in the past couple of days."

She nodded, understanding. "I have to go upstairs to change and fix my makeup."

"You look great, Cassie."

She squeezed his hand. "I have to put on Cassandra if I'm going to do this. She can extrovert. I can't."

"All right, Red. Whatever you need to do. Don't dress fancy, though. Casual is fine."

The doorbell rang, and she jumped. Ty didn't jump. He twisted around to look at the door, then got up and moved toward it far more silently than she'd have thought possible for a man as big as he was. He had a hand at his back, beneath his shirt, and she realized for the first time that he was carrying a weapon.

He looked out the peephole and dropped his shirt. "UPS," he said, opening the door.

He came back inside with packages. Cassie got up and followed him to the dining room as he laid them all out so she could see. She pulled up the list on her phone, checking them one by one.

"Not this one," she said when she came to one that didn't match her list. "It's not one I'm expecting, but that doesn't necessarily mean anything. I get free stuff from brands sometimes, because they want me to try the product."

He moved it over to the side. "Anything else?"

She finished checking the list. "No. That's it."

Ty flicked open his pocket knife. "Stand back, Cass. I'll check it."

The knife sliced through the tape with a *zzzzt* sound. She held her breath as Ty put it in his pocket and unfolded the flaps.

"Jesus Christ," he said.

"What is it?" Her heart resided in her throat. "Another rat?"

"No. Best if you don't look."

"I-I have to. My mind will make it worse if I don't."

He turned to her with anger-filled eyes. "Are you sure?"

She wasn't, but she nodded. He held the box out, the flaps pulled back. "It's fake," he said.

Cassie peered at the contents. And bit back a scream.

Chapter Fifteen

HE DIDN'T WANT TO SHOW IT TO HER, BUT HE understood what she meant about making it worse in her head. Cassie's face paled as she peered into the box and sucked in a gasp.

"It's not real," he reiterated.

"Good God, I would hope not," she breathed.

Ty set the box down, took his knife out, and poked around inside for an invoice. The bloody human heart was inside a clear plastic bag, looking gruesome as hell. It appeared as if someone had added fake blood to it, which meant they'd probably packaged it themselves. He doubted it had come from the store that way.

"We might get prints from this," he said. "I'll need to take it to my guys."

Cassie waved a hand. She wasn't looking at the heart anymore. "Please. Take it. Get it out of here." She shivered. "If I'd opened that by myself, I'd have screamed bloody murder."

"That was the intention, I'm sure."

She looked a little green as she met his gaze. "How do you know it's fake? It looks pretty real to me."

"There's a whiff of rubber in the box. And it's a little too perfect. If it'd been cut from a real person and sent via UPS, without being packed in ice, it would discolor and look different. This looks fresh, which means someone probably got it from a Halloween store. Do you have a grocery bag or something I can put this in?"

"Sure."

She retrieved a bag from inside the pantry and handed it to him. He put the box inside and tied the bag. He didn't think they'd get prints, but if there was the slightest possibility, then he had to try.

"Have you gotten more emails? Any new comments that were threatening?"

"I haven't checked today because I had to work, but there was nothing last night."

"Can you check before we leave?"

"You still want to go?" she asked.

"There's no reason to stay, Cassie. I'll take the box with us. After my guys go over it, we can take it to the police. Unless you'd rather not go anywhere."

She shook her head. "No, I want to get out of the house. I can't believe I'm saying that," she added as she retrieved her computer. She set it on the table while she logged in. Then she straightened. "You check for emails and comments, please. I want to go upstairs and change if you don't mind."

He nodded. "If you want me to."

"I do. I don't—I don't think I can face it if there's something nasty waiting for me."

He picked up the computer. "Is everything visible for me?"

"Yes. Check the tabs. Email, TikTok, and YouTube. They're all there. I can show you how to delete comments when I come back."

Ty carried the computer to the couch while Cassie went upstairs. He worked his way through the emails first. There was nothing. Then he went to YouTube and TikTok. There was nothing more than a few nasty comments about Cassie faking it, though her supporters leapt to her defense. He didn't need her to tell him how to delete comments, but he wouldn't delete any without her permission. He noted a couple, though nothing from Big Guns. She'd apparently blocked him since their last conversation.

He checked her follower numbers. She was over fifty-thousand now and heading toward sixty. The viral video was still racking up the views, which he imagined didn't make Kelly Cosmetics all that happy. Several of her other videos were starting to climb in views, which meant new comments on them as well.

Ty raked a hand over his head. It'd take a fucking village to watch all the comments until they caught this asshole. He picked up his phone and fired off a text to Dax about it. Dax returned shortly after with a brief comment: *I'm on it.*

Cassie came downstairs a short while later, dressed in a pair of dark jeans, ankle boots, and a black top that clung to her curves and showcased her beautiful cleavage in a tasteful way. The shirt didn't plunge, but it definitely hinted. She wore a single diamond necklace that winked against her skin, but no earrings. Her hair was loose, curled at the ends, and she'd done her makeup with care.

This woman was Cassandra, not Cassie. She was certain of herself, gorgeous, and confident. Fucking turned him on that she had these two sides of herself. He liked sweet Cassie and her vulnerabilities. He wanted to mess up Cassandra's lipstick and make her moan his name.

"What's wrong?" she asked as she stopped on the landing with two steps left to go. "Too dressy? Not dressy enough?"

He shook his head as he snapped the laptop closed and stood. "The only thing wrong is that we have to go spend the evening with other people."

She smiled as she took the other two steps down. "You invited me, remember?"

"I know, but now I want to spend the evening with just you and me."

She ducked her head shyly, and he realized Cassie was right beneath the surface. She was trying to think of something to say. He knew she wasn't entirely comfortable with compliments from him yet. He didn't want her to feel uncertain of herself or her response, so he didn't pursue it.

"We'll have fun with my people though. Promise. And Natasha is a mean cook, so we get a free meal out of it too."

"That's good. Will you tell me about everyone on the way over there? I'll feel less insecure if I know something about them."

"Sure. Be happy to."

She glanced at the computer. "Did you find anything I need to take care of right away?"

"There are some comments, but nothing too bad. And no emails."

"Good. I blocked Big Guns, like you said. I hadn't seen his comments until you mentioned him. Just another dudebro offended by a curvy woman trying to be sexy."

He didn't tell her that Big Guns and Glockman123 might be the same guy. He didn't know for sure. Besides, once the guy learned he'd been blocked, he'd send a blistering email if it was him.

"I hope you don't let those guys bother you too much. They're assholes."

She shrugged as she went over to rummage around in her purse for something. She pulled out a tube of lip gloss and painted it on while looking into the mirror hanging nearby. "I know. I was bothered at first, but the more I hung out in groups and learned what others go through, the more I realized it's normal. There really are a lot of angry men in this world who can't stand a woman being successful."

"Not all men. There are a lot of us who aren't threatened by a woman's success."

She closed the tube and put it away. "I know. It's just that when you do something that's about appearance, you get a lot of those ugly men who want to tear you down. I don't know why they're so angry, but they are. But then I look at men like Heath, who is surrounded by three strong-willed females, and he's there for it. He'd never tear down Kari or the girls, and he steps up to do his part as a dad every single day."

Ty smiled as he thought of his cousin-in-law. "Yeah, Heath's a good one. I give him shit because I can, but I know he'd do anything for Kari and their daughters. A strong man is one who stands with his mate instead of blocking her at every turn."

Cassie nodded. "I believe that. I grew up without a dad, and my mom was a hot mess, but I also got to see your Uncle Joe and Aunt Karen a lot when I spent the night with Kari. I know they aren't perfect, but I thought they were back then. They didn't get drunk and yell, and your uncle didn't chase your aunt from the house with a shotgun. Or vice versa, because Lottie did that about as often as her boyfriends did. Anyway, long story, but do you remember when your aunt decided to join the community theater?"

Ty shook his head. "I must have missed that." He'd spent a lot of time trying to excel at everything he did because his dad had demanded it, and he hadn't paid much attention to what others were doing unless he had to.

"Oh yeah, she did. And she was a terrible actress, really. But she wanted to practice her lines, and your uncle would sit there with her, patiently reading from the script and helping her. He never told her she was awful, and one time when Kari got mad and wanted to tell your aunt to just stop because it was embarrassing, he told Kari that it made her mother happy and it would be cruel to pop the bubble of her dream when it was harmless."

Ty was surprised at the lump in his throat. Uncle Joe was a great guy. How his own dad had turned out to be such an asshole still didn't make sense to him. Though his dad had always claimed he wasn't an asshole and he'd just been trying to toughen Ty up for life.

"Anyway," Cassie said. "I thought that was just incredibly sweet and I've never forgotten it. I think about Heath and your uncle when I need to believe in good men. It helps."

He hoped she'd add him to that list before it was all over. He intended to make sure she could.

"I'm glad. They're at the top of my list too. But I think you're going to meet some other men you can add to that list tonight. In fact, wait until I tell you about Ian and Natasha. Talk about needing to be secure in your manhood."

Cassie's eyes sparked with interest. "Sounds intriguing."

He'd have to tell her a sanitized version, of course. "It is. You ready to get going?"

"I think so."

"Let me take the box to my truck, then I'll come back and we can check the doors and windows to make sure they're secure before we go."

Chapter Sixteen

SHE WAS NERVOUS. CASSIE FUMBLED WITH THE BRACELET she'd put on and wondered why she'd ever agreed to go to Ty's boss's house. Ian and Natasha. She knew a bit about them now, thanks to Ty's story, and she was in awe.

Ian and Natasha were trained as combat operatives, and they'd been on opposite sides for the past few years. Until they realized they were in love, and now they were on the same side. Ian fully supported Natasha, and she was joining his company to work side by side with him. She was also going to head up a training program within his organization. A combat training program, which Cassie found intriguing. Apparently, Natasha had martial arts training and could take down a man Ty's size without trouble.

Cassie wished she was that skilled, but her skills lay elsewhere. She could make a man look like a gorgeous woman with makeup, but she wasn't going to karate chop one into surrendering if she was ever attacked.

After Ty pulled up to a thrift store collection site and

dropped the sealed box of sex toys, they headed to the Beltway and started the long trip to the Chesapeake Bay. When Ty had told her where Ian lived, she'd been a little surprised and a lot impressed. A house with a view of the Chesapeake. Must be nice.

The trip took a couple of hours because of traffic, though they'd started early enough that they didn't get caught in the worst of it. It was nearly seven when they reached an iron gate flanked by stone pillars and a gate house on one side. There were two men with rifles inside the gatehouse, but when Ty rolled to a stop, they grinned and exchanged a few words with him before the gates opened and they went through.

"Wow," Cassie said as Ty steered the truck up the drive. The house was big, sprawling, and when they reached the crest of the drive, there was nothing but inky black in the distance. The nearest lights were miles away.

"You can't see it, but that's the Chesapeake down there," Ty said, pointing behind the house and into the inky blackness.

"I'd wondered if it was woods, but water makes sense."

Ty parked in a small lot off to the side of the house. "You ready?"

She gazed at the stone facade of the house. "I'm feeling underdressed, Ty. You didn't tell me it was this fancy."

"You look great, Cassie. Trust me, this crowd isn't going for fancy tonight. It's about hanging out together and having a good meal with friends."

"Okay, but I'm still nervous."

"You'll be fine. Just be you."

She couldn't help but laugh. "You don't want me to be me. Cassie Dixon is tongue-tied and shy. I need to channel my YouTube persona if I'm going to survive this."

He grinned. "Whatever you need, I'll be right there with you. Now sit tight, Red, and stop babbling. I'm going to come around and open your door. Then we're walking to the front door and ringing the bell."

Cassie waited, then took Ty's hand and stepped onto the cobblestones. He squeezed her hand and she dragged her attention from the house to look at him. His eyes searched hers, and she found herself caught by the intensity of them.

"I'm considering distracting you with a kiss, just so you know. But it would be our first, and I'm not sure this is the right place for a first kiss."

Her breath caught. Her brain started to trip over itself, but she forced it to slow the heck down. "Where's the right place?" she asked softly.

He stepped into her and pressed her ever so lightly against the side of his truck. She could feel his body against hers, and she shivered.

"I don't know. Your house? Mine? Inside my truck? Where would you prefer it?"

"Honestly, Ty, I could use a distraction right now. I think you'd be a good one."

He grinned down at her, and a remote corner of her brain squealed that *this* was Tyler Scott, football star, most popular guy in school, and someone she had never in a million years had a chance with. This was Tyler Scott, and he was about to kiss *her.* Cassie Dixon. It was every high school dream she'd ever had come true.

He put a hand on her hip like he had in the hallway

at Elite's office building, and her heart skipped. He liked doing that, she thought. Anchoring her with one big hand firmly holding her. She had a moment's discomfort when she thought about how thick and wide she was there, but those thoughts fled when his other hand threaded along her jaw, cupping her face gently as he tilted her head back.

He took another step, pressing her tighter to him, and her insides melted at the contact. If she could hook a leg around his hips and rip his shirt off right there, she'd do it while the shy part of her looked on in abject horror.

Ty dipped his head toward hers in slow motion— and then his lips touched hers in the lightest of caresses. Cassie whimpered because it wasn't enough, then blushed to her roots because she'd whimpered.

"Patience, Cassie," he whispered against her mouth. And then he tickled her lips with his again before pressing a little harder this time.

Her heart hammered as his tongue slid lightly along the seam of her lips. She opened automatically —and his tongue slipped in to tease her own. Cassie realized she was clutching his sleeves. She loosened her grip and put her arms around his neck. It was a tentative move, but he made a noise of approval in his throat.

His tongue stroked deeper, demanding a response. Cassie arched into him before she realized she'd done it, meeting him stroke for stroke as their tongues tangled and danced. By the time he broke the kiss and took one step backward, she'd forgotten where they were.

But that step rattled her and her arms dropped away until her hands were on his sleeves again. She told herself he'd liked the kiss, but her insecurities flared, telling her the opposite.

Ty took another step back, twined his hand in hers, and blew out a breath. "I need to stand here for a minute or two."

"Okay."

He laughed when she didn't say anything else. "That's it? No sympathy for me?"

"I, uh…" Understanding dawned then. "Oh. Oh, I'm sorry."

She'd felt him pressing into her, but she'd been so blown away by the kiss that it hadn't quite registered. It did now, and a deep satisfaction flared within. *She* had done that. Cassie Dixon had made Tyler Scott want her.

"I'm only sorry we can't do anything about it." He let his breath out slowly, as if getting control. "But I want you to know, I don't intend to do anything about getting you naked for a while yet."

"Oh?" Did she sound disappointed? She thought maybe she did.

"Not because I don't want to, Cassie. I *really* want to. But I don't want you questioning my motives about any of this. I'm not rushing you. We've got time."

What he said was sweet, and yet it frustrated her too. Maybe she needed to just leap for once. Leap and see if she could swim.

She imagined it. Imagined ending up in bed with him tonight, naked, their bodies straining together—and knew he was right. She'd be a mess of insecurities if they did that. She'd be worried about what he thought of her, if he was disgusted by her soft body, if he was disappointed in the sex. In short, she'd ruin everything by overthinking it.

"I don't want to rush it either," she said. "I need time to get used to this."

He nodded. "Good. You ready? I think I can go inside without embarrassing myself now."

Cassie pulled in a deep breath, her nerves spiking again. "I'm about as ready as I'll ever be."

Ty took her hand. "It'll be okay, Cass. Promise."

Then he led her toward the house.

Chapter Seventeen

"So you and Ty are from the same town?" Natasha asked as she put the finishing touches on the cake she'd baked. The lasagna was on the island, cooling for a few minutes, and Cassie was standing nearby, glass of wine in hand, chatting with her hostess.

She'd been terrified when Ian had answered the door and asked them to come in. Terrified when she'd been introduced to the people who were all looking at her curiously. Terrified when the little girl named Daria had come over and asked Cassie if Ty was her boyfriend.

Natasha had put a glass of wine in her hand, shooed Daria away, and dragged Cassie to the kitchen with her while she told everyone else to mingle. Then she'd spent the next fifteen minutes soothing Cassie's nerves with small talk.

There were two other women present tonight. Libby and Maddy. Both were thin and pretty, but they both had kind eyes and they'd been friendly when they were introduced. They were in with the men at the moment, but Natasha said the ladies would chat after dinner while the men did dishes. She'd said it with a wink, and Cassie had warmed to her even more.

She liked Natasha's style. She was confident, and she was lean and pretty. Almost Barbie-like in her blond beauty. It was hard to believe she could kick a man's ass, but Ty had assured her that Natasha could. Cassie wasn't going to ask, though.

"Yes," she answered. "His cousin and I have been best friends since kindergarten."

"Ah," Natasha said with a sparkle in her eyes, "you have known each other since you were children."

Cassie twisted the wine glass in her hand. "Um, technically, yes. But I was very shy. I never spoke to anyone, especially not Ty. He was very popular in school, and I was nobody. He admitted just the other day that he'd entirely forgotten who I was when Kari asked him to help me."

"Oh dear," Natasha said. "Well, he knows who you are now. He hasn't stopped looking over here at you since you arrived."

Cassie felt the blush rising in her cheeks. "He's protective of me. For Kari."

Natasha took a sip of her sparkling water—because she was pregnant—and one corner of her mouth turned up in a smile. "Yes, I'm sure that's what it is. Tell me about this trouble you are in. Ian says you have a YouTube channel."

"Um, yes. I have a channel about makeup and clothing for bigger women like me. I mean anyone can learn from my makeup techniques, but the clothes are for plus-sized women."

"You're very pretty," Natasha said. "I can see you doing well."

"Oh. Thank you."

"You're welcome. Now, what about the trouble?"

Cassie found herself explaining about the emails she'd gotten, the pizzas, rat, sex toys, and now the fake human heart. Natasha looked angrier and angrier as Cassie went on.

"You need defensive training," she snapped out when Cassie was done. "Immediately. Ty!"

Ty came sauntering over, his gaze darting between them as he walked into the kitchen. He'd been talking to a couple of the men in the adjoining family room, but now his attention was on them.

"Yes, Boss Lady?"

Natasha seemed to soften when he said those words. "You must give Cassie some defensive training. Or bring her here and I'll do it."

"I think Ian might object if—"

"Ian isn't allowed to object. I'm barely pregnant, and I'm healthy. I can train Cassie to defend herself. Or I'll supervise you doing it."

Cassie was stunned and touched at the same time. This woman she'd only just met—a beautiful, lively woman who seemed to have all her shit together—was offering to give her defensive training.

A moment later, reality set in, and Cassie felt miserable that she would have to explain why she couldn't take her up on the offer.

"I'm not very athletic," she squeaked during a lull in the conversation. "I'm, uh, overweight and my stamina isn't good."

It shamed her to say it, because thin, fit people like

Natasha and Ty always thought it was a matter of willpower and diet. She had plenty of willpower, and she'd starved herself in the past to lose weight. It didn't work. She retained what she had because her body would not let go.

Natasha waved a hand. "You don't have to be athletic to defend yourself. You just need a few moves to surprise an attacker. We can do this, I promise. Ty?"

"I'll show her some things," he said. "And when she feels like she's mastered those, I'll bring her over. Will that work?"

Natasha looked fierce. Then she sighed. "Yes, of course." She reached out and touched Cassie's arm. "You must forgive my passion about this. I've been in situations where I've needed to know how to defend myself, and I want other women to know what I do. Especially when I hear that someone is threatening you."

Cassie was more touched than she could say. "Thank you. Really. I know you're right, and I want to learn. I don't like feeling afraid when some new thing arrives in the mail, or dreading getting another email."

Natasha nodded. "Good. We'll do this then. Ty will start with a few basic moves, and then we can expand on that. But first, dinner and more conversation. Will you help me carry things to the table?"

"Yes, of course! What can I take?"

"The garlic bread. Ty, can you get the pan of lasagna, please?"

Ty smirked. "It'd be my pleasure."

Natasha glared at him. "You take that pan anywhere but the table and I will skewer you with an ice pick. Understand?"

He laughed. "Got it."

"You aren't worried I put a Tide pod into your portion?" she asked teasingly.

Cassie threw a look at Ty as she carried the basket of bread. She didn't know what was going on between these two, but it almost sounded as if they didn't like each other. Except he laughed even harder than before. "Nope. Not anymore."

Ty glanced over. He must have noticed her frown. "It's a joke, Cass. Natasha and I didn't like each other at first. I thought she wanted to poison me."

"I did want to poison you," Natasha said, pouring water into glasses. "But you grew on me. Like a fungus," she added.

Ty threw his head back and laughed, and Cassie envied that he had friends like these. People he worked with, but who clearly cared about each other. She didn't know what they did, not exactly, but considering that Kari had told her Ty could protect her—and that Ty had told her Natasha and Ian were highly trained warriors—then it stood to reason that everyone gathered around the table was in the same profession.

She'd worked with the people at Elite Events for a year, and while she liked most of them, she didn't want to hang out with them after work. Ty wanted to be with these people. And the way Natasha had pulled Cassie in and offered to train her without knowing anything about her other than she was Ty's cousin's best friend, well, that was an amazing thing.

Everyone gathered around the table and took a seat. There were no place cards. People just sat where they wanted. The couples sat together, and Cassie found herself between Ty and Dax. Daria was between Ty and Natasha.

The meal was delicious, and Cassie relaxed as the evening went on. It was partly the wine and partly how friendly everyone was. They put her at ease. After dinner, the men cleared the table and started to do the dishes.

"That's real china, Ian. Hand wash, please," Natasha called out from her seat in the family room where the women had retreated. "And dry it and stack it gently."

The men groaned, but water started to flow from the sink.

Natasha looked at the three of them—Cassie, Libby, and Maddy—and grinned. "It's dishwasher safe, but they don't need to know that."

Libby snorted. "When I was growing up, it was the women who cooked all the food, set the table, cleared the table, and did the dishes. All the men had to do was show up. I'm totally onboard with this."

Maddy laughed too. "Jace is very good about helping out, but there are times... I think men come encoded with DNA that makes them slightly helpless whenever there's a woman around. Like they need to be told what to do or it won't get done."

Cassie thought of Lottie always catering to the men she'd brought home. None of those men had ever helped with dishes or laundry, and they damn sure hadn't cooked anything.

Natasha shook her head. "Don't let him fool you, Maddy. Our parents shared the cooking, and we cleaned up. He knows what to do."

Maddy sipped her wine. "Well, it's partially my fault.

I'm particular about certain things, and he waits for me to tell him rather than have to start over again. I should probably get over that."

The women chatted for a while as the men cleaned the kitchen. Cassie didn't say much, and they didn't press her, but they tried to include her in their conversation. She spoke when she felt she had something to contribute, otherwise she just listened.

Daria had gone to her room to get ready for bed, and she returned to say goodnight. She was a sweet little girl, and she seemed to really love Ty and Dax both. And why not? They doted on her, and she was no dummy.

Somehow, she managed to wrangle them both into reading her a bedtime story. Ty shot Cassie a look as he was led away by the hand, shrugging as he went. Cassie smiled to let him know she was fine.

"She adores them because they can't say no to her," Natasha said with a suspicious gleam in her eyes. She swiped her fingers beneath her eyes and smiled.

It only made Cassie like Ty all the more.

It was sometime later when the evening ended and Ty came to take her hand and lead her to the hallway where she could put on her coat. Ian and Natasha were there, saying their goodbyes to everyone as coats and scarves were donned. There were promises to do it all again soon, and then Cassie and Ty were walking into the cold night air, their breath frosting as they headed for his truck. He opened the door for her and helped her in, then went around to his side.

"Do you live around here?" Cassie asked him as they headed down the drive.

"About twenty minutes away."

She felt guilty that he had to take her all the way home. "Maybe we could go to your place and I could get an Uber from there," she said. "It's a long way to go for you."

He shook his head. "First rule of protection is that you safely deliver your protectee to her destination. Then you make sure everything's good and she's locked in before you leave her."

"It'll be after midnight by the time you get home."

"No, Cassie. I'm taking you home. Not negotiable."

She didn't argue because she knew there was no point. "If you want to stay, you can. I have a futon in the studio. You could sleep there."

He was silent for a moment. "I'd like that. Thank you."

Just like that, every cell in her body started to tingle. Ty was going to sleep in her house. A wall away from her bed. She wasn't sure she could get through the night without turning on her new favorite toy and pretending it was Ty's mouth making her bite back a scream...

Chapter Eighteen

TY WAS REGRETTING THAT HE SAID HE'D STAY THE NIGHT. Not because he didn't want to be close to Cassie, but because he wanted to be closer still. They'd made it back to her house a little after eleven. They hadn't talked on the way because Cassie had fallen asleep. He hadn't wanted to disturb her since he wasn't sure if she was sleeping all that well these days.

After they'd arrived at her house, he'd woken her with a gentle shake. He'd had her stay in his truck with the doors locked while he cleared the small townhouse and made sure it was safe. He planned to install a Ring camera system on her doors so they could monitor deliveries and visitors, but he hadn't been able to do it yet.

Still, the locks had been intact, there'd been no packages on the front or back porches, and everything looked as it had when they'd left a few hours earlier. He'd returned to the truck to turn it off and retrieve a yawning Cassie.

Now, he stood in the door to her studio and stared at the background that was familiar from her videos. She had hanging racks of clothing against one wall, but it was stylish and clearly done for the camera. The signature color she'd used in the room was pink. The futon was white, and she had fuzzy pink pillows against one corner. There was a light pink throw over the opposite corner. She'd put up wallpaper with a subtle gold diamond pattern on one wall, and all her accessories were either pink or white. There were also a couple of blue and white vases with bouquets of faux flowers that looked real until you touched one.

She'd draped a white sheet against another wall, and she had box lights that weren't currently turned on. There was a tripod with a digital camera—a DSLR, not a video camera—and a ring light. She had a desk with a computer that had two screens against one wall, and a printer. The room wasn't as big as it looked on video, but it was inviting.

And very feminine.

Cassie picked up the pink pillows from the futon and set them on her desk chair. "Sorry it's so girly," she said.

"I can handle a little pink, Cass. It's not a big deal."

She smiled. "Good."

He stepped into the room and went over to look at the camera setup. "Looks very professional."

"It's what a lot of YouTubers use. I got all the recs from other people's videos, and then I found the right stuff for me. There was a learning curve, but thank God for YouTube because I found videos on how to operate the camera."

"You film everything in here?"

"Yes. The white backdrop is for when I don't want anything to detract from what I'm showing, but I mostly use the room as the background."

"I think your videos are very professional and appealing, and I'd like to understand how you do it. Will you show me sometime?"

She ducked her head in that gesture he knew sprang from her insecurities. "I can do that."

He put a finger under her chin and lifted her head until their eyes met. "It's fine if you don't want to, but I'd really like to see how you do it."

"I want to, Ty. It's still hard for me to accept compliments sometimes. That's all."

"I wouldn't say it if I didn't mean it."

"Thank you." She straightened, suddenly businesslike. "Let me get a blanket and proper pillow for you."

She left the room and returned with the items she'd promised. Meanwhile, Ty had unfolded the futon. There wasn't much room to walk around with the mattress all the way out, and yet his feet were still going to hang over the edge. He was a king-sized kind of guy. Queen-size didn't do it.

He took the blanket and pillow she offered. "Thanks for letting me stay."

"It's the least I could do. I'm just sorry I don't have a proper guest room."

"It's fine. I've slept in places you don't want to imagine. Trust me when I tell you a girly room with a futon is heaven compared to that."

"I'm glad then. Not that you've had to sleep in terrible places, but that a little *frou-frou* doesn't bother you." She nibbled her lip. "Thanks for inviting me tonight. You were right. I did have fun."

"I'm glad. I told you everyone was great."

"They really are. You're very lucky to have such a good relationship with the people you work with."

He hesitated, and then he decided he wanted her to know. Especially if they were going to take this thing to the next level at some point. "There's a reason for it, Cassie. We do a dangerous job, and you have to know the person out there with you has your back. We literally trust each other with our lives. If I don't like them well enough to want to hang out with them when we aren't working, how can I trust that they won't get me killed when we're on the job?"

Her eyes had gone a little wide, and she blinked rapidly. But then she seemed to compose herself. "I didn't think of that."

He tossed the pillow she'd given him onto the futon and started to shake out the blanket. "Why would you? What I do isn't exactly normal."

"I'm thinking maybe I don't know what you do at all. You were a Marine, and now you work for a private security firm. I guess I figured you carried a gun and looked out for threats, but it sounds like it's more intense than that."

"It can be." He rubbed his temples with one hand. "Maybe now isn't the right time to bring it up."

She made a scoffing sound. "Too late now. You don't put information like that out there and *not* explain. Don't make me ask Kari."

"Kari doesn't know," he said, and her eyes widened again.

"Seriously?"

He took her hand and pulled her over to the futon, dragging her down beside him. Then he skimmed his fingers over her cheek and toyed with a lock of her gorgeous hair.

"It's soft," he said, lifting it to his nose. "Smells like jasmine."

Cassie put her hand on his wrist. "You're avoiding the subject, Ty."

"Am I?"

She nodded. "Yes. One minute we're talking about how great tonight was, and then you're telling me your life is on the line at work in a way that sounds more serious than providing bodyguard services to people like me who've gotten threats."

"I was in the military, Cassie. I'm a highly trained warrior, like most everyone who was there tonight, and sometimes what we do involves going into battle."

"Explain, please."

He liked that she was direct about it. Cassie was often unsure of herself or what to say, but not this time. "There are battles waged in this world every single day that don't involve national armies and tanks and borders. There are small, private armies that fight against drug lords, human traffickers, and terrorists on a regular basis. It's combat waged on the microlevel, with the possibility of death a very real consequence. That's what I do. What BDI does."

"Oh," she breathed.

"Those people—Ian, Jared, Jace, Dax, and even Natasha—are people I entrust my life to every time we head out for a mission. That's why we're close. There's no way we can do what we do and not be."

"I see." She drew in a breath. "You're right, by the way. Kari does *not* need to know about this. She was so relieved when you left the Marines that she didn't stop

talking about it for a solid month. She thinks you're a
private bodyguard with military training. This would
totally freak her out."

"Yeah, it would." He grimaced. "I guess I should
have asked if you were comfortable keeping a secret
from her before I told you."

"It's not my secret, Ty. I won't say anything."

He skimmed a thumb over her bottom lip. Damn,
she was sexy. How could she think otherwise? "Thank
you."

She frowned, her gaze dropping. "There's something
I didn't tell you yesterday."

Apprehension twisted inside him. "You can tell me
now."

"I said I was nervous at the police department
because of my mother and her history. Which is very
true, because nothing good ever came of those visits,
believe me. But there was another reason I didn't want
to go."

"They didn't arrest you," he teased. "So I'm
guessing you aren't wanted for anything."

He was trying to make her laugh, and she did, but
she grew serious again as she looked at him. Her eyes
were the deep green of summer. It struck him that he'd
never really made the comparison before.

"No, I'm not wanted." She huffed a breath. "I dated
Brian Woodruff. He was the officer who took notes and
didn't say anything when I made the report."

Not what he'd expected.

"Okay. How many dates? Was it serious?" He tried
to think about it logically, but when he imagined the
man he'd seen at the police station yesterday holding
Cassie close and kissing her, he didn't like it.

"It wasn't serious. We never, um, you know. I met him when he worked an event of ours, and he asked me out. We had seven dates, and he was nice enough, but he's a little too in love with himself. I decided I didn't want to be part of something where the things I was interested in didn't matter."

"Wow."

"Why *wow*?" she asked, frowning.

"Wow, because he could be so stupid." He skimmed his fingers down her arm. He didn't miss that she shivered at his touch. "Good for me. Bad for him."

"You aren't mad?"

"Why would I be mad? I mean, yeah, I wish you'd told me the truth yesterday. I'd have handled the situation differently, and now that I know you dated him, I have to add him to the list of people to check out."

"There's no way Brian sent me those emails. He's a cop, and he was never anything but decent to me. He never once did anything inappropriate. He just didn't show any interest in letting me talk, or asking me questions beyond a cursory *how was your day?* That felt like a relationship red flag to me, so I said I didn't think it was going to work out."

"How did he take it?"

She shrugged. "Fine. He said okay and that was it. I haven't talked to him since. Yesterday was the first time I've seen him in over a month."

Ty thought about the officer who'd taken notes while the other officer—Jones—asked questions. He hadn't seemed to look at Cassie in any particular way, but he'd had a bit of that puffed up aggressiveness that some military and law enforcement got. Like he wanted you to know he was an alpha male. Ty had chalked it up to his presence, but maybe it had been a little more than that. Maybe Brian Woodruff had been annoyed that Cassie had broken up with him a month ago and then showed up at the police station with another man.

Ty knew the way he looked and the vibe he gave off. He was big, muscular, and he had the coolness of a professional soldier. He was alpha through and through. Some men were threatened by that. Woodruff might be one of those, or he might have just been curious.

"I'll ask Dax to run a background check on him."

"Is that necessary?"

"It's part of the routine, Cass. He won't know about it, don't worry."

"Okay, I understand. I'm sorry I didn't say anything yesterday."

He leaned forward and pressed a kiss to her forehead. He really wanted her lips, but he was afraid that would spiral out of control far too easily. Foreheads were safe. Plump, kissable lips were not.

"It's fine. You said something now. Anything else you need to tell me?"

She shook her head. Then she pushed to her feet and stood over him. "I should go to bed. I've got a Zoom in the morning."

He leaned back against the futon on one elbow and propped his head against his hand. "Guess I'll see you in the morning then."

Cassie's nostrils flared the tiniest bit. Was it the bulge of his biceps? Or maybe the way his shirt stretched across his chest? A guy could hope.

"Um, yes. Okay. Right," she babbled.

He wanted to laugh. He knew better though. "Is there any particular time you like to shower?"

"Shower? Uh, about eight. Yes, eight. Why? Do you need it then?"

"Nope. Just want to be sure I'm not naked in your bathroom when you need to use it."

She swallowed. "Great. Thanks."

"You got eggs, by the way?" he asked as she headed for the door.

She turned around. "Yes, I have some."

"I'll cook you breakfast then."

"I thought you said you couldn't cook."

"I can scramble eggs and put bread in a toaster. I can also make coffee. A.k.a., breakfast."

"You're a man of many talents," she teased.

He grinned. "You've only scratched the surface, babe. Just wait until I show you the rest."

Chapter Nineteen

CASSIE SLEPT, BUT NOT WELL. SHE KEPT DREAMING about shadowy men following her down dark alleys, about being cornered and not knowing what to do. And then, right before the man's face was revealed in the single beam of light shafting across the alley, she woke with a start.

It took her a long moment to come back to herself, to realize she was in her bed in her house—and that her protector was in the next room. Ty wasn't letting anyone get inside the walls of her townhouse, and she was completely safe so long as he was there.

That made it easy to fall asleep again, but it wasn't nearly as easy to stay that way. Which was why, after the fourth time she'd startled awake, she sat up and flung the covers back. Ordinarily, she'd head to her studio and work on some video editing, but that was out because Ty was asleep there.

Cassie slipped into her robe, belted it tight, and headed downstairs to retrieve her laptop and get a glass of wine. At least she could sit in bed and go over her stats for a while. If she was lucky, she'd grow tired soon enough and get a little more sleep before it was time to get ready for work.

The house was quiet other than the hum of appliances and the occasional car that went by. She grabbed her laptop from the coffee table and set it on the kitchen counter while she retrieved a glass and poured some white wine from the box she kept in the fridge.

She was just about ready to go upstairs again when she noticed that a car was idling nearby. She was in a townhouse community, so there was nothing unusual about that since people worked different shifts, but she still crept over to the window and peered through the blinds.

A dark shape moved up the sidewalk, carrying something. When it turned onto the walkway that led to her house, Cassie's breath stopped in her throat and a chill slid over her. She wanted to call out to Ty, but she wasn't capable of making a sound just then.

The shape—a man judging by the size—was carrying something big and bulky. She lost sight of him when he reached the door, but she was too scared to go over and look out the peephole. When he walked back down the sidewalk, he wasn't carrying anything. He got into the car and drove away.

Cassie had been frozen in place the entire time, but now she moved. She ran up the stairs and knocked on her studio door, her heart in her throat. Ty was there in an instant, chest bare, wearing nothing but fitted boxer briefs that would have made her sigh with delight at any other time.

He looked as if he'd been awake for hours, but

judging by the mussed state of his hair, he'd been sleeping. "What's wrong?" he asked.

"S-someone came to the front door. They left something out there, but I don't know what it is. I d-didn't look."

He turned and tugged on his pants, but he didn't grab a shirt. Instead, he produced a weapon that he held in one hand as he hurried downstairs to the front door. He motioned her back, then pulled the door open a hair. When nothing happened, he pulled it wider.

Then he swore.

"What?" Cassie asked, standing well back from the door, her arms folded tightly over her chest. Her heart pounded as if she'd run a marathon, and fear raced along her nerve endings.

"Did you see them, Cassie?"

"I s-saw a man in black carrying something bulky. I should have screamed. I should have woken you."

Tears pressed against her eyelids, and she swallowed them furiously.

He shut the door and twisted the lock, then came over and hugged her tightly to him. "It's okay, Cass. You were scared."

"W-what is it?" She tilted her head back to look up at him. His expression was troubled.

"Flowers," he clipped out. "Just flowers."

"That doesn't sound so bad."

He hugged her to him again, rubbing one broad hand up and down her back. Despite her fear, a little flicker of heat kindled to life and started to blaze higher with every stroke.

"I want you to understand that someone is waging psychological warfare on you, Cassie. They're sending you shit, signing you up for shit, to rattle you and break your spirit. It's all about making you quit. Whether it's to quit your channel or your job, or to quit town, I don't know. But someone wants to stop you."

"I understand that. I'm not quitting, though." She said it fiercely because she meant it.

"I want you to come stay at my place for a while."

She pushed back until she could look at him again. There was something he wasn't saying. "Why? What's really out there, Ty?"

He looked troubled. "It's a wreath, Cass."

"A wreath," she repeated.

"On a stand," he added.

"On a stand." It took her a minute before she realized what he meant. "Oh my God. It's a funeral wreath. Someone put a funeral wreath at my front door?"

"Yes."

Anger flooded her. "I should have screamed. I should have done something. Maybe you could have caught him."

She closed her eyes, frustrated with herself for not *doing* something. Maybe if she'd had that training Natasha had talked about, she'd have flung open the door and caught the asshole herself.

"Why were you downstairs in the first place?"

"I couldn't sleep." She rubbed her forehead. "I kept having bad dreams about being chased in a dark alley, so this time I thought I'd grab my computer and a glass of wine. I was pouring the wine when I heard the car idling out front. I went to look and saw the guy come up the walkway carrying something."

"You didn't get a good look at him, did you?"

"No. The front door is at a bad angle from the window, so I didn't. He was big, wearing a hoodie, when I saw him in the streetlight. It's not very good here because of the oak tree out front. This row of houses doesn't get much of the light. Honestly, I thought he was one of my neighbors. People work shifts, and there's always someone coming and going. But then he came up the walkway, and I froze."

"It's understandable. But I think it's time you got away for a few days. Come stay with me while I try to find the asshole behind all this."

She wanted to, but she also wanted to film her videos. She was gaining followers every day, and if she wanted to keep the pace, she had to put out more content. More followers meant more revenue, which meant she was that much closer to being able to walk away from her day job and do this full time.

"My studio is here. You could stay with me," she said hopefully.

"Not good enough, Cassie. I need to get you out of the line of fire and work this case without having to worry about you whenever I need to go somewhere. We can take as much of your equipment and stuff as you need. I have a spare room you can use, and while I can't promise pink pillows and shit, we can hang a white sheet against the wall and you can use it the same as you do here."

She didn't like it, but she also didn't see that she had a choice. Because he was right about her staying. He couldn't be with her twenty-four hours a day, and she didn't want to be alone. She definitely didn't want to be alone at night, not after this.

"I hate letting this guy chase me away."

"It's temporary. We'll find who's doing this, and you can come home again."

She sighed. "Okay. But I can't go anywhere until after work. I have online meetings and phone calls to make."

"That's all right. I can pack up some of your equipment for you if you tell me what to get."

"I don't know if I can sleep again," she said. "What time is it?"

"It's just after three."

"Earlier than I thought."

"Take your computer and wine and go back to bed. I'll get rid of the flowers. In the morning, you can tell me what you want to take with you."

She shivered. She couldn't imagine what it would have been like to find a funeral wreath at her front door if she'd been alone. At least with Ty staying overnight, she didn't have to see it at all.

"What are you going to do with the wreath?"

"Call an Uber and send them to the nearest funeral home to deliver it."

She couldn't help but smile, in spite of the creep factor that was going to stick with her long after the flowers were gone. "That's thoughtful."

He shrugged. "Makes the most sense to me."

She went to pick up her wine and laptop, then stopped and turned to him. "Would you come talk to me when you're done? I don't think I can face the comments or emails right now."

He gave her a smile that made her feel safe and secure. "Yeah, I'll come. Give me a little bit."

Chapter Twenty

TY SENT THE FLOWERS TO A FUNERAL HOME, BUT NOT before taking a couple of photos. The wreath wasn't made of real flowers. It was silk, and there was a sash across it that he had not told Cassie about. It'd said *Rest in Peace* and there was a photo slot where someone had tucked in a photo of Cassie from her YouTube channel. It was a dual photo, though. The before and after from one of her videos. Someone had written, in permanent marker, the word *LIAR* in all caps beneath it.

He folded the sash and put it in his coat, then sent the pics to Dax. He'd already sent Brian Woodruff's name to him last night, even though that was a long shot. Ty didn't think the man was behind the harassment. Too risky for a police officer to do something so stupid. And for what reason? It wasn't like they'd been dating long or had a sexual relationship.

He needed to get some cameras installed ASAP. If he put in the Ring system like he'd planned, the asshole would see it. But if he got some tiny cameras from BDI and installed those, they might have a better chance of capturing the stalker on video. He'd get that done in the next couple of days.

He grabbed a bottle of water from Cassie's fridge and stood at the bottom of the steps, looking up. He'd promised to go in and talk to her, but he sure hoped like hell she was under the covers with her chin tucked beneath them. If all he could see were her eyes, all the better.

He knew she wasn't going to be tucked up like that, but a guy could wish for it. He trudged upstairs and went to the door she'd left open. Soft light spilled into the hallway, and he knocked softly on the wood to let her know he was there.

She looked up from her computer and removed a pair of tortoiseshell glasses that looked sexy as fuck on her. Her hair was piled in a loose knot on her head, and she wore the same pale blue satin robe she'd had on downstairs, even though her feet were under the blankets.

He stepped into the room and took it all in. Cassie was ultrafeminine. She loved pastels and flowers, but there were pops of darker blue as well. Her walls were builder white, but she'd hung pictures of flowers on her walls. She had cream curtains and a faded Persian carpet on the floor. Her bed was iron, and it was piled high with pillows and fluffy blankets. Also queen-size, he noted, just like the futon.

There was a wingback chair in one corner, next to a window, and he sat down on it after he moved two pillows out of the way. There was a footstool, so he propped his feet on it and leaned back.

"Aren't you cold?" she asked.

He glanced down and remembered he'd never put

his shirt back on. He hooked his fingers into the throw blanket hanging on one corner of the chair. "Not yet, but I've got this if I need it."

She twisted the wine glass in her fingers before taking a sip. "Thanks for humoring me. I was just feeling a bit out of sorts."

He lifted an eyebrow. "A bit out of sorts? Cassie, somebody walked up to your house at three in the morning and dropped off a funeral wreath. I'd say you're allowed to feel *out of sorts*." He nodded at the computer. "Did you change your mind about email?"

She clicked the lid closed, shaking her head. "I was shopping. It makes me feel better."

He didn't understand that, but it seemed to be something the women in his life liked doing. Mom, Aunt Karen, Kari. They shopped when stressed or annoyed. "You'll want to put a hold on mail for the next few days."

"I already did. But I've got some things coming UPS. I've asked to pick them up at the store, so I'll need to do that."

"We'll get it done."

She leaned back on the headboard and closed her eyes. "Everything about this feels surreal. I've always been a nobody, someone who can hide in plain sight. I stand next to the pretty girls, and I'm invisible—or noticeable, but only as something hideous—"

"Fucking hell, Cass, you're not hideous. Stop saying that."

She opened an eye and looked at him. Then she snorted, but it wasn't a dismissive sound. "I don't mean hideous like a beast. Just, you know, not skinny and perfect."

"Newsflash, babe, but there's no such thing as perfect. Skinny or not."

"I do know that, Ty. But that's how so much of our culture thinks. Fat is ugly. Fat is a moral failing. A sin. Well, some of us really don't have as much choice as skinny people seem to think we do. It's not always about eating bags of chips and copious amounts of fast food. Some of us are just superefficient at storing fat, and our bodies do not want to let go. I'm not saying it's not possible to lose weight, because it is, but it's damned hard too. And surgery? Not an option for everyone, and not a cure-all either."

"I'm glad to hear you say that, Red. It's a healthy attitude to have. But if you don't think you're one of the pretty girls, then you haven't been paying attention. You're fucking gorgeous—thick thighs, big tits, and all."

Her cheeks turned a pretty shade of pink. "I'm glad you think so. I don't always feel pretty, which is what the channel is about. Helping me by helping others."

"Have you ever shared that with them?"

She nodded. "I have, though it's been a while. Maybe I should again."

"Maybe so."

She plucked at a thread on her comforter. "I've never been the center of attention in real life. Not when my mother was showing her ass to the world, not when Kari was on the dance team and I was her plus-one for games and events, not even when I went out on a few dates with a cop. People don't typically notice me other than to dismiss me."

He felt a surge of anger for her. "First of all, they pay more attention than you think, whether you realize it or not. People notice you, Cassie, because you're beautiful, even if you aren't what they expect. If they don't talk to you, it's probably because you're putting off those *don't talk to me* vibes of yours."

She blinked. "I do have those, don't I?"

"You do. You always have. But maybe you should let people in a little more often. They might surprise you."

"I guess so. It's hard though."

"I know, Red," he said softly, remembering her as an awkward shadow at Kari's side. "But not everyone's a dick."

She sighed. "I loved the attention from my channel at first, because it was much easier than trying to talk to people face to face. I felt that thrill of finding *my* people. It was so amazing to be the one they wanted to talk to. But now? I don't want to stop what I'm doing, but I also kinda wish some of those people would go away. Most of them are great, but there are some who think you owe them because they watch your videos. Like without them you wouldn't be a success."

"Those are the kind of people who can take it too far."

She nodded. "I know. I just never thought I'd get that kind of fan, you know? I'm about body positivity, and being who you are, even though I struggle with it myself. I thought that being positive wasn't going to attract those kind of people—but I know better now." She toyed with one end of her robe belt. "Was there anything else out there when you took care of the flowers?"

"No. Just that."

He wasn't going to tell her. There was no reason for it. Not right now when she was already scared and weary. Maybe later. Or not.

She closed her eyes again. "I'm so tired, but every time I close my eyes, I see shadowy figures waiting for me."

He hated that she was scared. "I'll stay here while you sleep."

Her lashes lifted groggily. "It's not going to work, Ty. Once I start to fall asleep, the fear takes over. I keep waking up."

He got to his feet and went over to her bed. She gazed up at him in question.

"Then I'll hold you. We can sleep together, Cassie. Just sleep, because you need the rest—and because I'm not rushing you into anything."

"Okay."

He was surprised that she agreed, but it was a measure of how worn out she was that she did. She moved over, making room, and he kicked off the shoes he'd put on before disposing of the wreath. He thought about taking off his jeans but decided it was probably best to leave them on. Less likely to feel the softness of her body against his skin, which hopefully meant less discomfort in the long run. Less temptation.

She didn't say anything about the jeans, and he knew she was probably thinking the same thing he was. He lay on his back, propped against the pillows, one arm sliding around her. She was stiff at first, but he didn't move and she slowly relaxed, sliding closer to him as she did so.

She put a hand on his chest, curled her fist against his bare skin, and lay her cheek on his shoulder. Then she sighed. He rubbed his hand up and down her arm, slowly, softly. He didn't try to touch her hip, or her back, or anything but her arm. He knew that doing so would make her uncomfortable, but he thought it was a damned shame that she was so self-conscious about her lush body. Her curves were incredible and he wanted to explore them.

"Thank you, Ty," she murmured, her breath soft against his skin.

The whisper of it made the back of his neck prickle with the beginnings of desire. It'd been a long time since he'd lain in bed with a woman and done nothing. In fact, he wasn't sure he could remember the last time. Whenever he hit the sheets with a woman, it was usually for sex. There was no curling up together and going to sleep. He liked it, but he suspected it was more about the woman he was with than the cuddling.

"You're welcome."

"Guess you didn't know what you were getting into when Kari started calling, did you?"

"Not a clue," he said. "But from where I'm currently lying, it's not a bad gig. I'm just sorry you needed my help in the first place."

"I am, and I'm not." She tilted her head back, and he looked into her eyes. She was smiling. "This is pretty much right out of my teenage fantasy playbook, you know."

He could feel himself grinning and frowning in confusion at the same time. "Really? How's that?"

"I'm talking about this part, Ty. Lying with you in a bed—chastely, of course—and having you hold me close. I was terrified of the other because Lottie impressed upon me how it would ruin my life to get pregnant. Oh, and of course all the popular girls would know you were my boyfriend and that you had eyes for no one but me. They would look at me with longing then, and they'd want to be my friend. I'd be popular too, and everyone would think I was soooo cool. Like I said, complete fantasy. But it was fun to daydream."

He could picture her as she'd been back then—head down, shapeless clothes, hiding from the world—and he understood why she'd fantasized about him. He'd been the most popular guy at Bear Creek High School. Prom king, sports star, voted most likely to succeed. All that crap. Not that he cared about it, but his father had.

"My son is a Scott, and the Scotts are titans in this town. Don't forget that, boy."

He hadn't forgotten it. He'd joined the Marines to escape it, and he still hadn't forgotten all these years later. Especially whenever he went home and his dad couldn't hide his disappointment that Ty hadn't turned into the professional athlete he'd always dreamed his son would be.

"I'm sure you know this by now, but being popular in school doesn't magically fix everything."

"I know. I have only to think about Laura Charles and how sad she is that her glory days are over to know it didn't help her any. But it was my fantasy back then. I needed those to get through the days."

He stared up at her ceiling as she curled into his side again. His dick was very interested in what was happening here, but he was trying not to let it get involved. "I'm sorry life was hard for you in school. Kids can be pricks."

"They can, but it's part of the growing up process. Figuring out where you belong. I don't hate anyone from those days, but I don't want to move back home and be besties with any of them either. Except Kari. I miss her all the time."

"When was the last time you were there?"

"Last year before I left. I keep intending to go visit Kari and Heath and the girls, but I've been busy with the channel and work. What about you?"

"A few months ago." And he'd gotten out again as soon as he could. His mom was happy to see him. Kari and his aunt and uncle, too. But his dad?

Nope. Ty was a perpetual disappointment to his dad, who'd spent much of the visit in his shop. When he did show up for family meals, it was only to grunt and speak in monosyllables before he made an excuse to leave again. It'd been fourteen years, and he still wasn't over his son enlisting in the Marine Corp instead of earning a football scholarship to a Division One school.

He'd never been going to get that scholarship, but his dad had insisted all he had to do was work harder. Instead, he'd enlisted during his senior year right after he'd turned eighteen.

"You don't sound like you enjoyed it," she said, her voice very soft.

"I like seeing my family. I don't much care about the rest."

"I miss Tammy's. Best ice cream around."

"Oh, hell, yes. Okay, I miss Tammy's sometimes. And Granger's Diner."

"They have the best cheeseburgers and fries."

"Apple pie isn't bad either."

"Oh, God, no. Warm with fresh vanilla ice cream from Tammy's. Miss Lulu is the apple pie queen."

Ty laughed. "You're making me miss home. Just a little bit."

"Me too. Just a little bit." She yawned big.

"Go to sleep, Cassie. We can talk some more in the morning."

"Okay," she whispered. "G'night, Ty."

He pressed a kiss to her hair, feeling protective and way more possessive than he'd expected. Cassie Dixon was a surprise after all these years. For a guy who didn't like surprises, he was enjoying this one.

Chapter Twenty-One

Kari: You're going to stay at Ty's place? Good. I'll feel better knowing you aren't alone.

Cassie: He felt it was a better plan than staying with me. He's probably right since he actually has an extra bedroom. All I have is a futon, and it's not big enough for him.

Kari: I'm glad he's taking this seriously. I feel better.

Cassie: I do too. Thanks for insisting. He's been very helpful.

Kari: You know… I've been thinking.

Cassie rolled her eyes. *What?*

Kari: You and Ty.

Cassie glanced over at Ty, who was currently navigating traffic. She'd attended her morning Zoom meeting with Elite Events, where she'd discussed swag bags and other sources of materials for the conference, and then she'd informed Amelia she was going to stay with a friend for a few days. Amelia's face had twisted in a frown, but what could she say to that? She was the one who'd sent Cassie to work from home.

Cassie: Me and Ty what?

Kari: <eggplant emoji><water drops emoji> *Bowchick-awowwow!*

Cassie nearly shrieked with laughter, but she managed to hold it in. *Um, where did you get that idea?*

Kari: He's single. You're single. You're my bestie. He's basically my brother, even if he's my cousin. I love you both, and I think you'd be great together.

Cassie slanted a look at Ty. *In case you haven't noticed lately, your cousin/brother is smoking HOT. Like, Hollywood hot, with abs and everything. I have rolls, not abs. He's gonna want to bang someone with flesh as firm as his.*

Ty hadn't indicated anything of the kind, and she knew it. But it was an easy excuse to give Kari, plus it deflected the conversation away from deep, dark confessions about the feelings she'd once harbored for him. That was the only secret she'd never shared with Kari. It would have been too embarrassing and far too pitiful back then.

Kari: A) You're beautiful. B) He'd be lucky to have you. C) He's a man. He wants to bang a beautiful woman who says yes. And besides, I wasn't just talking about banging. I mean the two of you as a couple. Relationship. The time is right for you both.

Cassie: You're a nut and I love you. Gotta run.

Kari: Avoiding the convo. I see. Bye!

Cassie put her phone down. Ty glanced over. "What did she want?"

"Lots of things," Cassie said, waving her phone. "She's glad I'm staying with you. She also thinks we should bang."

Ty nearly choked on a laugh. "Holy shit, you guys *do* talk about everything."

Cassie's skin grew hot. Why had she said that to him? She was getting far too comfortable talking to him about stuff. And then she got embarrassed by her own big mouth.

"I didn't tell her anything about last night, or even that we've kissed. She came up with that on her own."

He turned off the main road and into an apartment complex. They were in Maryland, on a corridor between DC and Annapolis.

"I like the way she thinks," he said with a wink. "Here we are."

He parked in front of a building and together they got her bags and camera equipment. She followed him upstairs to a second floor apartment. It was an end unit with windows on three sides and a balcony in the back.

The living room contained a couch—leather—and a TV stand. There was also a wooden coffee table with remotes on it and one side table where a stack of coasters sat.

He took her to the guest room and put her things down. The room was bigger than the one she used as a studio in her townhouse, and there was room for her to film at one end. There was a full-sized bed with a plain comforter and a pillow, and a single nightstand.

"Not as pretty as yours," he said.

"I think it's great, Ty. Thank you."

"There are two full baths, so you can have your own shower. I need to go grocery shopping." He looked a little sheepish. "There's nothing in the fridge right now, so you'll have to tell me what you like."

"Can we go together? That way I can get what I want?"

"We can do that. I have to swing by work for a little while. I can pick you up then, or you can go with me and hang out in the Cove."

"The Cove?"

"The Pirate's Cove. It's a bar. Exclusive to BDI, so there's nobody there but us. There's Wi-Fi if you need to work, or you can play video games on the arcade machine."

"Wow, you have an arcade at work?"

He grinned. "Yeah. It's a great little bar, and it's all ours."

She thought about staying and setting up her equipment. But she really wanted to go with Ty. There was plenty of time to set up later, and she still had two videos on her computer that were nearly ready to post. She was definitely going to have to film something new very soon, but she could do it tonight.

"Okay, I'm in. I want to see this magical bar you have at work."

He flipped his keys around a finger. "Whenever you're ready."

She picked up her laptop bag and shouldered it. "How about now?"

He laughed. "Now's good."

———

"A FUNERAL WREATH?" Ian said, shaking his head. "Jesus, that's sick."

"Yeah."

The sash lay on the table in front of them. Ty's blood boiled just looking at it. Dax was on the computer, and Rascal sat looking at the photos of the wreath. Jared, Brett, and Jace were there too. Colt was on assignment in France.

"We didn't get any prints off the fake heart, but

maybe we can lift something from the photos," Ian said. "Let's get the lab on it."

Jared took out his phone. "I'll text the lab and ask Kenny to come get it."

Ian nodded. "What else do we know about this?"

"Not much," Dax said. "It could have come from an online retailer. There are some florists in the area who work with silk, but it'll take time to check them all for that specific wreath. I've asked support to start making calls."

BDI had an entire support staff that took care of the day-to-day tasks involved with running a private security company. They were invaluable, and Ty knew they would leave no stone unturned.

"Unfortunately, she didn't wake me until after the guy left," Ty said. "I was asleep in her guest room because we got back to her place late, and it's a long drive home."

Nobody questioned that. Not that he expected they would.

"So the guy walked up to her door and set the wreath, then got into a vehicle and drove away?" Rascal asked.

"Yep. Cassie said she couldn't see him because of the angle of the porch from the window she was standing at. All she could tell about the vehicle was that it was dark, maybe blue or black, and looked like an SUV. The person got into the driver's side, so he was alone."

"Are we sure it's a man?" Ian said.

"No, but Cassie said he was big, so I'm assuming. Whoever sent her the emails is writing from a male point of view as well."

"It could be a woman," Dax added, "but the program I ran it through indicates male voice. Syntax and word choice. Not that a woman couldn't mimic those things, because she could. But she'd need to be someone who works with words a lot. Considering the misuse of grammar and punctuation in those emails, I'm thinking she's either a fucking genius who's damned amazing at covering her tracks, or it's a disgruntled guy."

"Occam's razor," Rascal said. "The simplest explanation is the most likely one."

Ty couldn't help but grin. Rascal was full of surprises these days. First, he'd grown his hair back after years of shaving it off, which changed just about everything according to everyone who knew him, and now he'd gone from monosyllables to spouting philosophy.

"Precisely," Ian said.

"He says some pretty vicious things." Jace was looking at the emails that Dax had printed for everyone. "What a fucking prince of a guy."

"I watched some of her videos with Libby," Jared said. "They're kinda brilliant, really. Libby squealed when she did the reveals."

Ty felt unaccountably proud even though he'd had nothing to do with it. "Some men feel duped because she makes herself look so terrible at the beginning. Then she's a damned beauty queen, and they can't handle it. The women fucking love it."

"I'll be honest," Brett said. "I never realized how much shit women go through online like that. Or what kind of artistry can be achieved with makeup. It's astounding."

"Yeah, but it's also filming and angles," Ty said.

"You saw Cassie last night. She's a normal human being. She's not either of those extremes. But somebody's latched onto her videos hard, and they aren't happy. And it has to be someone she knows, or someone local, because what delivery service drops off wreaths at three in the morning?"

"Right," Ian said. "What about Kelly Cosmetics? Anything more on them?"

"Odin, otherwise known as Toby Belen, has been working as Debra Kelly's right-hand man for the past three years," Dax said. "He's recently divorced from his husband of five years, and he's got a mortgage that eats a good portion of his pay every month. Apparently, he kept the house after the divorce, but it was basically a deal where his spouse agreed to give up any rights to equity—meaning there isn't any—and walked away. He's expecting to make a killing on the IPO when Kelly Cosmetics goes public. He could very well view Cassie's video as a threat to a payday he desperately needs in order to stay solvent."

"I could see him sending all that shit," Ty said. "The pizzas, the rat, the human heart, the wreath, and the sex toys. But if he's strapped for cash, where'd he get the money for that stuff?"

"He has an expense account at work. He could have ordered everything from there. It'll take some digging to figure that out though." Dax held up a hand to stop anyone from speaking. "I'm already on it."

"Brian Woodruff," Ty said. "Anything on him?"

"Not really. He's new to the department. He came up from Williamsburg about six months ago. No idea why. His record looks clear, but there's one file I can't get access to. I've tried, but it's blocked."

"I'll put in a call to Phoenix," Ian said. "She'll be thrilled to unearth a Virginia cop's file for me."

He said it with a healthy dose of sarcasm, and they all laughed. The all-powerful Phoenix was a highly placed CIA officer who performed magic when they needed her to. Like when she'd managed to burn down Ian's house without really burning it down. She'd convinced the media it had happened though, and that had given BDI an edge when going to Vienna to rescue Natasha and Daria from the Gemini Syndicate.

"That leaves Dylan Webb," Ty said. "He's Cassie's ex. They broke up a year ago. According to my cousin, he moved to Richmond this past year. He told Cassie a month ago that he was getting married. She said she hadn't heard from him before that since she left Bear Creek."

"It'd be nice to know the wife—or perspective wife's—name, because she must be the one with the mortgage or lease. His address still shows as Bear Creek on everything I can find," Dax said.

Ty frowned. "So it could be the ex. But why wait almost a year to start harassing her?"

Jace was shaking his head. "I dunno. I mean the guy from the emails sounds angry that she's so different in the befores and afters. Presumably a guy who'd been in a relationship with her would know what she looked like without makeup already. This guy sounds downright offended."

Ian leaned back and put his hands behind his head. "Three possibilities then. Or it's none of them and her stalker is someone else. One of the—how many subscribers is she up to now?"

"Seventy-five thousand," Dax said. "I've got people

combing the comments and flagging any questionable ones, but it takes time with that kind of following."

"Okay, damn. One of seventy-five thousand and growing. Even though we can probably eliminate a lot of those people, we don't know when they subscribed. Do we?"

"It's in the channel analytics on YouTube," Ty said. "We can eliminate people based on when they subscribed."

"Though," Dax cut in. "You don't *have* to subscribe to view someone's content. If I disliked someone enough to threaten them, I wouldn't subscribe. I'd just check their channel every time I logged on."

"Good point," Ian said. "Let's not waste resources tracking subscribers then."

"What about Big Guns?" Ty asked. "He was the user that Cassie blocked."

"Nothing on him," Dax said. "Other than the tone of his comments is similar to the emailer's. But that could just be dude speak, if I'm honest."

Ty groaned. "So we're really nowhere with any of this is what you're telling me."

"A little farther than nowhere. But, yeah, this guy isn't leaving a digital trail I can find yet. He's careful."

"I want to put surveillance on her house in case that guy comes back in the middle of the night again. We can at least get him on camera."

"Do it," Ian said. "I presume she's staying with you for the foreseeable future?"

Ty nodded. "I've moved her into the guest room. She's working remotely at the moment anyway."

"If this guy gets wind she's not there, he might not

show up again," Ian said. "Be prepared to move her back and stay with her if that's the case."

"Got it, boss."

Ian got to his feet. "We good for now? Everyone's got their marching orders?"

"Copy," Jace said. He put his arm on Ty's shoulder as they were walking out of the conference room. "I like her. She's a little quiet, but I feel like she warms up when she knows you. Maddy said she didn't talk much when the women were alone, but she was polite."

Ty felt a rush of protective emotion. "Cassie was pretty shy growing up. Her channel is about the only place she doesn't let that stop her. She says it feels like she's alone and talking to herself, so that's why she can do it."

"Probably what makes it so genuine, too. Maddy watched some of it. She said Cassie is a freaking genius with makeup. Her words, not mine."

Ty laughed. "No, you'd have said *fucking* genius."

"Too right. You know, if she's going to be around for a while, you should bring her over to the house. Maddy would love to pick her brain about makeup and how it relates to art."

"I'll ask her. Fair warning, it'll be a couple of days. Last night's dinner took a lot out of her."

Ian had stopped in the hall to talk to his executive assistant, Melanie, but he glanced over at that. "Hey, I behaved myself. Natasha made me."

Ty laughed. "We all behaved. And she had a great time, but she's an introvert. She has to recover before she can people again."

"Amen," Jared said. "You extroverts give me a headache."

"You're marrying one," Jace said with a laugh.

"That's right. She can people for me, and I'll people when I have to."

Melanie gave an exaggerated sigh as she closed the folder she'd been showing to Ian. "Y'all all crazy," she said. "I can't believe I ever took a job here."

Ian laughed as she strolled down the hall. "But you love us!"

"That I do," she called back.

"I left Cassie in the Cove," Ty said. "I need to get those cameras from you, Dax. Then I better go see if she's managed to beat my high score on *Area 51*."

"Aw, man, *Area 51*?" Dax said as they headed for the IT section where the equipment was kept. "I love that game. We could play a round before you go…"

"Nope. I have to take Cassie to the grocery store."

"Look at you, getting all domestic," Dax said. "Next thing you know, you'll be moving in with her permanently."

Ty grinned. "You never know. Maybe you need to start looking for someone to share *your* life with."

"Nope, not me," Dax replied, shaking his head. "I've got my computers and all you clowns. Too busy for anything besides meaningless sex."

"That's a shame," Ty said, and meant it.

Chapter Twenty-Two

IT WAS A LITTLE STRANGE TO BE STAYING IN TY'S apartment rather than her own place, but Cassie didn't mind it as much as she'd thought she would. They'd gone to the grocery store and picked up some things, with Cassie paying her share, though she'd had to insist, and then they'd returned to the apartment to put the groceries away and settle in for the evening.

Ty had a couple of cameras to install at her town-home, but it was getting too late in the day to do it now. He said he'd go tomorrow while she worked.

Cassie stood in the guest room and wished she'd brought her loose pajama pants and baggy sweatshirt, but the last thing she'd wanted as she'd packed her bags was for Ty to see her looking like a shapeless lump ever again.

She sighed as she put on the leggings and loose T-shirt she'd brought instead. The tee had more structure than she wanted right now. If she was at home, she'd have put all her baggy stuff on and to hell with it. Now she felt like the shirt was clinging to lumps and bumps she'd rather it didn't.

But a check of the full-length mirror she'd brought with her for filming told her she was fine. In fact, she looked cute, and when she slid her feet into her fuzzy flip flops, even better. Casual, comfortable, and not sloppy.

When she emerged from the guest room, Ty wasn't in the living area or the kitchen. She went to the fridge and started to pull things out to fix one of her favorite, healthy dishes—black bean tacos. She was in the midst of chopping onions and tomatoes for salsa when Ty appeared.

Almost literally appeared because she gasped. Thank God she wasn't actively slicing at that moment. "You scared the heck out of me."

"Sorry," he said. "I should have said something."

"You're like a cat without a bell."

He grinned. "You want me to wear a bell now? Kinky."

Cassie shook her head, though she was grinning too. "Apparently, I'm all kinds of kinky if the variety of adult newsletters hitting my inbox is any indication."

"Have you gotten more?"

"No, just the ones I already told you about."

"That's good." He came into the kitchen and peered at the cutting board and bowls. "What are you making?"

"Black bean tacos. I promise they're good," she added at the way he wrinkled his nose.

"Can I help?"

"Get some plates and silverware? It won't take long, and I swear you'll like them. Oh, and get some of that store bought salsa for the chips, please."

He pulled out two of everything, poured chips into a bowl, and added salsa to another bowl. In the meantime, she'd finished the salsa for the tacos and moved on to cooking the filling.

"Damn, smells good."

Cassie threw him a smile. "Told you they were good."

"Do you cook a lot?"

"I try to," she said as she moved the poblano pepper and onion around in the pan. "I like to control the salt and fat if I can. So much takeout food is made with too much of those things. Especially salt. High blood pressure runs in the family. Or at least for me it does. Lottie said my dad had it and that's where I got it, but who knows if she's telling the truth or not? Of course her blood pressure is fine, even with the crap she eats and all the drinking."

She wasn't bitter. Much.

"Why do you call her Lottie?"

Cassie added tomato paste and spices and swirled them around. "That's what she wanted when I got to be about eight. Said she was too young to have a kid my age."

It'd been hard for her to go from Mom—because Lottie had never allowed Mommy—to Lottie, but she'd done it.

Ty was frowning when she glanced at him. "That's a shitty thing to do to a kid."

"Yes, well, Lottie Dixon is a force of nature unto herself, or some such shit. She always did what she wanted. And your Aunt Karen let me call her Mom, so I was fine."

Mostly.

"Cassie, you weren't fine. You know you weren't."

Sudden tears pricked her eyes. What the heck? She sniffed. "Okay, no, I wasn't. I didn't entirely understand, but it was because of the men in her life. She didn't want them to know she had a kid. She told them I was her sister's kid and she was just taking care of me. Didn't seem as permanent that way."

He came over and put his arms around her from behind while she stirred the beans into the mixture. The urge to turn in his arms and hug him tight was strong, but she wasn't going to burn dinner. "I'm sorry," he whispered in her ear, his warm breath sending shivers of awareness along the column of her neck and into her spine.

"Thank you. I'm used to it now, but it was hard then."

"It's no wonder you were so quiet all the time. You were hiding from everyone, even back then."

He was right, and it rocked her that he'd seen it that easily. "Hiding was what I did best."

"I don't want you to hide from me, Cassie. I want to know all your secrets."

She closed her eyes as emotion threatened to over-whelm her. "You really need to let me go, or I'm going to burn this."

His arms loosened and then he stepped away. "Okay, but we aren't done with this conversation."

"Can you warm those tortillas for me?" she asked, her throat tight.

"I can, but you have to tell me exactly what to do. Not familiar with tortilla warming. Can't cook, remember?"

She loved that he moved back to lighthearted

conversation as if nothing had happened. It was what she needed right now. "Wrap them in a paper towel, and put in the microwave for fifteen seconds. If they aren't warm enough, do another ten."

He tore off paper towels. "How will I know?"

"You'll know."

He did as she said, and she removed the black bean mixture from the heat. When Ty finished the tortillas, she put them onto plates—four for him and two for her —and filled them with black beans, shredded cheese, sour cream, a squeeze of lime, and the salsa she'd made. He carried the plates to the small dining room table and they sat down to eat.

Ty's eyes widened as he bit into a taco. "Whoa, you were right. This is good."

"Told you so."

"And it's just vegetables, right? No meat?"

"No meat. You can have a delicious and satisfying meal without meat."

"Damn," he muttered as he polished off one taco and picked up another. "You aren't a vegetarian because you ate the beef at the Korean restaurant and the lasagna last night."

"I try to limit meat, but yes, I still eat it. I have some other go-to veggie dishes I make."

"I want to try them all." He closed his eyes and made a noise much like a moan. "Damn, I love good food. Especially when it's homemade."

"Your aunt's a great cook. So's Kari. And I know I had your mom's homemade apple pie at least once, so I'm assuming she is too. Why didn't you learn how?"

He gave her a look. "My dad is a lot like your mom.

He's an asshole who thought his son didn't need to learn a girly thing like cooking."

"Wow. I had no idea."

"How could you? He seems normal on the outside. Trust me, he's not."

She hadn't expected that. She'd never talked to his dad, but then she hadn't talked to much of anybody back then if she didn't have to. Still, he was Kari's uncle and he'd seemed normal enough. Guess you never really knew about people sometimes. "I'm sorry. I didn't know."

"I don't think anybody did. Well, not many people. Kari knows we don't get along, but she doesn't know everything. My dad doted on her like she was his own daughter. But she's a girl, so the expectations weren't as high."

Cassie must have made a face because he hurried on.

"I mean *his* expectations. Kari just had to be cute and sweet. Me? If I'd cured cancer and rocketed to the moon, it still probably wouldn't have been enough."

"Jeez. My mom expected almost nothing out of me, and your dad expected everything out of you. If we could've put them into a pot and stirred them together, we'd have probably found the right mix." She snagged a chip and ate it. "What did he want you to do with your life? Wasn't he proud you were a Marine?"

"He wanted me to be a professional athlete." Ty flexed the biceps in one arm. "I was destined to play football or baseball. Win a Heisman trophy, maybe. Get a couple of Super Bowl rings. Or World Series rings. Didn't matter to him which."

"Did you want to be a pro?"

He snorted. "I wasn't good enough, Cassie. I was good enough to be a star in Bear Creek. But to play for Alabama or LSU or Ohio State at that level? No. Wasn't happening. I could have probably gotten a partial scholarship for football because of my size and the fact I played decently, but a school like that would have eaten me up. And I just couldn't take four years of my dad's bitching about me not getting enough play, or needing to toughen up, or whatever." He shrugged. "I went to the Marine recruiter the day after I turned eighteen and did a delayed enlistment. My dad was furious."

She reached out and put a hand on his arm. "Guess we both had our reasons for wanting to leave Bear Creek. Except you did it a lot sooner than I did."

"I was scared as shit; I'm not gonna lie. But I survived Parris Island, and then I felt like I could do anything."

She knew Parris Island was where the Marines went to bootcamp. She'd looked it up after Ty had joined. There was a bootcamp in San Diego as well, but he'd gone to South Carolina because it was closer. She also knew that all female Marines went to Parris Island as well. She didn't know why, and the idea of her joining had never been serious, but she'd pictured herself there in her late night fantasies about losing weight, getting strong, and showing absolutely *everyone* that they'd underestimated her.

Turned out there were more ways to do that than joining the Marines. Thank God.

"You were decorated. That's what Kari said."

She thought he looked troubled before he spoke. "A Purple Heart and a Bronze Star with V device. One is for being wounded in action and the other is for heroism in combat with valor."

Her heart thumped. "Combat. Wow. That sounds intense. And scary."

He shrugged. "It was intense. There's not enough time to be scared when it's happening, but after—yeah, it catches up to you."

"Why did you leave?"

He didn't say anything at first, and she wondered if she'd blundered into something she shouldn't have. If she'd taken their nice meal together and made it awkward.

But then he blew out a breath as if he'd made a decision. "I like having a measure of control over my fate. I didn't have it in the Marines. The day I got that Bronze Star, half my team died in an ambush. I don't know that it was anyone's fault, not specifically, but nothing about that day felt right. Yet we had no choice but to obey orders. If something doesn't feel right these days, I don't do it. My opinion matters as much as the next guy's, including Ian's. I prefer it that way."

There was a hard knot in her throat. "I'm sorry about what happened to your team. That had to be difficult for you."

He nodded. "It was. We were all highly trained, and we all knew what could happen to us. Still, losing men I'd served side by side with for so long—" He shook his head as if clearing it. "Takes time to get over that. Though I'm not sure you get over it so much as you learn to live with it."

She reached over and took his hand in hers. "I'm really sorry, Ty. I don't know what that's like and I can't pretend I do. But I can see it hurts you, and I wish I could fix it for you."

He lifted their clasped hands to his mouth and pressed a kiss to the back of hers. "Thank you. It's sweet of you to say that."

Her skin was starting to tingle, and she grew instantly wet between her thighs. Simply from the touch of his lips to the back of her hand. Such an innocent touch, and her body was acting like he'd slipped his fingers into her panties. Wow.

"Dessert?" she practically yelped, her voice sounding high and strained. She hoped he didn't notice, but she was pretty sure he had by the way he gazed at her for a moment before he let her go.

"What did you have in mind, Red?"

Hot things. Dirty things. Things she could never say out loud. She pictured them naked together, pictured his head between her legs instead of the vibrator…

"Cassie?" Ty snapped his fingers. "Earth to Cassie."

"I, oh, sorry."

What were they talking about again?

"Dessert?" he prodded.

"Right, yes! I'm sorry. Is it hot in here? I feel hot. Oh my."

He lifted her hand to his lips again. When his tongue slipped along her knuckles, she had to suppress a whimper. He let go and grinned at her, and she knew he'd been teasing her on purpose.

Tyler Scott was so much better in real life than he'd ever been in her dreams.

Chapter Twenty-Three

TY WATCHED CASSIE BLINK RAPIDLY. HER CHEEKS AND neck were a little pink, and she looked as if she'd been daydreaming. All he'd done was kiss the back of her hand—and lick her knuckles—and she looked as if he'd stroked an erogenous zone. As if she were fighting off arousal.

He wanted, more than anything, to press her on it. To lift her hand and suck one of her fingers before kissing his way up her arm and over to her sweet, luscious lips. But he knew he'd freak her out if he did. He had to give her time to breathe. Time to accept what he knew was inevitable between them.

He wanted her, but there was a right way to go about it. She had to trust him, and he wasn't entirely sure she did just yet. Not with this.

He wasn't offended by it. She trusted him to help her, but she wasn't ready to trust him with her body. He got that. A lifetime of being self-conscious about her appearance wasn't going to disappear overnight. When they finally ended up naked together, he wanted her to know that he craved every inch of her.

How could she be so uncertain of herself when she was fucking gorgeous? It would have frustrated him if he hadn't known where she'd come from and what she'd endured as a kid. Even if she'd been an outgoing child, having her own mother make her pretend they weren't parent and child had to be a serious mind fuck.

"Um, how about frozen yogurt with caramel sauce?" she said when she found her voice again. "I'm afraid I got the lite version though."

"Sounds good to me. How about we finish dinner, then I'll clean up the dishes while you get bowls."

"Oh, you don't have to do that. I made the mess—"

"Cassie," he interrupted.

"Yes?"

"You cooked dinner for me. Least I can do is clean up. But first I want to finish these delicious tacos, eat some chips and salsa, and talk to you about random shit."

Her smile was a little tentative. She dipped a chip into salsa. "What kind of random shit?" she asked before popping it into her mouth.

"Favorite TV series."

She blinked. "Is that a question?"

"Yes."

"*A Discovery of Witches.* All three seasons."

"Don't think I've heard of that."

"Really? It's about a witch and a vampire, and they fall in love, but falling in love is against the rules—" She waved a hand. "There's a lot going on. But it's a romance at heart, and I adored every episode."

"Okay, guess I'll have to watch it and see why you like it so much. Favorite color?"

"Wait a minute. You didn't tell me your favorite series."

"*Doctor Who*. Tenth Doctor is the favorite, but I like them all, really. Every actor brings something to the role."

She was grinning. "I like *Doctor Who*. Not that I've watched them all. Some of them are a bit intense when you live alone."

"And a show about vampires and witches isn't?" He loved watching her face when she talked about things she liked. He also loved to tease her.

"There are demons, too. It had some moments, but I read all the books so I knew what was coming. After I watched the *Doctor Who* episode with the weeping angels, I had to take a break. I couldn't turn the lights off for days!"

He chuckled. "Yeah, that one's creepy as fuck. That's as far as you got?"

She nodded.

"Man, you've got a long way to go then. And there are more angels. Just warning you now."

"Great," she deadpanned, rolling her eyes.

"We could watch together. You can hide your face against my chest at the scary parts."

She took a chip and broke off part of it, chewing slowly. "Maybe. But only if you watch *A Discovery of Witches* with me."

"It's a deal," he said. Because he wasn't stupid, and anything that got him cuddled up on the couch with Cassie squeezing against him was a good thing. "We can start tonight if you want."

She scrunched her face adorably. "I want to, but I really need to make a new video."

"Okay. How long does it take, and can I help?"

She ate another piece of the chip. "It depends. The raw footage can take a couple of hours if I'm changing clothes a lot, and then I have to edit everything—but the editing doesn't need to happen tonight. If you managed the camera for me, that would cut down on the amount of footage I have to edit out." She made a face again. "But it's always been just me, and I'm not sure I can do it with you watching. I'm afraid it'll make me stiff and robotic if you're there."

"That's the last thing I want. Maybe we could try, and if it doesn't work, then I'll leave you alone to do what you do."

"I'm sorry," she blurted. "It sounds so stupid, but I've always filmed alone, and I just don't know if—"

He put his fingers over her mouth. Gently. She blinked at him but she also stopped speaking. Her lips were soft against his hand. He shoved the thought out of his brain before his dick got the message and started to react.

"It's okay, Red. Don't apologize for being who you are."

She smiled as he took his hand away. "Thanks for understanding."

"I'm here for you, babe. Whatever you need."

"I appreciate that. I know you only came to my rescue because Kari insisted, but I'm glad you did. And glad you stuck around."

"I'm glad too. I want to catch whoever's doing this to you, Cassie. I want you to feel safe again."

"I feel safe with you."

That gratified him more than he could say. "I'm glad. And, hey, I still need to teach you some self-defense moves. Natasha isn't wrong about that."

She frowned. "Couldn't I just buy a gun?"

It was his turn to frown. "A gun won't do you a damned bit of good if you can't keep someone from taking it away from you, Red. You need to know how to defend yourself."

Her gaze dropped to her lap. "If it involves a push-up, I'm doomed."

He put a finger under her chin and made her look at him. The look in her eyes sent a hot shard of desire straight to his groin. It wasn't a sexy look. It was a vulnerable one, and it made him want to wrap her up and protect her.

Jesus, this girl. She was hell on his psyche.

"No push-ups. No running. Just some jabbing in unexpected places and maybe some twisting too. You can handle it."

"You must think I'm pitiful. But I do walk, Ty. I go to the gym at my neighborhood community center, and I walk for at least an hour on the treadmill. Sometimes more if I have time. Not that I've done it lately."

"Do you want to know something?"

She nodded.

"You're more fit than you think. It takes core strength and strong bones to carry extra weight, plus the muscle strength involved. People don't realize that. They look at someone heavy and just see an unfit person. But, damn, if you didn't have a strong core and back, you couldn't carry your weight around. You'd buckle under the pressure, same as I would with all this extra muscle.

You're strong, Cassie. You can handle some self-defense exercises just fine."

She smiled at him, and his heart flipped in his chest. He resisted the urge to rub it.

"You really are good for my self-esteem, you know that?"

"I'm just telling it like it is, Red. You're strong, you're sexy, and you're fucking gorgeous. You need to own it and stop letting other people's opinions chip away at your confidence."

"You're right."

"I know I am."

She leaned forward and kissed him. His pulse sped up, and his dick throbbed to life. He wanted to drag her to him and kiss the living daylights out of her, but he let her set the pace. He hoped she'd take it to the next level, but she pulled away and gazed at him.

"I appreciate that you want to take it slow with me, Ty. And that's good for right now—but I don't think it's going to last. I think, soon enough, you're going to make me snap and agree to anything just to ease the ache inside."

He caressed her cheek with the back of his fingers. "I damn sure hope so. You're worth the wait, but I'm not gonna lie and tell you it doesn't physically hurt."

"I'm sorry."

He grinned. "I'm not. Because when we do get together, Red? Fucking epic."

Chapter Twenty-Four

THEY SETTLED INTO A ROUTINE OVER THE NEXT COUPLE of days. Cassie worked on Elite Events projects in the morning, and then filmed her TikTok or YouTube videos in the afternoon. She let Ty observe to start with, just to see if she could do it, and discovered that she *could* do the makeup videos after she got used to his presence. The clothes were different. For some reason, she had a harder time with those, probably because clothes made her feel more vulnerable than makeup did.

She knew what she was doing with makeup. It was art, and she was good at art. Clothing was guesswork, though she was pretty sure she'd figured it out for herself. There were still missteps sometimes. She tried to be honest with her viewers when she got something that didn't work, and to show them why. Not every outfit choice was a good one, and people needed to know what worked and what didn't.

Ty seemed to be interested in the process. The first time she'd sat down in front of him with a clean face, bright lights shining at all her flaws, her heart had been in her throat. She didn't tell him what it cost her to let him see her in person that way, but he seemed to know. He was gentle with her and complimentary. She explained how to angle the camera and lights for the worst possible effect, and he did so. Then he told her she was a genius for doing it that way.

She'd had to inform him she was not, that she'd copied other influencers, but the formula worked so she kept doing it. Then she set about painting her face with the new palette she'd gotten from a cosmetics company who wanted her to try it out.

"Holy shit," Ty said after it was over and he'd pressed stop. "That's really kinda amazing how you do that."

She felt the glow of his praise all over. "It's just using lights and shadows to bring out what's already there."

"It's more than that," he told her. "It's you."

She didn't have an answer to that, but his words meant a lot.

After the videos were done, Ty showed her some self-defense moves. They stood in his living room, the coffee table pushed out of the way, and he taught her how to attack with her keys, how to gouge at eyes, and how to stomp insteps and get out of chokeholds. It wasn't easy, and she worked up a sweat while they practiced, but he was right that she could do it. She felt a sense of accomplishment when they were done, and she headed for the shower where she let hot water pour over her aching muscles.

She had some bruises and soreness, but it was the price for learning how to take care of herself. The first time Ty saw a bruise forming on her wrist, he'd apologized profusely. She'd put a hand over his mouth and told him it was okay. More than okay. It was necessary. He hadn't seemed happy, but he'd accepted it.

And when he'd tried to back off the intensity the next time, she'd called him on it and made him do it as if he were a real attacker. He still hadn't pressed as hard as he could, but he'd pressed her hard enough that she felt it in her body later that night when everything started to ache.

In the evening, they watched television together. At first, Cassie sat stiffly beside him, but he encouraged her to lean against him—so she did. If felt natural to curl up next to Ty on the couch and watch an episode of one of their favorite shows. She suggested they alternate, but he said no, they'd do all hers first. They were still watching it three days later.

Staying with Ty was easy. Maybe too easy, because she thought about what it would be like when she went home again. She'd be alone, which she usually liked, but the thought of being alone without Ty wasn't appealing. He'd ruined being alone for her.

Not that she intended on telling him that. They had an easy relationship right now. Enjoying hanging out together was one thing. Telling a man you were beginning to dread spending time without him was quite another.

She didn't have a lot of experience with men, but she was pretty sure that was the kind of thing that made them nervous.

She should have known that being with Ty every day would make her want things she couldn't have. He'd said he wanted to get to know her, and that he was attracted to her, but he hadn't tried to kiss her since the night she'd kissed him and told him he could make her snap. He just put his arm around her as they watched television. Then they went their separate ways without even a goodnight peck on the cheek.

It was very confusing.

On Monday, Cassie had the usual morning meeting. Her work email contained no new surprise subscriptions, thankfully. There would be no packages because Amelia had put a hold on them in the mail room. Anything Cassie needed for work, like product samples, she had sent to Pamela. Hopefully, Ty and his buddies would catch whoever was doing this, and she could get back to normal. Until then, she was thankful not to get any panicked messages about giant boxes of sex toys.

Pamela texted her during the meeting. *How's the sexy boyfriend? Still can't believe you didn't tell me about him. Last one you mentioned was the cop.*

She started to say it was complicated, but then she decided to roll with it. Why the hell not? Big girls could have fun, too. And sometimes they could get the best looking guy in the building.

Cassie: He's great. It happened so quickly and I didn't want to say anything in case it didn't work out. Still might not, but the sex is off the charts. The cop was a phase. We didn't have a lot in common.

She blushed hard at the lie about sex, but so what? Pamela had always been great to her, but she was another of those women who thought all you had to do was go to the gym every day, eat salads and a little bit of protein, and life would be great. It was a matter of willpower to thin women. They just didn't get how hard some women fought and still couldn't lose much weight, and they never would. To them, it would always be about not wanting it badly enough.

Well, Cassie wanted it, always had, but her metabolism did not. She was Rubenesque, and that hadn't been such a bad thing during the Renaissance when all the painters had wanted to paint women with generous bodies, had it?

Pamela: Does he have a brother? Because wow that man is fine. Where did you find him?

Cassie: He doesn't have a brother, and we grew up in the same hometown. There's history.

On her side, maybe, but not his. She'd lusted for him, and he hadn't known she existed. Yet another thing she wasn't telling Pamela.

Pamela: Oh, old boyfriend then?

Cassie: We didn't date then. It's complicated.

There, she'd said it. "It's complicated, Pamela," she muttered. "Stop asking."

"What's complicated?"

Cassie squeaked at the sound of his voice. He'd gone to the apartment gym to run on a treadmill, and she hadn't heard him return. She set her Zoom screen to *Away* and took him in. He wore gym shorts and a black tank, and he was sweating from head to toe. Why was that sexy?

"Sourcing swag for Kelly Cosmetics. There are a lot of choices out there. It's complicated to go through them all and choose the best ones."

She hoped that sounded reasonable because she didn't want to tell him she'd been exaggerating about their relationship to a coworker.

"Which you still want to do, despite how they treated you."

"Well, yes. It's my job."

"I have to shower, but do you want to grab lunch

after? We could go pick up that package you had held at the UPS store."

Her heart thumped at how easily he included her. "Yes, that sounds great."

"Cool. I'll be out in ten. When's the meeting over?"

"Any minute, I hope."

He strolled toward his bedroom, and she watched the play of muscle in his thighs and ass as he walked. Damn, he was fine. Nothing jiggled on the man. Nothing at all.

"Cassie, are you there? Where did you go?"

It was Amelia's voice in her ear, sounding sharp. Cassie unmuted the microphone and turned the camera back on. "Here. Sorry."

"I need those projections on my desk by five. We're finalizing the budget for the conference. Oh, and I need you all to start thinking about ideas for the spring festival in Alexandria this year. We need to get moving on it ASAP. Cassie, since you're enjoying yourself at home, collect everyone's thoughts and have those to me by week's end. Thank you, everyone. This was very productive."

The screen went dead. Amelia had ended the Zoom for anyone calling in from elsewhere, but she was no doubt still talking to those in the conference room. Cassie rolled her eyes.

Not her circus, not her monkeys. Except that she now had to get everyone's thoughts for the spring festival and send them to Amelia. Busy work.

Cassie dashed off an email asking for everyone's thoughts, then typed another to Amelia and attached the documents she'd been working on with the projections. Amelia thought she was sitting around with her thumb up her ass or something, but *au contraire*. She had the information.

"Take that," she said as she pressed send.

Once she finished the work emails, she opened up her personal email to check for anything new. There were emails from some followers and from a couple of companies wanting to send her products, which was awesome.

But then she saw the all-too-familiar handle, and her stomach twisted. Glockman123's email stared at her, it's bolded subject line daring her to open it.

Liar!

Her belly ran cold and then hot. Anger made the blood throb in her temples, her throat, her wrists. She didn't deserve his hatred, or his abuse.

She was just a person trying to make a living, and this asshole took it personally. Though she knew she shouldn't, Cassie clicked the email with a muttered curse and started to read.

Chapter Twenty-Five

TY FINISHED HIS SHOWER AND HURRIEDLY DRESSED. HE was hungry, and he needed to get out of the apartment for a while. He'd been cooped up over the weekend with Cassie, and it was driving him crazy.

Crazy because he wanted to touch her. He'd decided to keep his hands off her and take it slow, but he really wanted to mess up her hair, dominate her mouth with his, and make her scream his name as she exploded beneath him. Every night when they lay on the couch together, watching television, he fought his desire. It was getting harder—pun not intended, ha, ha, ha—not easier.

She fascinated him. She was such a natural in front of her camera that it was hard to believe she was the same girl who'd hidden her face when they were growing up. She still wouldn't let him help with the clothing videos, which didn't make a lot of sense to him since it was clothes and not skin, but whatever.

Her face without makeup was beautiful. He didn't think she knew it, though. He'd tried to tell her. She had plump, full lips, rounded cheeks, and the most beautiful green eyes. With no makeup, her eyes were the first thing you noticed. Then her lips. When she put on her makeup, it depended on what she wanted to highlight. Some days she did her eyes so that you couldn't stop staring at them. Other days it was her lips that stood out, lined and painted and puckered. So fucking kissable.

It was driving him crazy not to kiss her. Crazy not to peel off her cute outfits and lay her down on his bed where he could explore every beautiful curve she had.

That's why he needed to get out. Take her to lunch somewhere and just talk for a while. Go get her damned packages and check on her place, which meant a long drive in traffic in both directions, and then by the time they got home it'd be time for dinner and an episode of her show. She'd fall asleep on him, because she often did even if she insisted that she'd been awake the whole time, and he wouldn't wake her because he liked the way she felt there.

Then it would be time for bed, and he'd walk back to his room like a fucking Victorian gentleman. He'd stroke his cock and relieve some pressure before falling asleep and starting all over again the next day.

He'd been on the phone with Dax and the team. There was nothing definitive on Cassie's stalker yet. No prints on the photo from the wreath, no digital trail, no sign of Dylan Webb yet, and they still didn't have Brian Woodruff's file.

Basically, they had fuck all to go on.

He'd installed the cameras at her place, aimed at the front and back doors. He'd had to silence notifications because of all the dog walkers and other people moving around the neighborhood, but he checked the feed regularly. He'd noticed this morning that the one trained on the back door had gone off-line. It happened sometimes, but he needed to go over and see what the problem was.

Ty raked his hands through his damp hair and shrugged on a button down over his T-shirt, which he left open because he was still hot from the run and the shower, even if it was in the thirties outside.

When he walked into the kitchen, Cassie was sitting at the counter like she'd been when he'd passed by earlier. But her face was pale and she stared at her screen. His senses started to tingle.

"What's wrong?" he asked.

She looked up at him. Tears trembled on the edges of her pretty eyes. She sniffed them back, her face a mottled red. As if she was angry instead of scared.

Okay, angry was good. He hoped.

"He's back. The guy who sent the emails."

Ty's blood ran cold. The desire to kill the son of a bitch flooded him like acid. "Let me see."

She turned the computer and he skimmed the email before going back and reading it from the beginning. If he could get his hands on this guy, he'd be one dead motherfucker.

YOU'RE A FAT, *ugly bitch and u need weight watchers. You think ur pretty hot shit, don't you? You aren't. You're trash, Cassandra Dixon. Trailer trash from bumfuck virginia. You're a nobody. I wouldn't fuck you with a stolen dick. I wouldn't fuck you if you were the only pussy left on earth.*

You got a bodyguard now, but he won't save you when I come for you. The bigger they are, the harder they fall. You ever hear that one? I'm gonna prove it to you, bitch. Then I'm gonna make you suck my cock. You suck it good enough, I might keep you around and let you do it some more. But if you don't? Bang-bang, you're dead.

TY HAD to reach deep for his professional cool because he was about to blow a fucking gasket. "You okay?" he asked.

She nodded, but her eyes still glittered. He stepped closer and tugged her against him where she sat. Her face pressed into his chest, her arms lifting to wrap around his waist. She trembled, and that fucking killed him.

"You realize he's wrong, don't you? About everything. He's a small man, Cassie. That's how small men behave. They try to intimidate and frighten from afar. They stir shit and say things they'd never say in person because they don't have the guts."

He also knew that men like this one were capable of doing harm, but he didn't say that aloud. She might already know it, or she might not, but he wasn't adding that thought to what she was already processing.

"I know. But how does he know I lived in a trailer, Ty? I've never said a word about where I grew up on my channel."

He'd been wondering that too. "Are you sure it's not Dylan?"

"I'm not sure of anything. I don't know why he'd harass me like this, though. Not now. He was pissed when I didn't stay in Bear Creek and keep worshipping the ground he walked on, but it's been a year. Seems weird that he'd start acting all unhinged now."

"Not if he's jealous of your success. Or envious. Maybe he thinks you're getting rich off your channel and he's pissed about it."

"I guess it's possible. I just feel like he'd call me to ask for money, though."

"You could be right. But I had to ask. It does sound like the guy knows more about you than the average subscriber—but if he's good enough, he could find the information on the web."

"Even the fact I lived in a trailer?"

"Address, Cassie. If he found your old address and used Google Maps, he'd know. He could even do the street view to see it."

"I didn't think of that."

He stepped back without letting go of her. She looked up at him. Her eyes were less watery now. "You want to stay home? We can order something and watch your show."

He could see her thinking about it. Then her jaw thrust out stubbornly and she frowned. "No. I want to go out, Ty. I want to get my packages and see what the companies sent for me to try, and the things I ordered. I need to keep filming new content."

He admired her dogged determination to keep doing the thing she loved. "We'll go, then." He grabbed his jacket off the chair he'd lain it over and shrugged into it while she tidied up her space. "How many subscribers do you have now?"

"I think it was at ninety-five this morning. I'll hit one-hundred thousand sometime in the next day or two. I think."

"Oh, I think you will." He grinned. "Do you drink champagne?"

"On occasion."

"I think this is an occasion, Red. We'll get a bottle while we're out, and we'll pop the cork when you hit a hundred thousand."

Her smile was big and genuine. "That sounds great. Thank you."

He loved seeing her smile. He wanted to tell her that she was completely fuckable in his book, but he thought that might be going a little far for the moment. He was definitely going to tell her. Better yet, he'd like to show her. But… patience.

She got her coat and he took it from her, holding it so she could shrug into it. "Would you have done anything to celebrate?" he asked, settling the coat on her shoulders.

"I'd have called Kari and squealed, probably," she said as she turned and draped her crossbody purse over her shoulder and torso. "And I'd probably do a video thanking everyone. I mean I *will* do that. Oh, I probably should give away some gift cards or something. I haven't had time to think because it's all happened so fast."

"What about the Kelly Cosmetics video? Is that still getting a lot of views?" He could have asked Dax, or he could have looked at it himself, but he hadn't checked since yesterday.

"Over a million," she said, eyebrows scrunched adorably. "I still don't get it, but it's popular."

"You realize people like negativity, right? You trashed the product, even if you weren't snarky about it."

"I sometimes wish I'd never done it. But I can't deny it's been good for visibility. I didn't do it for that reason, though. And I wouldn't, either. It's just a bad product, and they can do better. I didn't know we were about to get the Kelly account for the convention, or I might not have posted it when I did."

He locked the door behind them and turned to face her. "Don't second-guess yourself. You did it to save people money, not to make Odin and his boss happy. Fuck them. If they don't like it, they can make a better product."

She smiled at him, and his heart did a slow flip in his chest. "I like that you're always on my side. Just like Kari. I don't know how I lucked into the Scott family, but I'm so glad I did."

He put his arm around her and started walking down the hall. "Me too, Red. Me too."

Chapter Twenty-Six

HE WAS DOING THINGS TO HER AND HE DIDN'T EVEN know it. Cassie's heart pounded every time she looked at him. Ty's hands on the steering wheel were sexy. Long fingers wrapped around the wheel, and she thought of them stroking her skin. What would that feel like?

She imagined it would feel amazing. And yet she'd have to be naked for it to happen, which was a little worrisome.

Okay, a lot worrisome. What if he didn't like what he saw? For all his talk of her being beautiful and sexy, what if he only said it to make her feel good? Because he hadn't tried to kiss her in days now. He'd said her online harasser was wrong, but he hadn't said more than that.

Cassie closed her eyes and told herself to stop. Just stop. She was going in circles, and for what? Ty was helping her, if nothing else. Protecting her. He didn't do his job for free, she was pretty sure, but he hadn't asked for money.

Oh shit, should she ask him? Maybe he hadn't said

anything because of Kari, but she should offer to pay him. It was only right. She really missed the obvious sometimes, didn't she?

They grabbed lunch at a pizza place, then drove to the UPS store near her townhouse and picked up her packages. All of them were ones she was expecting. Then they swung by her place so he could troubleshoot one of the cameras that had stopped working last night. Ty made her wait in the truck, but when he came back, he was tight-lipped. She knew something was wrong.

"What is it?"

"Someone's been inside," he growled.

Cassie's heart dropped to her stomach. "How do you know?" She could barely get her voice to work.

He reversed out of the parking space. "I rigged trip-wires just in case. The trap on the back door was sprung."

Cassie's pulse rocketed. That was where the camera that had stopped working was located. "Could it be a mistake?"

"No. I used thread. I tied it low, a couple of feet into the entry, so it'd come loose if someone walked through it. It was gone, Cass. Probably wrapped around the intruder's leg and he didn't even know it."

"Oh, Jesus. And you don't want to call the police?"

His expression was hard. "No. I want to get you out of here, not sit around and draw attention so that someone watching can tag us when we're distracted. Besides, it's just the thread that's disturbed. There's not enough evidence for the police."

"And the camera?"

He shot her a troubled look. "Looks like a squirrel chewed the wire. But that'd be a hell of a coincidence."

Cassie was cold. She wrapped her arms around herself and shivered.

Ty glanced in the rearview mirror as he drove. He took side streets and detours, and she knew he was trying to avoid being tailed. It all seemed so surreal to her. She was Cassie Dixon, big girl, YouTuber. She wasn't freaking Lady Gaga or Jennifer Lawrence. She was a nobody in the grand scheme of things, not a celebrity.

"You doing all right over there?" he asked after a while.

"I think so. I'm with you, and I feel safe. Though I'm creeped out too."

"I understand, and I'm sorry." He flexed his hands on the wheel. "I need to call the team. See if we can get someone over there to gather evidence."

She nodded. He punched a button on his steering wheel, then said, "Call Dax's cell phone."

The computer voice answered him, then dialed the number. A moment later, Dax's voice said, "Hey, man, what's up?"

"Someone broke into Cassie's place. The rear camera looks like an animal chewed the wire, but I doubt it."

"Fuck. Where are you?"

"We're in the truck and I'm taking her back to my place. I took evasive measures, and I don't see a tail."

"Good. What do you need?"

"Need a team to get over there and see if they can find any DNA evidence. He didn't turn the place over, but the thread I rigged is gone."

"Got it. I'll let Ian know, and I'll send a forensics team."

"Thanks. Got anything else for me?"

"Not yet. I'll call when I do."

"Thanks, man."

Ty ended the call and Cassie bit her lip as they drove through the streets. He took the route through DC instead of around it, and she thought that was to make it harder to follow them. Though it was the tail end of rush hour, and everything was still somewhat slow.

"I've never asked how much I owe you," she said, her voice sounding tentative to her own ears.

He whipped a glance at her. "Owe me? You don't owe me anything, Cassie."

"But this is your job, and I'm taking you away from it to help me. For free. Those cameras cost money, the forensics team—everything. I can't let you do that."

He shook his head but didn't look at her. "You aren't taking me away from anything. There's nothing I have to do right now—though there will be at times, and I hope you'll be okay with me being gone. It'll be a couple of weeks at a time, sometimes longer, and I won't be able to talk about it. But right now—right *fucking now*— my only responsibility is *you.*"

"But it's not just you. It's Ian and your whole crew. They don't really know me from Adam, so why would they do all this for me—use all their resources—for nothing? You can't run a business that way."

He snorted. "First of all, Ian is a fucking billionaire. He can do what he wants. Second, we *help* people. It's what we do. If Ian looked at it like he'd only help those who could pay him, I wouldn't be working for him. Don't get me wrong—there are people who pay, and pay a lot—but it's not someone like you, Cassie."

"I'm not broke," she said indignantly. She wasn't

rich either. Not even close. In fact, she spent most of what she made on her living expenses, with a small amount set aside to hopefully buy her own place one day. As her channel grew, so too did her savings. But she wasn't swimming in money just yet.

"I didn't say you were. But you're not the kind of public-facing client that BDI takes. We protect rich people. Captains of industry, pop stars, heads of state—and we make them pay handsomely for it. It's how we fund the real work."

"Real work?"

He shook his head again. "I can't talk about that yet, but one day I will. If the things I hope happen *do*."

"I don't understand."

"It's okay. You will eventually. I'll tell you everything when the time is right, but not yet. You just have to trust me."

She wanted to know, and yet she knew she couldn't push him on this. Not yet. "I do trust you, Ty. I thought that was pretty clear. I've done everything you've told me to do, and I left my house a few days ago to go with you because you said so. I trust you with my life if that's not clear."

He reached over and wrapped her fingers in his. "I know, babe. But I've asked for a lot, and I just wanted to be clear with you."

She decided to be bold for a change. She lifted their clasped hands and pressed her lips to his skin the way he'd done to hers so many times before. "Thank you, Ty. For everything."

"You're welcome, Red. For the record, I'm still picking up champagne. We're going to toast your success. Not letting some asshole ruin that for you."

Her eyes prickled with happy tears. He was perfect, and he didn't even know it. She was just as much in danger of falling in love with him as she had been when she was a teenager.

No—*more* in danger. Because that had been an unrequited love borne of awkwardness and wanting what she couldn't have. But this time?

This time it had everything to do with how beautiful a soul he really was. In the midst of everything, he still thought of her comfort and her triumphs. He cared about how she was feeling, and she knew it wasn't fake. It might only be because Kari made him care, but she couldn't spend a lot of time thinking about that. If she did, she'd lose her joy.

And she didn't want to lose her joy. She wanted to wallow in it. With Tyler Scott, former Bear Creek heart-throb and current perfect man material.

Because she deserved joy for as long as it lasted.

Chapter Twenty-Seven

HE BOUGHT THE CHAMPAGNE. FUCKING *DOM PERIGNON*, because she was worth it, and then they went back to his place—after he took a few more detours—and he found a bowl big enough to put some ice in. Then he nestled the champagne into it.

Cassie seemed overwhelmed, but touched by the gesture. "You didn't have to do that," she said with her soft voice.

"It's not much. Sorry I don't have a real ice bucket."

Her smile was everything. "I think it's perfect. I'll remember this more than I'd ever remember an ice bucket. The day Tyler Scott put ice in a mixing bowl for a bottle of champagne just so it'd be ready if I hit the magic mark tonight."

"You will hit the magic mark tonight," he said with utter confidence. "And I could have put it in the refrigerator to keep it chilled, but that's not nearly as dramatic, is it?"

"No." Her face was pure happiness, and he was

glad. After that email she'd gotten earlier, and then the news of the break-in, Cassie deserved to be happy.

He was still fucking pissed about the camera, about someone violating her home, and about Glockman123's email. The three things had to be connected. *Had* to be. And when he found Glockman123, that asshole would wish he'd never so much as blinked in Cassie's direction.

Until then, he had to be cool and take care of his girl. He went to the cabinet where he kept glasses and reached into the top to pull out two champagne flutes. They weren't fancy, but they were actual champagne flutes made of glass.

"Don't know when or where I picked these up, but I have four of them for some reason. I keep them because you never know." He set them on the counter beside the homemade ice bucket and grinned at her. "We're ready."

"You're really sweet to me. I appreciate it so much."

"You deserve all the sweetness life can give you, Red. You don't deserve the shit you're getting."

She shrugged, but he knew it bothered her. "Shit happens to everyone, and I'm not immune."

He took her hand and pulled her into his arms because he wanted to hold her and he didn't want to deny himself. He'd been careful, but, dammit, he'd been on edge since discovering someone had broken into her house.

What was the reason the person had done so? What had they been planning to do? That's what Ty didn't know, and what sent a chill down his spine. The break-in must have happened after the camera went out, which was at 2:07 a.m. this morning. Had this person known she was gone, or were they expecting to find her there?

He didn't like to think about what the plan might have been if she'd been home.

Ty could have asked her to go inside with him and see if anything was missing, but his gut had told him to get her the hell out of there as quickly as possible. That's what his team was for. Rascal, Dax, and Finn McDermott, newly returned from Europe, were heading over there, along with a couple of lab techs. They'd go over the place with a fine-tooth comb. Dax was going to be looking for bugs and cameras, too.

It was entirely possible the fucker had broken in just to place recording devices so he could spy on Cassie. Ty wanted the asshole's balls in a vise. He wanted the man sitting in a holding cell in BDI's state-of-the-art headquarters, fearing that he'd made the biggest mistake of his life.

Because he had. Coming after Cassie was like attacking Bambi or something. And Ty wasn't letting this stalker asshole get away with it.

Cassie put her arms around his waist and her cheek against his chest. She wasn't stiff in his arms, and he liked that. Meant she wasn't overthinking it or worried about what came next.

He knew what he wanted to come next, but that wasn't happening yet. Not until he was positive she was ready. However long it took. Because, damn, there was something about Cassie that he couldn't quite get enough of. Something that made him want more of her —more smiles, more conversations, more sitting on the couch and watching whatever in the hell she wanted to watch.

Even if it involved people in historical costumes, because she'd mentioned some romance novel show to him called *Bridgerton*. What the hell, he'd watch that too. If it made her happy, he'd do it. He wasn't sure what that said about him, but he suspected he was pretty damned entranced with Miss Cassie Dixon—and they hadn't even had sex yet.

Other than on the phone. He still hadn't gotten over that night, but he hadn't tried to repeat it. So much had happened in the days since that it hadn't seemed quite right.

"You hungry?" he asked, his lips against her silky hair.

"Still full from lunch, so that's a no."

"Okay. We can eat later. Whenever you're ready. Or maybe we can have popcorn with your witch show."

She laughed. "Popcorn sounds good. It's more than just witches, Ty."

"I know. I just like hearing you laugh when I pretend like I haven't got a clue. You ready to start watching now, or do you have to work on your channel?"

She sighed. "I should edit a video, and I need to do an unboxing for the stuff I just got. I'll film the unboxing now, then the trying-on-outfits part tomorrow."

"Then you'll cut it all together with music and voice-over, right?"

"Right. You're learning."

"You sure you don't want to take a break, Red?"

"I need to be busy, Ty. If I have something to do, I won't dwell on it."

He wanted to give her something to do all right, but he refrained from saying it. He eased his hold on her and she stepped back. Disappointment flared, but he'd get over it. Eventually.

"I should call Dax, and see what's up with the team. And I gotta keep the ice fresh on the champagne. I'll be watching your follower count, so if you hear me whoop, you'll know why. Or should I not whoop, just in case you're filming?"

She laughed, but he could tell it wasn't completely natural. "I'll text you when I start and when I stop. How's that?"

"That'll work."

He was still holding one of her hands. When she tried to step back again, he tugged her forward, spread his fingers over her cheek, and tilted her head up. Then he slanted his mouth over hers and kissed her the way he'd been dying to do.

He'd told himself it would only be a brief kiss, that she'd pull away, and that he'd let her. But she didn't pull away, and he wasn't ready for brief. Her mouth opened beneath his, and he dipped his tongue inside, teasing hers. She made a soft sound, a moan, and his gut twisted with desire. His dick was harder than stone within an instant.

He wanted this woman so fucking badly. She was in charge of the journey, but that didn't mean he couldn't tempt her with previews of the destination. He closed the distance between them, as small as it was, and wrapped an arm around her. The other stayed on her face, gently holding her in place. He wanted her to know she could leave if she wanted. She could step away and he'd let her go.

But he also wanted her to know that he had her safely within his arms. That he intended to protect her with everything he had. He didn't know what all these

emotions inside him were, but he knew she was important and he wasn't going to fail her.

Not the way he'd failed his team that day. He hadn't
listened to his gut, hadn't fought for them, and he should
have. He would fight for Cassie. For her safety, for the
right to worship her body the way she deserved, and,
yeah, even for her heart.

Because he believed, now more than ever, there was
something here. Something between them that made the
craving that much stronger. It wasn't a fad or a phase.

It was Cassie Dixon and her sweetness. Her vulnera-
bility, her drive, her loyalty. His cousin had been onto
something all those years ago when she'd befriended
Cassie. Kari had known a real friend—a lifelong friend
—when she'd seen one.

Ty knew it now, too. And he wasn't letting her go.
Not without a fight.

He slanted his mouth over hers and asked for a little
more. She slid her arms up his biceps and around his
neck. Then she gave him what he wanted. She was the
one who pressed into him, the one who flexed her hips
against his and made his cock ache. He knew she
couldn't mistake what he was feeling, so when she did it
again, he growled low in his throat.

A warning, maybe. Or a plea.

And then, because he couldn't take much more of
this torture, he cupped her face in both hands and broke
the kiss. She blinked up at him, confusion and maybe a
little pain written in her expression.

"I can't keep doing this, Cassie. I want you so much
it physically hurts. I know I'm the one who started it,
and I only have myself to blame, but, hell, I want more
than a quiet evening on the couch with you. I want that

too—don't get me wrong—but I also want to strip every last piece of clothing off your body and lose myself in you. I want to spread you out on my bed and lick your pussy until you scream, then I want to do it again and again until you're limp and satisfied.

"And then I'd like to ease my cock into your wet heat and fuck you until I explode. I want to hold you close while we catch our breath, and then I want to do it again. And, shit, I might as well say it—I want to lick champagne off your nipples, and I also want to give you a celebratory orgasm when you cross that hundred-k threshold. After that, maybe some of your witches and popcorn. Then we fuck some more, fall asleep together, and then I get to take you doggy style in the shower in the morning while I stroke your clit and make you see stars before breakfast."

He ran out of words, or thought better of them, because her eyes were wide and her mouth was open and he wasn't quite certain if she was shocked or offended or both. He'd meant to take it easy with her, and he had been, but then he'd had to go and tell her all the dirty things he wanted to do to her.

Okay, maybe not all of them. And maybe he should have said he wanted to make love instead of fuck, though God knew he wanted both those things. But women sometimes had funny reactions to being told a man wanted to fuck them.

And, oh shit, there were those sick messages she'd gotten where the guy had used that kind of language, but not in a good way. Yeah, he was an idiot, and he'd just fucked this whole thing up with Cassie, hadn't he?

But then she smiled, though it was a little tentative, and licked her lips. Just a quick dart of her tongue over her luscious lower lip, but he felt it all the way to his balls.

"I want you too, Ty," she said softly. He started to gather her up again, but she put a hand on his chest, blocking him. He stopped and waited, his dick and brain throbbing together. "I'm scared. I've never been with anyone but Dylan. It wasn't great. For the longest time, I was too aroused to know any differently. Everything worked, and I got off too. But later…"

She hesitated, and his heart was breaking for her. Anger simmered inside him, too.

"Later, he didn't even care about making it good for me. So long as he got off, he was good. If I could, I had to finish myself off—silently—in the bathroom with the door locked."

"It's not going to be that way with me. Because I know the most important thing in a sexual relationship is *both* parties having fun. If you don't enjoy it, then what's in it for me? A man can get his rocks off easily, but to satisfy his woman while doing it? How is that not the ultimate high? Not going to vow I'll never come before you do, but I can promise you my goal is to make you come first."

"There are other reasons I'm scared," she said, her gaze dropping away from his.

"Cassie Dixon, I think you're a fucking siren. A beauty queen. I think you've got curves that don't quit, and I *ache* to see them. To explore them. I don't care if you think you're fat, or if some dumb fuck made you think you were ugly—strike that. I *do* care, but only because someone hurt you. But I sure as shit don't think you're ugly."

"You don't jiggle, Ty. I do."

He tilted his head to study her like she'd just said the most asinine thing. "Oh, Red. Shit, I want to see your tits jiggle. Badly. And anything else that wants to jiggle, I'm there for it. If your ass jiggles while I fuck you from behind—Jesus, don't make me picture that right now because I don't want to come in my pants."

She laughed at that, and he was glad. He'd been at least a little serious, but it was good to see her laugh. "You're crazy, Tyler Scott. Batshit crazy, but you do know how to make me feel better."

"You're killing me. I want to see you. Explore you. Taste you. Make you come. I *need* these things in my life. Hard-ons don't lie, and you know you make me hard. You've felt it. Just now."

She nodded. "I did. I liked it."

Thank God for that. "I'm glad." He blew out a breath. "Go make your video, Cassie. I won't say those things again. I just want you to know that Dylan Webb was a stupid fuck, and the asshole sending you those emails doesn't think you're ugly at all. He wants you, and he's pissed that you aren't his. It's not about you being ugly, because you aren't. It's about you being gorgeous and unattainable. Never forget that, honey. You're worth waiting for, so I'm gonna wait."

She smiled shyly. "Thank you for saying, well, everything you just said. It helps, even if you don't think so."

"I hope so. I feel like I maybe went overboard."

She giggled, and relief unfurled inside him. "Are you kidding me? What woman doesn't like to hear she's a siren? Or that a gorgeous man wants to see her jiggle? I mean that still worries me, but I think you mean it."

"I definitely mean it."

"Somebody told me today that they wouldn't fuck

me with a stolen dick. You pretty much just made my day with your declaration."

"Glad I could help."

She stood on tiptoe and kissed his cheek. His cock throbbed.

"You definitely helped."

"Go make that video, Cassie. Or I swear I'll carry you to my bedroom and have my wicked way with you right damn now."

Her eyes widened a fraction. He hoped she'd stay, but she didn't. She fled.

Chapter Twenty-Eight

CASSIE STARED AT HER PHONE. SHE WAS IN THE GUEST room, door closed, but she wasn't filming a damned thing. It wasn't that she was hung up on the fact someone had broken into her house, though that definitely worried her. She'd even considered filming a video about it, about what was happening to her, but she couldn't quite bring herself to do it yet. She was trying to stay positive, and sharing her problems with her audience felt more like asking for attention than being positive.

Besides, Ty and his team were handling the situation, and she knew she couldn't ask for anything more.

Instead, what she was hung up on at the moment was what had just happened with Ty, and trying to decide whether she should text her bestie for advice or not. Ty was Kari's cousin, after all, and even though she'd said she thought Cassie and Ty should get together, that didn't mean she wanted to hear the details.

But who else did Cassie have? She started thumbing the screen. *Need advice.*

Kari: Really? About what?

Cassie: Ty.

Kari: Ooooh, do tell!

Cassie: He kissed me. It got a little hot.

Kari: I knew it! So then what? Did you do the nasty?

Cassie laughed. Good lord, leave it to Kari. *Um, no, we did not. I'm scared.*

She hit send before she could think too hard about it. She bit her lip until the three dots appeared.

Kari: I want to call and talk through this, but I'm at a gymnastics practice for the girls and it's loud as shit. Plus I think you wouldn't talk as freely as you'll text. Why are you scared?

Cassie: C'mon, K. You could bounce a quarter off your cousin's ass. Mine's like a marshmallow—pillowy and soft.

Kari: Honey, my ass is like Jell-O these days. Heath doesn't care. He cares that he's getting laid.

Cassie: You aren't helping. You're saying Ty just wants to get laid and won't care about my ass.

Kari: <peach emoji> Oh, he'll care, heh heh. But not the way you think. Cass, listen. My cousin can probably have any piece of ass he wants, it's true. And I can't guarantee in any way that he'll want more than that from you. But he's not kissing you out of pity. Ty doesn't need to kiss anyone out of pity. He also doesn't need to get busy with you because he can't find anyone else. He can find plenty of partners. So if he's trying it with you, he's not doing it for any reason other than he WANTS YOU. There. I don't know how much plainer I can be. What did he say about it?

Cassie stared at the big swath of text, nibbling her lip as she did so. Jeez, she was being silly. Ty had said a lot, and none of it had been anything but arousing. She was still so wet her panties were soaked, and her clit still ached with the need to be stroked. He was in the next damn room. And he'd said he planned to lick her clit, not just stroke it.

Cassie bit back a moan as she typed. *He said a lot. It was dirty and hot, by the way.*

Kari: Oh jeez, don't tell me. I don't want to know the specifics. All I know is I love you both, and I selfishly want you together. And maybe it won't work out that way, but damn, honey, don't you think you ought to get back on the horse and go for a good, long ride? Dylan was a dumb fuck. I don't think Ty is, but I admit I'm blind to his faults.

Cassie: He's not a dumb fuck. He's sweet, and he said a lot of beautiful things. I ran away. Typical, right?

Kari: <eyeroll emoji><laughing emoji> I know you didn't leave his place because he wouldn't let you. So if you think you can handle this without emotion, get back out there and saddle up, girl-friend. But don't tell me any specifics because, eww, my cousin.

Cassie: You're crazy.

Kari: Yep. Oh crap, gotta go. They're about to do the big pyramid and I have to film.

Cassie: Go. Much love to you all.

Cassie set her phone down. She was kinda glad Kari had to go because she hadn't planned to tell her friend about someone breaking into her house, but she'd have felt guilty if Kari had asked if anything else had happened. Thank goodness for the big pyramid.

Cassie sighed. The sticking point was handling this thing with Ty without emotion. That was the part that worried her. Because she'd always been so damned in love with Ty—from afar, yes. Teenage unrequited love, yes. But it had hurt at the time, and it'd been angsty, and she'd wallowed in it.

And maybe a little bit of her fear was that real Ty

wasn't going to live up to fantasy Ty. Oh, she didn't doubt he'd be good at the sexy bits—he hadn't sounded at all like a man who only cared about his own orgasm —but what if he broke her heart after? Fantasy Ty would never break her heart.

"Oh, for fuck's sake, Cassie," she muttered. "You have a real man out there who says he wants you. And maybe it won't last more than one night, but that's a lot better than the nights you've been having. Go throw yourself at him and let him prove that he can do all those things he said."

She stood. Her pussy throbbed and her heart raced. She took a deep breath. But instead of heading for the door, she peered into the mirror. She could touch up her makeup. Change into that silky pajama set she'd ordered but hadn't filmed for the channel yet. She kept meaning to do a video about getting ready for your man, but she just hadn't done it. She knew she had ladies who wanted to see that. Ladies who wanted ideas for how to be sexy in the bedroom.

As if she knew. Seriously, Ty was out there right now. He'd told her he wanted her. He'd told her the things he wanted to do to her. And she was contemplating making a video about pajamas?

"Come on, Cassandra," she said into the mirror. "You can do this. Live in the moment and stop worrying about the damn channel."

Except she couldn't. She stared at herself, frowning. She sighed in defeat, then sat down to do her makeup. When she was finished, she got the box of clothes she'd ordered and pressed play on the camera.

Time to film the unboxing.

———

TY'S PHONE rang an hour later. It was Dax.

"We found a camera in her bedroom, and one in the living room. There were listening devices too. Oh, and a pizza got delivered while we were there."

Ty's gut twisted. What the actual fuck? He knew that DNA evidence would take longer, but maybe they'd get a hair or something. "What kind of pizza?"

Dax snorted. "Supreme. It was a big one. We ate it."

"You ate it?"

"Yeah, it was a local place, and Rascal called to make sure it was legit. It was. Someone called to order it an hour before. Said where to drop it, and they'd pay when it arrived. So we paid and chowed down."

"You think he's watching the place? Sent the pizza as a fuck you?"

"Who cares? It was good. Added that joint to my list for when I'm over this way."

Ty tapped a finger against his leg angrily. Not at Dax or the guys. He'd have eaten the fucking thing too. But the audacity of this motherfucker. Breaking in, placing listening and recording devices, and then ordering a pizza? Damn.

"Okay. Thanks for telling me. I'm guessing no prints on the devices."

"Nope. But they have serial numbers, so we'll run those. Might find something."

"Thanks. Let me know when you do."

"You got it, dude. How's Cassie doing?"

Ty looked over at the bedroom door. She'd been in there for two hours now. He'd heard her moving around, heard her talking—filming—but she hadn't emerged or texted to tell him she was done. "I think she's all right. Working on one of her videos now."

"Those videos, man," Dax said. "Some of them are kinda hot. Or is it just me?"

Ty's hackles rose. "Dude, not cool. She's off limits."

"Is she? Why? Are you interested?"

Dax knew he was after their last conversation. But Ty wasn't getting into it right now. "Fuck you."

Dax laughed like an idiot. "Damn, just last month you were on Ian's ass about Natasha—and look at you now. Getting wrapped around the axle over a woman."

"It's not like that," he growled. Lying his ass off and they both knew it. "I've known her since we were kids."

"Yeah, so you said in Colorado when we went out there to help Ian fake his own death. In fact, you specifically said you'd pissed off your cousin because you couldn't remember Cassie."

"You don't have to bring that up."

"Yes, I do. It's fun."

"Fine. I'm interested. You happy?"

"Not really. Means I can't ask her out now."

"No, you fucking can't. Don't even think about it."

Dax laughed again. "You're a goner, Ty. I can hear it in your voice."

Ty looked at the bedroom door. "You've seen her. How couldn't I be?"

"Yeah, I get it. I really do. She's sweet and sexy and vulnerable all at once. Hell of a combination."

Ty wasn't exactly thrilled with his friend noticing all that, but he knew Cassie would be. He'd have to tell her. The girl lacked confidence, and she needed to hear it. Hopefully she'd believe him when he told her.

"You know, I said you can't ask her out—and you

216

can't—but do you think the next time we're all together, you might find a way to tell her you'd be interested if she wasn't with me?"

"So you can kick my ass? No way."

"I'm serious, Dax."

He could almost hear the wheels of curiosity turning in Dax's head. "I suppose I could. Why?"

"It doesn't come across on her videos, but Cassie has a lot of baggage from her childhood. She doesn't think she's all that remarkable. She worries about her weight and her appearance, and I want her to know it's not just me who thinks she's beautiful."

There, he'd said it. Put it all on the line.

"Damn," Dax said. "That's not what comes across on the videos. Yeah, I'll find a way. Just don't punch me when I do, okay?"

Ty laughed. "Don't try to kiss her or anything and we're good."

"Got it. No kissing. Can I pinch her ass?"

"Dax," Ty growled.

Dax laughed. "I wouldn't do it anyway. It's disrespectful. Unless you're in a relationship with someone."

"Just tell her she's beautiful and you'd be into her if she was available. Which she won't be," Ty added.

"Hey, you don't know. What if you fuck it all up?"

"Not fucking it up."

"Good. Because I think you need someone, and she seems like the right someone."

"How can you know that? You've barely talked to her."

"Don't have to. It's the way she looks at you. Like you put the moon in the sky just for her."

"Isn't that a little poetic for you?" Ty asked. But he

liked the sound of it. He hadn't a clue how Cassie looked at him when he wasn't looking at her.

"Jared isn't the only one who reads around here. I've been known to dabble in a book or two. Just picked up a romance novel, in fact."

"A romance novel? Didn't see that one coming."

"Me neither, but Ian told me to. I think we're about to get a novelist for a client."

"Interesting. And he picked you, huh?"

"Looks that way. She's getting death threats over a book. Sounds stupid to me, but hey, who knows what winds people up?"

"Hard to say sometimes." Ty's smart watch tapped him on the arm. "Gotta run, man. I have to check Cassie's stats. I've got champagne chilling in case she hits a hundred thousand followers tonight."

"I'll let you know if we get anything else, but I don't think we will until tomorrow."

They said goodnight and Ty woke his laptop so he could refresh YouTube and see the count. One hundred and three. She was still recording so he didn't whoop, but he closed the computer and waited. He got her text a few minutes later—and whooped loud enough to make her yank the door open and emerge with a big smile on her face.

"Really?"

He took the champagne from the bowl. "Really," he said before twisting the top off with a subtle *pop* sound. He poured it into two glasses and handed one to her. "To you, Cassie Dixon, for being a badass, sexy fucking babe who's gonna take over the world of beauty with your channel."

Chapter Twenty-Nine

THE CHAMPAGNE BUBBLES WEREN'T THE ONLY THINGS fizzing tonight. Happiness fizzed and popped inside her as she clinked glasses with Ty and took a tentative sip. She wasn't really going to take over the world of beauty, but the fact that he believed in her made her feel pretty damned awesome.

Cassie coughed as the bubbles got into her nose, and then she laughed when they nearly made her sneeze. She held a finger under her nose until the danger was gone. Ty was grinning at her like a fool.

"Tickles your nose, huh?"

"I don't drink champagne much." She thought about it. "In fact, I don't think I've ever had the real thing before. From France, I mean."

"This is it, babe. Wait until you meet Colt and Angie. They're getting married soon, and Colt's a French count. His family makes wine. He doesn't, but he grew up with it. Anyway, if you want an education about French wine and champagne, he's the guy."

"Wait… he's a French count? What's that mean? All I know is the Count from Sesame Street. And Count Dracula."

Ty snorted, but luckily he wasn't drinking champagne at that moment. "Oh, he's going to love that. It's like an English earl. Apparently, if you read historical romance novels, you understand this stuff."

"I used to read romances. I don't remember any counts in the ones I read. Guess I should start again."

Ty took her hand and led her to the couch. Then he went and retrieved the bottle. "Maybe you should. But tonight, we're toasting you, Cassie. Congratulations again on hitting one-hundred thousand subscribers on your YouTube channel. That's pretty amazing."

Her heart was happy. Despite all the trouble, the threats, the lingering nastiness that was always online, she was happy right now. In this moment, with Ty. She couldn't imagine anything better.

"I'm very grateful. There's a lot of content on YouTube, and people can watch anything. To know that so many people find my videos entertaining or informative—well, it's so much more than I ever thought possible when I started uploading."

He leaned over and kissed her. It was a light, sweet kiss—but she found herself wanting to lean into him in turn. Wanting to put her hands on his chest, wrap her fingers into his shirt, and drag him down on top of her.

Oh, now, that was a thought…

He leaned back again, grinning as if they were toasting his success too. She loved that about him. That he could be so genuinely happy *for* her. Dylan had never been happy for anything she'd accomplished. When she'd worked for Jessica back home, planning events and learning the ropes, he'd never congratulated her when she'd signed her first client, or planned her first event, or gotten an Employee of the Quarter award. Unless it was about him, he hadn't really engaged.

Looking back on it, she couldn't believe she'd stayed with him for so long. She'd bought into the lie that nobody else would ever be interested in her. And even if it hadn't been a lie, she now knew that being alone was far better than staying with someone who made you feel small.

"What do you want to do now?" Ty asked. "We could watch television, or you can talk to me all night about how this makes you feel."

She smiled as she took another sip of champagne. "Why are you so good to me, Tyler Scott?"

"Why wouldn't I be?"

She shrugged. "Dylan was never interested in my success. All he cared about was dinner on the table and his underwear neatly folded in his drawer."

"He didn't deserve you."

Another wave of happiness flooded her. Or maybe it was the champagne. "No, he didn't. I wish I'd realized it sooner."

"You figured it out, and you left."

"Sure did." She felt like she was grinning stupidly. Maybe she was.

"Careful with that champagne. It goes to your head."

"I know. But maybe that's what I need, Ty. Just that little bit of bravery to tip me over the edge."

He looked wary. "Regarding?"

"You." He didn't speak or move. She pressed her

palm to her chest, felt her heart fluttering. "You. Me. All those things you said earlier."

"I want that very badly, Red. But I didn't give you champagne to lower your inhibitions. And I don't want you to regret it after."

Would she? Maybe. But right now she felt like she could conquer the world. Because of him. Because of his belief in her.

She set the champagne on the coffee table and knee-walked her way over to him as he sat back on the couch and waited. He tilted his head back to look up at her. She took his hand and pressed it to her chest. Over her heart.

Her crazily pounding heart.

"Yes, I'm still scared of what it all means. Being naked with you. The aftermath when you might just think once was enough and you're done. But I've been cautious my whole damn life. The only thing I've ever thrown myself into was my channel—and look how that's turning out. Aside from a stalker trying to make me quit, I mean."

He was still watching her. Not moving. He hadn't pulled his hand away though. He just gazed up at her hovering over him and waited for something. She wasn't sure what, so she kept talking.

"I think maybe I overthink stuff. It took me five years to leave Dylan. Well, two really since I thought the first three were the way it was supposed to be. And then it took me a couple of months to start my channel because I figured I had nothing to lose. And while I don't think I have nothing to lose with you—hell, I have everything to lose, including my heart—I also think maybe I shouldn't be so afraid that I never try."

He glanced over at her glass, then back at her. His eyes sparked with heat and humor. "You didn't even drink half that glass. You can't be drunk."

"I'm not drunk, Ty. I'm finally waking up."

He carefully placed his glass on the table. Then he pulled her across his lap in a move that had her on her back and looking up at him in surprise. They weren't that far apart, but he'd managed to flip them so he was dominant.

She melted inside. Everything simply melted.

He traced a finger down the vee of her shirt, against the swells of her breasts, and she pressed her lips together to stop herself from gasping.

"This is what I've been dreaming about for the past week, Cassie. You, in my arms, like this. Trusting me to make you feel good. I will, you know. Whatever you've experienced in the past, any disappointments with sex, that's over. If you don't like something, tell me. If you like it and want more, tell me. Don't let me do *anything* you aren't comfortable with. Don't keep your mouth shut and think it'll all be fine if you just let me do it. You can't offend me or disappointment me. I'm already hard thinking about all I get to do with this luscious body of yours. If it takes all night, or only takes fifteen minutes because we go up like a Roman candle, I don't care. Fair warning, though—if it's over in fifteen, we're doing it again as soon as we're able, because you deserve a lot more than a fifteen minute quickie. Blink if you understand me."

She giggled, and he laughed too. "I mean it, Cassie. I know you've always been quiet and shy, but don't be that way with me. Not about this. It's too important."

In that moment, she knew she could love him

forever. Maybe she was crazy, but she didn't care. Dylan had been her first lover, but not the first or last man she'd ever dated. Not one of them had ever treated her like Ty did. Like she mattered. Dylan had at first, but she recognized now just how superficial his attention had been. He'd ask her where she wanted to eat, then have a good reason why they should try another place. Or he'd ask her what she wanted to do, but there would be a reason why they needed to do that thing another day.

In short, she'd very rarely gotten to do what she wanted or go where she wanted. Ty, however, made her wants and needs a priority. She didn't doubt he would do the same thing in bed.

"I promise to tell you what I like and what I don't," she said. "And maybe this isn't the way to begin, but I'm not going to like the lights on. I'm not saying pitch black, but very dim would be good."

She knew he had Wi-Fi bulbs that he could control with his phone.

"I'll let you change the level to one you like," he told her. "But I think we've talked enough. I need to kiss you."

She tilted her face up to his, and their lips met with exquisite gentleness. She could feel her blood beating in her ears, her throat. Ty kissed her tenderly, but it didn't matter. Her body was on fire anyway.

Beneath her hip, she could feel the hard press of his cock against her. It thrilled her. Aroused her. A man could lie about a lot of things, but he couldn't lie about desire. She didn't feel like she'd ever be the sort of woman to parade around naked in front of him, but maybe she was wrong. Knowing she affected him in this way was incredibly satisfying.

Exciting.

His tongue slipped into her mouth, and she wrapped her arms around his neck, kissing him desperately. Kari had told her to go for it. She was going for it, and she wasn't going to stop. If it went wrong tomorrow, then she'd deal with it then.

He shifted her further, until her ass was on the couch and he hovered over her. His mouth didn't leave hers as the kiss grew more intense. They sucked each other's tongues, their lips meshing, devouring. Her body grew impossibly hot, so hot she was ready to beg him to remove her clothes.

But instead of pushing her further, he gentled the kiss. His hips settled in the cradle of her thighs, and his impressive cock pushed against her right where she wanted to feel him. Lightning streaked across her skin, driven by the press of him against her sensitive clit. The seam of her jeans provided more delicious pressure as he flexed his hips.

She didn't know how long they spent like that, just kissing, his hips flexing periodically and reminding her what she had to look forward to, but the result of all that teasing was a bone-deep need that wanted to move this thing to the next phase.

Cassie slid her hands down his muscled arms, his sides, and gripped his ass. She no longer cared about taking it slow or what he might think about her grabbing his ass like she owned it.

His response was a low chuckle in his throat, along with another flex of his hips that sent those pulses of heat throbbing through her again. Her panties were soaked. Her jeans were very likely wet too.

Ty broke the kiss and trailed his mouth over her jaw and down her throat. "You want more, babe?"

"What gave you that idea?" she panted.

He slid further downward, and then his hand slipped beneath her shirt at the back—she was thankful it was the back because she'd worried about him touching her stomach—and up to the clasp of her bra. He unsnapped it easily, then lifted himself and grabbed his phone to hand it to her.

"You need to select your light level, honey. Because I need to see these beautiful tits."

Cassie took his phone with shaking fingers and slid the bar all the way to the bottom. It was dark, but there was a hint of light. They could see each other, and would see more when their eyes adjusted, but it wasn't like the sun was out or anything.

"The bedroom, too," he said. "Because that's where we're headed."

She slid the bar to the bottom and gave him the phone back. He tossed it to the table, then reached for the hem of her shirt and tugged it up. She stiffened for a moment, and he stopped.

"What's wrong, Cass?"

"I—I'm just, um…" She closed her eyes. "You're so beautiful, Ty. Not an ounce of fat on you. I'm afraid you aren't going to like what you see."

"Baby, you have to give me more credit than that. I'm aching to see you. I want you. Can't you tell how hard I am for you? My dick would really like me to hurry up and thrust into you so it can get on with the program. But I want to build the anticipation. And, shit, I want to make you feel so good you beg me for more."

Butterflies swirled in her stomach. She had to believe him. It was the only way this would work. "Okay."

He lifted her shirt and bra at the same time, tossing them aside, and Cassie closed her eyes. This was it. She was exposed and there was no turning back. Best to know now, right?

"Look at me, Cassie."

She cracked an eye open. Ty ran his hands over her not so flat torso and cupped her generous breasts in his palms.

"These are the most beautiful boobs I think I've ever seen."

She laughed nervously. "Seriously, Tyler? Don't bull-shit me."

He grinned. "Okay, fine. I love boobs. I'm totally a tits man, and I've seen a few. These rank at the top. Definitely among the most beautiful I've seen." He picked up the bottle of *Dom*. "You ready for what comes next?"

"I... Maybe."

He bent over and licked one of her nipples. She gasped. Then he poured a cold stream of champagne on it and lapped it up before sucking her nipple into his mouth and tugging. She hadn't quite realized how sensitive her nipples were before, or maybe it was just Ty, because she hadn't felt this same tingle of sensation from her nipple to her pussy ever before.

But she felt it now, and she wanted more. She arched her back, thrusting her breast into his mouth. He licked a trail to the other nipple and repeated the process until she was a quivering mass of sensation.

"You know where else this champagne would taste great?" he purred, looking at her through slitted eyes.

Desire was a physical ache that overrode the chattering of her brain. "Where?"

He got to his feet and held out a hand. "Let me take you to the bedroom and show you."

Chapter Thirty

"You," she blurted when they reached his bedroom. The lights were dim, but she was lacking a shirt and bra and he still had on all his clothes. He turned to look at her questioningly.

Stupid brain.

"You need to take off your clothes," she clarified, arms wrapped around her naked breasts. And her stomach. Lord, why did she eat that pizza today? She'd had no idea she'd be naked in front of him later.

As if avoiding a single afternoon of pizza would have made a difference.

He set the champagne on the nightstand and shrugged out of his button-down shirt that he'd worn open over a black T-shirt. Then he reached behind him and tugged the shirt over his head one-handed.

Cassie could only stare. He had a tattoo on his shoulder, and one on his pec. She thought it might be a phoenix, and the Marine Corp symbol. There was also some writing. She reached out to trace it, mesmerized.

"The names of my teammates," he said. "The ones who didn't come back."

"Oh." She hurt for him, but she didn't know what to say. The curse of being an introvert was that you didn't always have the right words. Or any words.

He lifted her fingers to his mouth and kissed them. Then he pushed her hand down to his waistband. "Take them off for me," he said softly.

She had to lower her other arm from her chest to do it. She hesitated only a moment, then tackled the button and zipper of his jeans. Then she shoved them down his hips until he stood in his boxer briefs. Damn, he filled those out fine.

She could see the outline of his cock, and she reached out to touch it. Ty groaned as she did so, and it made her bolder. She pulled the briefs down, freeing him.

Holy hell, was that a tattoo? Not on his dick, but close. Right beneath the waistband of his briefs, he had a coiled snake with a tail that ended right above the root of his penis.

"That had to hurt," she said.

He snorted. "A little."

"Why?"

"Why did I do it?"

"Yes."

He shrugged. "Seemed like the thing to do at the time. Besides, it reminds me that you can't always see the danger that waits for you, but you'd damn sure better expect it."

"That's an interesting place to put it."

"Kind of an important place though, right?"

She laughed. "Definitely." She touched the snake

and he hissed in a breath. "It's surprising but also pretty."

"My dick or the snake?"

"Both."

"Can I take your jeans off, Cassie?"

She swallowed. "Yes."

He reached for the button, and she was glad she hadn't worn Spanx. She'd thought about it, but she hadn't. He undid her jeans, then pushed them down her hips. It wasn't as easy for him as it'd been for her because her jeans were meant to cling. Still, he got them off and she kicked out of them. Then he pushed her panties down to join them.

She stood before him utterly naked, and it terrified her. At least it was mostly dark. Still, she could see the tight muscles of his chest and abdomen, and that amazing Adonis belt where he didn't have an ounce of fat over the blades of his hipbones. She'd imagined things like this, but she'd never seen it in person. Dylan had never had abs you could see or a stomach you could bounce a quarter off.

"I don't know what you're thinking, Cassie Dixon, but if it's anything other than I'm about to rock your world, you need to stop."

How did he know?

He took her hand, gently, and wrapped it around his cock. "You feel that?"

She did. It was hot, and hard, and really big. Bigger than she'd expected. Though not so ridiculous it was meant for someone without a cervix. She thought of the giant dildo someone had sent her and nearly giggled nervously. But she managed not to.

"Yes," she whispered.

"It doesn't lie, Cassie. You can't trick it. I mean, yeah, it's a dick and it could be forced to react to direct stimulation. But that's not what's happening. You didn't hold me down and stroke me. You didn't suck my cock to make me hard. All you did was let me kiss you and lick your pretty nipples. I'm hard because of that and because I want to bury myself in you. This is need—*for you*—plain and simple. So if you're having doubts about that, you need to stop."

She couldn't help but give him a little squeeze. He sucked in a breath. "You're right," she said. "I'm doubting myself. You're perfect, Ty. And I'm not—"

She didn't get to finish the sentence because he dragged her against him, naked skin to naked skin, and slanted his mouth over hers. And then, when he had her limp from his kiss, he put his hands on her ass and picked her up as if she weighed nothing at all.

His strength shocked her. Somehow, she didn't ruin it. Somehow, she managed to wrap her legs around his hips. That move opened her to him, and his fingers skimmed along her wet slit. Her doubts and fears were quickly melting beneath the onslaught of pleasure.

The world tipped, and she found herself on her back in the middle of his bed. He hovered over her, still kissing her, his skilled fingers dragging from her slit to her clit. Cassie moaned into his mouth as he worked her, his fingers sliding, circling, pinching, until she was on the edge and dying for release.

He didn't let her come, though. Instead, he dropped his mouth to her throat, dragged it to her nipples, and then down her abdomen. She lay with one fist clenched around the covers, the other hand covering her eyes, her breathing uneven and needy.

And then he licked her. Licked her pussy like nobody had ever done before. Cassie had to open her eyes. Had to look down and see him between her legs. It was the most amazing and erotic thing she'd ever seen. It was her teenage dreams come true, only way better because she'd really had no clue back then.

Ty's gaze met hers, and he winked. Then he reached for the champagne bottle. A cold stream of *Dom Perignon* dribbled from the top of her pussy to the bottom, and Ty licked it up, uncaring that he got some on his bed.

Cassie closed her eyes again and arched her back, unable to hold off the orgasm barreling toward her any longer. It hit hard and she cried out as Ty sucked her clit into his mouth. He made her come for long moments, licking and sucking and pouring champagne onto her pussy as he lapped it up.

But then he kissed his way up her body again, his mouth taking hers in a slow, hot kiss that made everything inside her tighten with need once more.

"Just a sec," he said, levering himself off her and heading for the living room. He was back a moment later with their glasses. He handed hers to her. "Sip."

She did, and he set the glass on the bedside table.

"Why did you do that?"

He tugged the table drawer open and produced a box of condoms that he tossed onto the bed before he pushed her back and stretched his big body over hers. He held himself above her, and she realized that he managed to make her feel dainty.

"Because you didn't get to finish yours," he said, his tongue darting out to lick her nipple, "and I've been drinking more than my share from your pretty body."

Pretty body.

She traced his mouth with a finger, and then she traced his scar. "You're too good to be true," she said softly.

"Exactly what a man wants to hear when he's making you come." He waggled his eyebrows and she laughed. Then he dropped his gaze down her body before meeting her eyes again. "Fucking gorgeous," he said before kissing her again.

He took his time stoking the flames, kissing her, circling her clit with his fingers, building her up until her body hurt with the need to have him inside her. He groaned as she wrapped her hand around his cock and squeezed.

The sound of his voice in her ear, mirroring the need she felt, made her bold. She reached for the condoms and dragged a strip from the box. Ty shifted so she could use both hands. She ripped one from the strip, opened it, and rolled it onto him with fingers that only shook a little.

He pressed her into the bed this time, no longer hovering over her, but letting her feel the power of his body as the tip of his cock pressed into her.

"We still good?" he asked.

"You have to ask?"

"Yes, I do. If you tell me we are, I'm pushing inside you and I'm not stopping until we're both satisfied. If you need more time, or you've changed your mind, then I'll change tactics."

"I think if you don't start moving, I'm going to scream. Out of frustration, I should add."

"That's all I needed to know," he told her before he thrust into her body.

Cassie gasped. She had a vibrator. She'd used it. Fucked herself with it, though not too often. But Ty made the vibrator seem inadequate. He was big, and it took her a moment to accommodate him. He didn't move beyond the initial thrust, and she knew he did that for her.

"I'm sorry, Red. I should have been more careful."

"I'm okay," she whispered against his shoulder. Against his tattoo. "More than okay."

He took her mouth in a kiss as he started to fuck her, his hips moving slowly at first and then faster as the tension began to tighten inside her. Cassie lost herself in the powerful drive of his body. She ceased thinking about anything but the way it felt to have Ty inside her, pounding into her, pushing them both to impossible heights.

She'd never had sex like this before. There was all-consuming need. Desperate desire. The pleasure/pain of the tension building inside her, winding tighter and tighter. To want someone so much it physically hurt was a new thing for her.

She'd never made noise during sex in the past, but she did now. Needy, desperate sounds in her throat. Moans. Sighs.

Cassie closed her eyes and let the feelings wash over her. The pleasure. The need. The love.

There was no way she couldn't love him. Not with the way he put her feelings and needs first. She'd loved him as a teenager only because he was gorgeous and unattainable. Not really love, though of course it had felt like it to her at the time.

She loved him now because of who he was inside. The outside didn't hurt, but it was the inside that mattered. And Tyler Scott was everything that was beautiful on the inside.

The tension inside her snapped as her orgasm crashed into her. She cried out, her mouth on his shoulder, the salt of his skin on her tongue. He bracketed her face between his hands and kissed her hard and deep, fucking her the same way, drawing out her orgasm as he hit all her pleasure points.

When she thought she couldn't take another second of the intensity, he stiffened and drove deep. The groan in his throat told her he was coming. It went on for long seconds, and then his body seemed to relax. He kissed her softly before making his way to her ear and nibbling her lobe.

"That was fucking fantastic," he whispered. "You're amazing, Cassie. Hot, sweet, and sexy as fuck."

Every word out of his mouth was a drug to her senses. He told her she was sexy, but he also made her *feel* like she was sexy, and that was an incredible feeling for her. She knew—*knew*—she was pretty. But she didn't often feel sexy. Not even when she was making her videos and telling other women like her they had the right to be sexy too.

She knew she had the right. She just hadn't felt it before now.

Ty put his forehead on hers as he propped himself on his elbows above her. "I don't want to move, but I have to take care of this condom."

"Okay."

Her body was cold when he left. She curled into a ball and tried to process everything that'd just happened. Ty was back quickly. He pushed the covers down and helped her beneath them, and she pulled them almost to her chin. Her eyes had adjusted to the light, which meant his had too. She watched the tight muscles in his ass as he turned and poured champagne into her glass. She wanted to bite that ass. Eventually. If he let her.

He slipped beneath the covers, but he didn't lie down. Instead, he propped up the pillows on his side of the bed and leaned against them. Then he helped her do the same and handed her the glass of champagne. He took his own and they clinked.

"To you, Cassie. To your success."

They drank. He lifted his glass again. "And to my good fortune in getting to celebrate it with you the way you deserve. In case you don't know what that is, it's being worshipped head to toe like the goddess you are."

She was blushing like a fool, but she knew he couldn't see it in the dim light. "You're ridiculous. But thank you."

"I'm serious," he said. "And honored that you trusted me enough to let me touch you and taste you. And while I don't think I should have to say it, I'm going to anyway—I'm not disappointed. I'm fucking delighted. I can't wait to do it all again, though I was planning to give you a reprieve while we watch an episode of your show. But once those credits roll, you're mine."

What kind of idiot would argue with that? Cassie clinked her glass with his and took a swig. "You're on."

Chapter Thirty-One

IT WASN'T EASY KEEPING HIS HANDS TO HIMSELF FOR AN hour, but he managed it. As soon as the credits rolled, Ty dragged Cassie down to the mattress and rolled on top of her. Then he proceeded to kiss his way back down to her pussy before making her moan while he ate her out.

He loved the sounds she made, the way she tasted, and the sated look in her eyes when she recovered from the three orgasms he wrung from her. He knelt between her legs, rolled on a condom, and then lifted her to him so he could fuck her from that position.

He loved watching his cock disappear inside her body, loved the sounds they made together. She was so fucking wet, and she squeezed him tight as he pumped. He wished he'd asked her if she'd brought that clitoral vibrator with her because he'd love to watch her use it while he fucked her like this.

He put it on his mental list of things he was going to do with Cassie. Because no way was he done after tonight. She made his balls ache, and she made him crazy with need. He loved kissing her, eating her, burying his cock in her. He was going to love grabbing handfuls of her ass while he did it from behind, and he was really going to love sucking her tits while she rode him.

One thing at a time, though. Right now, he had to make her come hard. He wanted to be the one who made her see stars, not some damn purple dong. Not that he thought she'd kept it. But he was kind of dying to know what else she'd kept besides the little vibrator. He wanted to use them on her.

After she stiffened in his arms, her legs shaking, her head rolling back on the pillow, his name on her lips—not loud, not forceful, not anything other than a very Cassie-like gasp—he let himself go, rocking into her until his climax exploded through him, draining him of every last ounce of energy and semen he had.

He would have collapsed beside her, but he had to get rid of the condom. When he returned, she was beneath the covers again, her arm across her eyes, her chest rising and falling a bit faster than it had been before he'd dragged her beneath him.

Her hair spilled over the pillows, long and dark in the dim light. He wanted to run his fingers through it, play with it. He got in beside her and pulled her against him. She was stiff for only a second before she turned into him and put a leg over his, her palm on his chest and her head against his shoulder.

"In case it's not clear, I want you to stay with me. If you prefer to go back to the guest room, I won't stop you. But it's not what I want."

She tilted her head up to look at him. "I'd like to stay. But I need to get something to sleep in."

He wanted her to sleep naked, but he knew that waking up with him might be a bit much for her. He hated that she was so self-conscious, but he also knew she needed time to realize he thought she was banging. How she didn't realize it, especially since she seemed to when she made videos, astounded him.

"Want one of my T-shirts?"

"I, um, I'm not sure it'll work."

"It'll work. I weigh two-fifty, Red."

He didn't wait for a reply. He left her to grab a T-shirt and tossed it to her, then he got into bed again. She sat up and unfolded it. "Okay, this will work."

"Told you."

She shrugged into it, though he'd hoped she would wait a while longer. When her head emerged from the neck, he thanked his lucky stars he'd grabbed a V-neck because it meant he could easily reach inside and play with a breast if he wanted.

He was definitely going to want to do that.

Cassie lay beside him again, her knee going over his leg, and he wrapped an arm around her and squeezed her ass.

"Thank you, Ty," she said softly.

He was beginning to feel sleepy. "For what?"

"For everything. For being you."

He jolted a little at that. He wasn't used to someone thanking him for being who he was. He'd spent a lot of years trying to be better because his father had demanded it, and then when he'd finally accepted that he was just fine the way he was, he'd discovered new challenges to his sense of worth.

The loss of his team had been a huge one. Why hadn't he protected them better?

"Thanks," he said, because Cassie didn't need to hear all that.

She put her hand on his jaw and turned him to face her. Then she kissed him sweetly. His dick stirred, but it wasn't real interest since he was spent. But if he had the energy, he'd be inside her again in a flash.

She traced his scar. "How did you get this?"

Everything inside him went still. It was a long damn time ago, and it still made him feel like a frightened ten-year old sometimes. "A bat," he said.

"It shattered. That's what Kari said."

"Yes, it shattered." He remembered that day like it was yesterday. "My dad got pissed that I couldn't hit the ball the way he wanted. He took it away from me, hit a few balls with it, and then threw it at me. It hit the shed and splintered into pieces. I don't think he expected it to break. Anyway, one of the shards hit me in the face and did this. I was ten."

"Oh, Ty. I'm sorry."

She put her head on his chest and hugged him tight. Anybody else, and he'd want to escape. Anybody else, and he wouldn't have told. But Cassie understood. She had a bitch of a mother who'd treated her like shit. She got it better than anyone he knew. It felt right telling her.

He squeezed her to him. "I know, babe. Kari doesn't know how it happened. I think there are only three people who do, now that I've told you."

"I won't say anything."

"I know. I trust you."

He really did. But he wasn't sure if she trusted him yet. With her life, yes. With her heart? Probably not.

————

CASSIE WOKE BEFORE TY. It was still dark out, but she could see the beginnings of light behind the curtains. She lay still for a moment, listening to him breathe. Last night had been incredible. The most amazing sex of her life. She already wanted more, though she could feel a little bit of soreness between her legs.

Their glasses were on his nightstand, empty, and the bottle was there too. Her first time drinking real champagne was definitely memorable, and for more than one reason. One hundred-thousand followers and hot sex with Ty. She thought of the way he'd poured a stream of expensive champagne on her body, like it flowed from an endless river instead of a pricey bottle, and lapped it up as if she were the finest crystal.

Memorable.

She wanted to text Kari and tell her all about it, but she figured some details were better kept private. If Ty had been anyone else, she might spill. But he was Ty, and aside from the awkwardness of him being her best friend's cousin, there were things she wanted to hold inside for her own. Analyzing his behavior might lead to doubts, and she didn't want to go there.

Right now, she was happier than she'd been in a very long time. And Ty was a big part of that happiness.

Cassie eased from the bed and tiptoed across the room. Ty's room was bigger than the one she was in, and it was about as sparsely furnished as the rest of the apartment. He had a king-size bed, two nightstands, and a chest of drawers. There was a generic piece of art on the wall that she thought had probably come with the apartment, but otherwise the walls were empty. The curtains and carpet kept the room from echoing too badly, however.

She slipped through the door and back to her room, then gathered up some clothes and headed for the shower, doing her best to be quiet. Ty had fallen asleep before she had last night, but she still didn't want to wake him.

After she took a quick shower and threw on clean underwear, leggings and a sweater, she pulled on thick socks and made her way to the kitchen. Ty was there, and she crashed to a halt as her heart thumped at the sight of his broad back—shirtless—and tight ass in boxer briefs. He was spooning coffee into a filter when he turned and grinned at her.

"Morning, Red. Did you sleep all right?"

Seriously, had she died and gone to heaven? Because he could not be more beautiful, even with his hair seriously messed up and his eyes still looking as if he wanted to go back to bed.

She forced herself to move until she was inside the kitchen with him. "I did. How about you?"

He popped the filter into the basket, slid it into place, and turned on the coffee pot. Then he caught her around the waist and pulled her against his big, warm body. So warm. His mouth came down on hers, and she sighed. He tasted minty, like toothpaste, and he sucked her tongue lazily before he lifted his head again.

"Like I had fantastic sex with a hot babe who wore me out."

"I guess I should offer to cook breakfast, then. To get your strength up," she teased.

He arched an eyebrow. "I won't turn it down. What were you thinking?"

"You have eggs and cheese. Bread. And a package of bacon."

"Sold," he said, and she laughed.

"Okay, then how about egg and cheese omelets with toast and bacon?" She might even allow herself one piece of bacon this morning. She usually didn't eat it because it was salty and bad for her blood pressure. One or two pieces wouldn't kill her, though.

"Sounds terrific. Tell me how I can help."

"All right. Do you have parchment paper?"

"Uh, what's that?"

"Going with no then. A baking pan?"

"Maybe."

She gaped at him. "How do you not know if you have a baking pan?"

"I rented this place furnished and it came with kitchen stuff. I don't really cook, so I've never looked."

Cassie sighed exaggeratedly. "Okay, I'll look. You get the stuff out of the fridge and I'll search your kitchen for cooking implements."

"I have pans. And spatulas. Won't those work?"

"They will," she said, opening a cabinet. "But cooking bacon in the oven is better."

"Really?"

"Crispier and less splatter. Though it'd be even better if you had a bacon pan, or that parchment paper. Aha," she said when she'd opened the third cabinet door. "A baking sheet!"

She took it out and set it on the counter, then got a pan for the eggs and a bowl to crack them in. Ty disappeared to put on a shirt, and returned to lay the bacon in strips on the pan the way she told him. Cassie preheated the oven, shoving the pan inside when it was time. When the bacon was close to done, she prepared the omelets. Ty was in charge of toast and coffee.

When they sat down and Ty took the first bite of his crunchy bacon, he grinned at her. "Damn, Red, you were right about this bacon."

"I'm glad you like it."

He tried the omelet, closing his eyes and sighing. "So good. I'm in heaven."

"It's just an omelet, Ty. I didn't do anything special."

He eyed her as if she'd just said the most ridiculous thing. "You cooked it. That's special to me. I only get home-cooked meals if I go to Ian's these days. Natasha can make a seriously tasty meatloaf, and her mac and cheese is to die for."

Cassie laughed. "What you're telling me is that the way to your heart is most definitely through your stomach."

"Damn straight. Food is my Kryptonite."

"I'll remember that. I try not to make mac and cheese all that often, by the way. Carbs. But I have a lower fat version I like. And I can definitely do meatloaf."

"I think I'm in love," he said with a grin.

Those words pricked her heart. Cassie forced a laugh because she knew he was joking around and she didn't want him to know he'd hurt her. He wouldn't like that he had, and he'd apologize.

But she didn't want an apology because it would highlight the differences in how they felt. She was in too deep, and he wasn't. She didn't need that reminder.

Instead, she needed to be careful. Being with Ty, having sex with Ty, was exciting and thrilling and more than she'd ever thought could happen—but it was temporary. He was helping her with a problem, not building a relationship.

No matter how pretty the things he said to her, how thoughtful and wonderful he could be, she had to remember that he hadn't promised her anything. A week ago, he hadn't even remembered who she was. Today, he was making jokes about being in love because she knew how to make a meatloaf.

Yes, he'd told her about his scar and said she was the only other person who knew. But sometimes a person needed to say a thing aloud to take away its power to gnaw at them, so that didn't make her special. It just put her in the right place at the right time.

She needed to remember this wasn't a relationship in the true sense of the word. It was something they'd fallen into because of proximity and desire, and it was something they could fall out of the instant her life returned to normal.

"Goodness," she said, tearing off a piece of toast, "if only I'd known I could impress you so easily."

He took the toast from her fingers and fed it to her. Then he leaned over and kissed her, a quick peck on the lips. "You impressed me before you ever turned on a burner."

Her lips tingled, and her body started to soften just thinking about what he could do to it. "Must have been when I shut the door in your face."

He laughed. "Close. It was before that. When I watched your videos. You have a real talent for talking to the camera. I was mesmerized."

A warm glow started inside, rising to the surface and spreading over her skin. She was still nursing her hurt, but she was determined to ignore it as much as possible.

She'd been having a good time, and she wasn't going to let negative thoughts ruin it. She'd enjoy the fun while it lasted. That's all you could do sometimes.

"You don't have to sweet talk me to get into my panties, Ty. We're past that stage."

He grinned. "Thank God. Because I need to get in there again soon." He stabbed a piece of omelet. "Did you bring any of those toys with you?"

She blinked, her cheeks growing hotter. "Um, just one."

He went still. "Please, *please*, tell me it's that clitoral suction one."

"Okay, I'll tell you that's the one."

"But is it really?"

"Yes, really."

He closed his eyes. "Oh, fuck me. This is going to be good."

"What did you have in mind?" Was she really asking that with a straight face? And did she honestly want the answer?

He shook his head. "Nope, can't talk about it right now. If I do, we won't finish breakfast."

Chapter Thirty-Two

FOUR DAYS WENT BY AND CASSIE WAS STILL AT HIS PLACE. Not that Ty minded. She'd started sleeping in his bed by default, and he loved waking up with her body next to his. She still insisted on wearing clothing once they went to sleep, but he didn't mind it if it made her feel better. Didn't stop him from lifting the bottom of her T-shirt or nightie and sliding his cock into her wet heat from behind while he stroked her clit.

Didn't stop her from responding with those little gasps and moans he'd come to love. He loved every moment he got to spend with her. They watched all the episodes of her witch show, then started on *Doctor Who*. He loved the way she snuggled up to him during the parts she found creepy—and the way she clung to him in bed those nights.

Unfortunately, Ty and his team were no closer to figuring out who was sending the threatening emails than before. The recording devices they'd found in her apartment came back untraceable, bought from a third party supplier with cash. None of the neighbors had spotted the intruder, so they didn't have a description. The camera pointing at the back door hadn't caught anything before it'd gone dead, other than a squirrel on the fence where it was located, and nothing had arrived at the front door since they'd stopped the mail.

There'd been no deliveries at all. It was as if the guy knew Cassie wasn't there. Ty didn't like that thought, but her stalker was clearly watching her house. He'd seen her leave with Ty. He had not seen her come back, which was why he'd laid off sending shit.

Cassie had put a hold on her mail at the post office, and her work mail was being routed to the mailroom. One of the guys picked up her packages, both work and post office. Ty figured that Ian had used his CIA connections to get that second one done. The USPS didn't randomly hand out packages to people who weren't the legal recipients of said packages.

Her work mail was distinct from her house mail, which was completely normal and filled with bills as well as small boxes from companies wanting to sponsor her. In her work mail, there'd been the usual stuff she expected, plus a few BDSM magazines, a Barely Legal magazine, a Big Mamas magazine, and a variety of fat fetish magazines. The magazines made Cassie's eyes flash angrily as she dropped them in the recycle bin. She was past the humiliation stage and had moved on to abject fury. He figured that was a good thing.

He'd considered hiding them from her, but it was her mail and he couldn't do that. He didn't have a right to do that, though he wanted to. Him and his damned honor. Because whenever she got something that had to do with body size, he knew it hurt her. It hurt because of her childhood and her damned mother, the way she'd been taught to think she wasn't good enough because she was too heavy.

The same way he'd been taught to think he wasn't good enough because he couldn't hit the hardest fastball or catch the farthest-thrown football. Not good enough based on a parent's inadequacies and hang-ups about their own life.

He tried to show her that shit didn't matter by worshipping her body with his. She was still shy sometimes, but she was coming out of her shell. Her mother was a skinny, drunk bitch most of the time. He knew because he'd asked Kari to tell him what she knew about the woman. She'd said that Lottie Dixon had once been voted Most Beautiful in high school, and she'd been Prom Queen during her sophomore year. Ty hadn't realized that.

Lottie had spent her life hung up on her teenage accolades while she'd chased men and drink and, yes, soft drugs like marijuana. She was forty-eight now, and she looked malnourished and far too thin, as if the alcohol was starting to take it out of her. She smoked, worked part-time at the Piggly Wiggly as a cashier, and partied her way through weekends.

She'd had Cassie when she was eighteen. She'd even married Cassie's father for a short time. He was a bit older than she was, a casual drug user who'd gotten hooked on pain pills. He'd left town two years after Cassie was born and never returned, which left Lottie to scrounge and scrape for the money to get by. That's where the random men came in and how Lottie eventually cooked up the scheme to tell them that Cassie was her sister's kid she was taking care of. Nobody from Bear Creek believed it, but there'd been plenty of plant workers moving in and out of the town who didn't know better.

All of it added up to Cassie being a beautiful, vibrant young woman with serious hang-ups about her worth. Hang-ups that Ty knew he wasn't changing overnight. Cassie had an entire channel dedicated to making women who weren't quite the Hollywood ideal believe they were beautiful, and yet she still doubted it about herself. Drove him crazy, but he knew that you didn't just get over the things that'd happened to you. Cassie's channel was her way of controlling those demons she hadn't yet conquered.

When he walked through the door that night, she had dinner on the table. Ty loved it, and yet it bothered him too. He knew that she'd felt duty-bound to cook for her ex, and he'd stressed to her more than once that she didn't have to do it for him. They could order in or go out. Though, truth be told, he loved the food she made. Most of it was healthy stuff, and most of it was vegetarian. Didn't matter because she managed to make it taste great. And she still knew how to make a meatloaf with mashed potatoes that made a man cry.

"How's the gang?" she asked with a smile.

He'd asked her to go with him, but she'd had to work on a new video. Apparently she had some sponsored products to try, and she'd been eager to get started.

"They're good. Everyone says hi. Ian says that Natasha's cooking again this weekend. We're all invited. Oh, and just so you know, they're getting married at the end of February. Might want to block that out on your calendar."

She blinked at him. "Really? I'm invited?"

He tugged her against him and kissed her. "You're my date, Red."

"That's more than a month away."

"And?"

"Um, well, a lot can happen in a month."

"Yes, it can. But one thing is sure; you're going with me to a wedding."

She dropped her gorgeous green gaze to the spaghetti sauce she ladled onto his plate. "Okay."

A flash of anger flared inside at the tone of her voice. Like she didn't believe it. He tipped her chin up and forced her to look at him. "Do you have other plans?"

"No."

They stared at each other, and he felt that same desperate tug of emotion that he always did when he gazed into her eyes. He cared about this woman. A lot. And she acted like she was only biding time. It pissed him off and made him feel a deep sense of panic at the same time.

"Good. Did you hear from Kari today?"

"Yes."

"Did you tell her about us yet?" He could have said something to his cousin, but he felt like it was Cassie's news, not his. Kari was his cousin. Cassie was her best friend. They talked about shit, the way besties did. It wasn't his place to get into the middle of that.

She glanced away. "Not exactly. It's awkward."

"How so?"

Her eyes flashed. "What am I supposed to say, Ty? *Hey, Kari, I'm banging your cousin and he's got a big dick? What do you want to know?*"

Ty snorted. He was annoyed, but she amused him too. "A big dick, huh? Tell me more."

She pushed his shoulder then handed him a cheese grater and a small wedge of parmesan. "Yes, Ty. You have a big dick. Like the rest of you, it's impressively large. But you already know that."

He grinned. "Doesn't mean I don't like hearing about it."

Cassie rolled her eyes, and things felt right again. For now.

"Men," she said. "So focused on their dicks."

He twirled hot spaghetti and took a bite. "Can I focus my dick on you later?"

Heat flared in her eyes. Even when she was annoyed at him, she wanted him. That was something, anyway. "I'll be disappointed if you don't."

"This is delicious," he said. "But you don't have to cook for me, Cassie. I don't expect it."

She studied her plate as she twirled noodles from her much smaller portion. "I know you don't. Sometimes I like it, though."

"I'm glad. But when you don't want to, or don't like doing it, don't. We'll order something, or we'll go out. You aren't my personal chef."

"I'm not, but consider it a trade."

"A trade?"

"For all the work you're about to do for me in bed."

She arched an eyebrow and he laughed. "Honey, that's not work. It's my pleasure to make you moan and beg."

"And you wonder why I haven't told Kari." She shook her head. "I honestly don't know what to say that won't sound supremely dirty. I mean she knows we kissed, but she hasn't asked any questions since the night she told me to stop being an idiot. I think she's respecting my privacy. I should just say it, but I keep expecting her to ask."

"Just tell her we're together and I'm the best you've ever had. No need to say more."

"The best, huh?"

He tilted his head to the side innocently. "Aren't I?"

She leaned over and kissed him, and the thought of food almost flew out the window. But then she sat back again and continued to eat. "Yes, you definitely are. Now stop fishing for compliments."

"You know something, Red?"

"What?"

He leaned toward her. "Are you listening? Really listening?"

"Yes," she said a touch breathlessly.

"You're the best I've ever had, too."

Chapter Thirty-Three

CASSIE HAD BEGUN TO THINK OF WHAT THEY DID together as lovemaking. It was for her. Ty didn't say so, but she hoped he felt the same. When they were together in bed, he sometimes talked dirty to her. He told her was going to fuck her hard and deep, and she creamed at the growly way he said it. She liked that he said it, but when it was all over, fuck was not the word she thought of.

He taught her many things about herself between the sheets. He taught her that she liked it when he spread her legs wide and pistoned his cock into her body, catching the nerve endings in her clit and her G-spot just right. The wider he spread her, the better. It was like magic every single time.

That night, he taught her that getting on her knees with her ass in the air and the pillow clutched to her mouth while he dominated her body from behind was another kind of heaven. She could hear the slap of his balls as he fucked her, and when he pressed that little clitoral vibrator into her hand and told her to use it, she seriously almost screamed. She wasn't a screamer at all, but the suction of the vibrator and the drive of his cock nearly did it.

When he slid the tip of his finger into her ass at the same time, she came so hard the stars didn't stop spinning for a good five minutes. How the hell was she supposed to tell Kari about any of this?

She wasn't, and she couldn't. Not without dying of supreme embarrassment.

Ty finished soon after, groaning as he clutched her hips and jerked inside her. He took her down to the bed with him and rolled them to the side, his cock still inside her.

"My God, Cassie," he said, his mouth beside her ear, his breath whispering across the sweat on her skin. "That was perfect. So damned perfect."

"Mmm," she said, because she couldn't speak. Her body still tingled. Her pussy clenched around him involuntarily, and the stars were still spinning. Her heart pounded almost painfully. It was the love she felt for him that hurt so much. She couldn't say it aloud. She didn't dare to.

"I hope you know I've got it bad for you, Red. Everything you say on your channel about being sexy and attractive and capable of rocking a man's world— it's fucking true. You're rocking mine every night. I want you to believe that."

She did believe it in that moment. But it wasn't the same thing as a declaration of love. It wasn't an invitation to forever.

He slid from her body and left the bed. When he returned, he dragged her into his arms and held her tight. But he never said the words she most wanted to hear. The words that would really make her believe.

When he fell asleep, she slipped from his arms and dragged on her sleep shirt. Her phone lit up with a message and she picked it up, thinking it was probably Kari. If so, it was time to tell her friend that she and her cousin were a thing. However long it lasted.

But it wasn't Kari. It was Dylan.

Been thinking about you. How are you?

Cassie frowned. She hadn't heard from him since he'd told her he was getting married a couple of months ago. She thought about ignoring him, but with everything else going on in her life, she didn't want one more dangling thread. Best to deal with him and get it over with. Like ripping off a Band-Aid.

Cassie: What do you want?

Dylan: Jesus, Cass, we were together five years. You don't have to be a bitch just because I want to know how you are.

Cassie gritted her teeth. He was such a fucking jerk. How had she missed it for so long? How had she ever let his flashes of anger, like this one, cow her into submission? But she had. Worse, she knew why. Because she'd thought she'd been lucky he was even interested in her.

She'd been far too hard on herself for far too long. Ty slumbered beside her. He'd told her she was the best he'd ever had, that what they did together was perfect. Even better, he was actually interested in *her*. What she wanted, what she thought, what she had to say. He made her feel special every single day, and had almost from the moment he'd crossed her threshold.

That was what she deserved in a man—and always had. She was coming to realize it finally, thanks to Ty.

Cassie: I repeat, what do you want?

Let him stew on that. He wouldn't expect her to be anything but submissive, so he was likely staring at his phone in shock right that moment. She almost wished she could see his face.

Almost.

Dylan: I just want to know how you are. How things are going. I saw your channel. You look amazing, Cass.

Cassie rolled her eyes. She'd known there was more to this from the moment she'd seen his name. *I'm fine, thanks. How are you? How was the wedding?*

She watched the dots for a long time as he either wrote a damned novel or erased what he'd said and started over a few times. Finally, the answer came.

Dylan: Didn't go through with it. She's not the right one for me.

Cassie felt like the anonymous woman had dodged a bullet with that one. *Sorry to hear it.*

She wasn't. Not at all.

Dylan: Are you really? Because I miss you, Cass. Really miss you.

Anger throbbed in her belly. He missed her being a doormat for him. Missed the free labor, and the extra money she'd brought in with her job. He'd always managed to be a bit short when it came time for his portion of the rent or utilities, and she'd always had to make it up for him.

Cassie: I'm sorry, Dylan, but I have a boyfriend. It's getting serious.

For her, anyway. She wasn't sure about Ty. She couldn't deny that, at a minimum, he loved having sex with her. He wasn't faking that.

Dylan: He can't love you like I do. We were good together. We could be again.

Cassie gaped at her screen. Was he serious? They'd either lived a different reality, or he'd rewritten everything in his mind so that it looked rosy in hindsight. Which, for him, it had been. But not because he'd loved her. Anger motivated her as her fingers flew over the letters.

Cassie: I'm sorry, but I'm not interested. I wish you the best.

Dylan: Can I at least see you? Talk to you?

Cassie: Why? I've just told you I'm not interested in revisiting the past. I've moved on. I thought you had too.

Dylan: Jesus, you aren't making this easy. Fine. I need a loan, baby. A small one. I'll pay you back. It's just to help me get back on my feet.

Cassie stared at her phone. Of course. She should have known it was money. He'd seen the YouTube channel, and he'd either figured it out, or someone had told him, that people made money on those. He wanted a piece of it.

Cassie: I'm sorry, Dylan, but I can't help you. I don't have any money to lend. It's expensive living in the city, and every dollar is spoken for. If I had it, I'd lend it to you.

That last was a lie, but she didn't mind saying it. He didn't deserve the truth anyway.

His reply was swift and predictable. Dylan always lost his temper and said nasty things when he didn't get his way.

You're a lying fucking cunt, Cassie. I hope you fuck off and die!

Cassie put her phone on the nightstand with a sigh and slid down into the covers, burrowing next to Ty. He slipped an arm around her and pulled her close. "Red," he murmured.

She put her hand on his cheek and slid it into his hair. "I'm right here, Ty."

For as long as he wanted her.

Chapter Thirty-Four

"Dylan Webb sent a threatening text to Cassie last night," Ty said to the gathered team before summarizing the exchange for them. They were in one of the conference rooms at BDI Headquarters. BDI had some persistent fires going on in other parts of the world right now, but they'd still managed to get together for a quick meeting about Cassie's situation.

Ty didn't think the text was a serious threat, but they had to treat it as if it were. Webb had wanted money, and he'd gotten angry when Cassie had told him she didn't have it to give.

Cassie hadn't wanted to show Ty the text exchange, but she'd done so when he'd told her it was important. He'd looked at her in confusion after he'd read it. "Aside from that shit he said to you, what's so bad about this that you didn't want me to see it?"

She'd been a little evasive before she'd finally admitted it was the part about having a boyfriend and getting serious with him. Ty had taken her in his arms, tilted her head back, and told her she hadn't said anything untrue. It *was* getting serious, at least for him.

She'd blinked rapidly and he'd realized she'd been blinking away tears. "Okay," she'd said.

He knew that word held a wealth of emotion for her. Cassie often said *okay* when she didn't know what else to say, when she couldn't find the words or she was too shy. He still couldn't figure out how she flipped a switch for the camera and became outgoing and confident, but that was just Cassie.

He'd pressed her, though. "Is it getting serious for you, too?"

"Yes," she'd finally said.

He'd kissed her so thoroughly that they'd ended up back in bed for another hour before they'd finally gotten it together enough to make the trek to BDI. Cassie was in the Cove with her laptop and some video editing because he'd promised her lunch after he was finished.

Dax looked up from his screen. "He's not in Richmond anymore. Phone records indicate he texted Cassie from Arlington. He was within a mile of her place at the time."

A chill went through Ty, followed by a flood of protective anger. If he got his hands on Dylan Webb, he'd knock the shit out of him for what he'd said to Cassie. And if he was the one who'd sent her the threats? Ty would snap his fucking neck.

"He could be the one sending the packages and other crap," Rascal piped up. "Maybe he wants to fuck with her mental state a bit. Or maybe it's a way to soften her up so she's more likely to turn to him if he tries to waltz back into her life. He was clearly trying that tactic before she told him she had a boyfriend."

"Maybe so," Ty said. "Not the way I'd go about trying to win a woman back, but then I'm not stupid."

"Debatable," Dax said with a grin.

"Fuck you," Ty replied mildly.

Dax snorted.

"All right, kids," Ian said. "No fighting."

Jace laughed. "Practicing for when you've got two children in the house as opposed to one?"

Ian arched an eyebrow. "Are you kidding? Running BDI has been training me to wrangle children for years. I'll be ready."

"I dunno, man," Rascal said. "My sister has three, and she says it's brutal. Like *Fight Club* every day."

"You have siblings?" Ty asked. "I thought you sprang fully formed from the earth or something."

Rascal laughed. "I have three sisters. Trust me, I've paid my dues."

Ian waved a hand. "My children will be well-behaved. Daria is already a perfect little princess."

Rascal shook his head. "Sure, boss. Whatever you say."

"Okie dokie," Ian said. "We know Webb's in the area. It could be him behind everything or just some of it."

That was the problem with having an increasingly high-profile online. More than one person could stalk you at a time. And Cassie's follower count was still rising. Her videos were going to a wider audience now, and she was giddy over the revenue she was generating. If it kept going, she'd be able to work for herself full time.

Ty figured that if Dylan Webb knew she was making good money at the videos, he wasn't going to give up so easily. Hell, he might even think she owed him. That might be enough to threaten her with, though it seemed like he'd send the threats *after* she turned him down, not before.

"Since he wants money from her, wouldn't he be less likely to send emails telling her to shut the channel down?" Ty mused.

"Unless it's not really money he wants," Jace replied. "Or not all he wants. If he's after revenge or wants to teach her a lesson, then he could be sending the emails to scare her. Maybe contacting her now is just a way to find out her mental state while he tries to make her fragile enough to give him what he wants."

They sat, frowning, all of them thinking. The variables were bigger than usual based on the viral nature of Cassie's channel and the Kelly Cosmetics video. Some of the people trolling her were vicious, but most of them were garden-variety kooks. It made the truly dangerous ones harder to spot in the crowd. Dax had an entire IT team looking at comments when they could spare the time from other work.

It was a slow process and a frustrating one.

"I got the closed file on Officer Woodruff this morning," Ian said. "He was disciplined for the use of excessive force during a routine arrest over a year ago. He transferred up here about six months ago."

"Nothing earthshaking," Dax said thoughtfully. "Not very likely he's sending threatening emails or other crap to a woman he dated briefly."

"Precisely."

"Shit," Ty said, raking a hand through his hair. "I feel like we've got nothing at all to go on. We're just waiting for this asshole to fuck up."

Ian steepled his hands on the table. "If we had more

people to spare, I'd tell you to take her back home for a while. If the stalker knew she'd returned, he might step up the harassment again." He sighed. "It'll have to wait a week or so until things return to a more normal tempo around here."

Ty was relieved to hear it since he didn't actually want to take Cassie back to her place. Of course he'd have stayed with her, and there'd have been a team watching the outside of the house, but if he was at Cassie's place, he wouldn't relax enough to enjoy being with her the way he could now. He'd be too focused on protecting her and too unwilling to let down his guard for a single moment.

Their relationship would suffer because Cassie would think he was aloof or uninterested. Even if he told her otherwise, he suspected she'd believe it deep inside.

"Thanks for the help," Ty said to the team. "I appreciate it so much."

"That's why we're here, Ty," Ian said. "To take care of each other and the world. Going to need all hands on deck tomorrow, speaking of the world. Feds have got a rumor of a drug dealer negotiating for a tactical nuke in Venezuela. Got a DEA contingent headed over to brief us. Everyone be here at eight a.m."

The meeting broke up, and Dax sidled in next to Ty as they headed out. "How's it going at home?"

Ty shot him a look. "Why? You hoping you've got a chance?"

Dax shrugged. "Hey, I wouldn't say no if your sexy lady wanted me instead—but no, that's not why I was asking. You seem, I don't know, more relaxed than usual.

More natural. Less like you're holding something in and trying to keep it from chewing you up inside."

Ty stopped and turned to face his friend. He hoped he didn't let his shock show. "What makes you think something's chewing me up inside?"

Dax leaned back against the wall and shrugged. "I can't be a pretty face and perceptive too?"

"Pretty to your momma maybe."

Ty was ribbing the other man. Even he had to admit that Dax had a pretty face. Almost ridiculously so. Like he should be in Hollywood instead of working as a mercenary.

"Ha, you wish," Dax said. Then he held his hands up. "It's none of my business. I know that. But whatever you've got going on with Cassie, it agrees with you. Just wanted to say that. In case you were clueless or something."

Ty started walking again. "Clueless?"

"Wasn't it Jace who decided he shouldn't see Maddy because she was too good for him or something stupid like that? And then he was a fucking asshole because he'd made the decision to walk away from her? Wasn't until he admitted the truth to himself that he begged her to take him back—or something along those lines."

Ty laughed. "I don't know if it was quite like that. But yeah, I think he had some idea he didn't need to be in her life because it was going to be bad for her if he was."

"Like I said. Clueless."

Ty reached the elevator and hesitated. "No, I'm not clueless, Dax. There's something going on between Cass and me. I think it's love, but I've never been there before so I'm not quite sure. I feel like if she told me she loved me, I'd trip over my tongue to say it back. But I don't want to scare her by saying it to her first. So, I'll wait."

Dax nodded. "Maybe don't wait too long, huh? Sometimes you have to take the chance, or you risk losing everything if you don't."

Ty gave the other man a curious look. "Sounds like experience talking."

Dax shrugged. "Maybe so."

Ty stepped into the elevator and looked at his friend's dour face. "Hey, how's the romance reading going?" he asked to lighten the mood.

Dax grimaced. "It's not a bad book, but damn, there's not a man alive who could live up to this woman's standards. It's no wonder she's getting death threats."

"Death threats over a novel? Wow."

The elevator doors started to slide closed.

"Tell Cassie you love her," Dax called out. "Don't be an idiot!"

Chapter Thirty-Five

TY SEEMED PREOCCUPIED. CASSIE WATCHED HIM AS THEY ate burgers and fries at a local diner. Well, hers was a veggie burger, but it was still good. And her fries were sweet potato fries without salt.

"I think I can give notice to Amelia in a couple of months," she said.

Ty's gaze slewed her way. "Really? That's awesome, Red!"

She glowed with his praise. "Revenue is way up, and my stats are growing. I mean I worry that something will happen and it'll all fall off again, but I think if it stays this way for two or three more months, and I'm putting out regular content and it's getting the views I'm getting now—well, I think I'll be safe."

"That's awesome, honey."

"I might have to move to a cheaper place, but that's okay. I wanted to live closer to work when I found the townhouse. If I'm not commuting, it won't matter."

She could even move to Maryland. Live closer to Ty. She wouldn't say that, though. She didn't want to make him think she was pushing him to make plans with her.

"You could move in with me."

Cassie's heart thumped. Talk about turning expectations upside down. "Isn't that a little quick?"

She thought a shadow passed over his face, but then it was gone before she could be sure.

"Not for me. Stay with me until you figure out if it's going to work with your channel. We can get a bigger place later."

She felt like a fish gasping for air. "You want to move in with me?"

He took her hand and kissed it. "Cassie, babe, haven't you noticed how much fun it is when we're in the same apartment together? I can live with a lot more of that in my life. A lot more of you."

"It's only been two weeks, or thereabouts," she said a touch wonderingly. "You can't possibly want to move in with me so soon."

"I know what I want. I see no reason to act like I don't. I want you. In my bed, on top of me, under me, surrounding me. I want to wake up and do dirty things to you in the mornings, and then I want to do it again at night before we go to sleep. Do you want to return to your townhome and live there alone?"

She didn't really have to think about it. She liked the place, but she didn't own it and it wasn't her dream home or anything. "No, not really. But I would, because that's what grownups do. And I do miss being at home. I miss my studio and my things."

"I know, Red. We're trying to fix that for you."

She ate a sweet potato fry. "I know. I appreciate it." He hadn't told her everything they'd talked about in their meeting, but she knew they didn't know who was sending her the threats yet. Whoever it was, he was cautious. He hadn't turned up at her house again, and she'd gotten no emails. It was as if he knew they were searching for him and he'd decided to back off.

She also knew that Dylan was in town instead of back in Bear Creek or in Richmond. That had surprised her, but she really didn't think he was the one threatening her. He was smart, but not so smart he knew how to evade a group of professionals searching for a link between him and the deliveries to her house.

Besides, she was pretty darn certain there was no way Dylan would have spent the coin required for some of that stuff. Especially the sex toys that'd been delivered to her office or the funeral wreath someone had left on her front doorstep. Not to mention the money he'd have needed to buy spy cameras and the risk of breaking into her house to place them.

Though, to be fair, she couldn't be absolutely certain. She'd seen Dylan mad before, and she knew he sometimes went to extraordinary lengths to get back at someone who'd slighted him. It'd never been anything illegal, but he'd done mean things like replacing powdered coffee creamer with protein powder, which gave his boss the shits for a week until he figured it out. Not nice, but not dangerous. Petty.

Still, Dylan was in town. And he was pissed at her— or at least he had been last night. He might be willing to harass her if he thought it would fuck with her head and make her miserable for a while.

"I'll help you set up your studio in the guest room just like you have it in your townhome. We can disassemble the bed and store it. Give you more space." Ty snatched one of her fries even though he had plenty regular fries of his own. "If you want to, Cassie. I'm not trying to force you, and I don't expect you to take care of me either. We'll keep our money separate, and you don't have to tell me a thing about how much you're earning. I'll pay for the rent and utilities and everything because I already do, but if we move somewhere together, we can discuss how to do it equitably."

His last sentence shocked her. "I can't let you pay for everything just because you already do. That's not fair."

"Will it get you to your goal faster?"

"A little bit. But that's not the point."

He shrugged. "Up to you. I'm just offering. I want you in my bed every night, but if you need your own space, then we'll figure that out too. And if you want to keep your townhome while you're still commuting, I'll make the drive to see you. I won't like you being so far away, but I'll do it."

"Why are you so good to me?" she whispered past the tightness in her throat. "You weren't supposed to be this way."

She didn't know what she'd expected, really. Her fantasy Ty had been a great lover and he'd been obsessed with her, of course, but she'd never considered the real Ty could be so much better than her romantic dreams had ever been.

He moved his chair closer to hers, until he could put his arm on the back of it and cup her face with his other hand. "I don't know what I was supposed to be like, but the truth is I care about you. I like who I am with you, and I want more of it. I don't care if it's only been a couple of weeks. I know how I feel. And before you think this is the way I operate, I've never asked a woman to move in with me. I've never told one I need her in my life and in my bed. But I *need* you."

"You need me? It seems so fast," she said, her voice barely more than a whisper. Her heart hammered like crazy as she tried to process everything he said.

He raked a hand through his hair. It stood up adorably on one side before subsiding into something tamer. "Hell, Red. I know it's crazy. I *know* it. I don't know if it's love. I don't know what it is because this is the first time I've felt like this, but if this is what love feels like, then yeah, I'm in love. And I damn sure know I don't want to take you back home when this is over and say goodbye like none of the stuff between us ever happened. I think it'd kill me if I had to do that, but I would if it's what you wanted."

Happiness swelled inside her. She couldn't help but run her fingers over his cheek, across his lips. His eyes grew darker, but he didn't move. "I loved you back home in Bear Creek, Tyler Scott. But that was teenage infatuation brought on by a desperate desire to be someone I wasn't. I know the difference between that and what I feel now, and I know I'm in love with you. I'm amazed you could feel the same way about me. It doesn't seem real. I keep thinking I should wake up."

He tilted his head to the side like a dog who'd heard something strange. "Why would you be amazed, Cassie? I'm nobody special. Just a former football jock from the same hometown as you. I wasn't smart enough to pay attention to you back home, but I am now. Thank God." His gaze dropped from her eyes to her chest. "I really, *really*, want to take you home and make hot, dirty love to you right now."

"I want that too," she said. "With the emphasis on dirty."

Ty arched an eyebrow. "Oh yeah? What did you have in mind?"

She glanced over at the waitress, who'd been shooting them not-so-subtle glances for a while. "I'll tell you in the truck."

Ty took money from his pocket and laid it on the table. Then he grabbed her hand and tugged her to her feet. Cassie laughed as he started to pull her toward the door.

"Wait! It's my turn to get it, not yours."

He shot her a look. "Sorry, no time to spare, Red. You can get it next time. I've got somewhere important to be."

Chapter Thirty-Six

Ty was doing everything he could to make this last, but Cassie was driving him insane. Apparently, she'd brought more toys with her than just the clitoral vibrator, no matter that she'd originally told him it was just the one. The way her cheeks reddened when she brought out the dong with the suction cup, he knew why she hadn't said anything. He was shocked she'd kept it, but now?

Now he was fucking glad. He'd suctioned it to the dresser, his heart beating out of his chest as he'd lowered the lights like she asked. Cassie had backed onto the dildo while he'd watched it disappear inside her, her moans doing things to his balls that didn't bode well for his stamina.

He'd watched her fuck herself for a few moments before pinching her nipples and sucking her tongue. Then he'd stood in front of her so she could take his cock in her mouth.

He was currently in that state of pleasure/pain that had him wanting to drive down her throat and make it last all at the same time. He dragged her hair to the side so he could see her mouth wrapped around him.

"Fuck, that's hot, Red. So hot. Holy shit, I love you."

She answered him with a moan that vibrated down his shaft and into his balls. When she'd told him what she wanted to do, he'd been stunned at first. A willing participant, hell yes, but stunned just the same. It was a bold move for sweet Cassie.

And yet she was clearly into it, both hands wrapped around his dick, her tongue swirling around the head. He closed his eyes and leaned back, fighting the urge to fuck her mouth. He knew she was good at sucking him because this wasn't the first time, but it was the first time she'd done it while riding a big dildo.

So. Damn. Hot.

He fucking loved this woman. He didn't doubt it in the least. And he was eternally grateful he'd taken Dax's advice and somehow managed to get it out there in the open. Because this beautiful, sweet, sexy, amazing woman loved him back. He probably didn't deserve it, but he was going to take it.

Later, after he came in her throat and then knelt beneath her so he could lick her clit while she rode the dildo—her orgasm was epic if the way she trembled and cried out was any indication—he coerced her into the shower with him. It wasn't a big shower, but it was big enough. He didn't turn on the overhead light, only the one above the sink.

They washed and kissed and touched until he turned her and slid into her pussy from behind after hurriedly rolling on one of the condoms he'd put on the ledge. Then he took his time, slowly moving in and out, pinching and pulling her soapy nipples, sucking her earlobe, stroking her clit lazily, until she begged him to let her come.

He fucked her hard as she pressed back against him, riding him just as hard, their bodies slapping together as their breathing turned into moans and cries. Cassie came first, shuddering and shaking, her pussy clenching him tight. He circled her back entrance with his finger, pressing lightly in and out, and her moans turned to choked sounds. He wasn't sure what that meant, so he stopped doing it just in case she didn't like it.

"Don't stop," she gasped, and he pressed a little deeper that time, triumphant. "Oh my God, Ty. I shouldn't like that, but I do. Yes, like that—oh my God…"

She was still coming when he let himself go deep inside her.

It was long minutes before they finished showering. The water beat down on them as Ty turned her and they stood together, arms wrapped around each other as they just held on and let their heartbeats slow again.

After they toweled off and dressed—well, Cassie dressed in a slinky leopard print nightie that barely covered her ass, but Ty was naked—they went back to bed and fell asleep.

When Ty woke later, it was from a dead sleep, and he was sweating. He blinked into the night, taking stock of where he was. His bedroom. Cassie was there because he could hear her. He listened hard, but there was nothing in the apartment except the usual sounds.

It wasn't like someone could get inside quietly anyway. But he still had a cold feeling of dread that took up residence in his gut and wouldn't abate. He recognized it almost instantly. It was the same feeling he'd had before his Force Recon team had gone on that final mission. Then, he'd known something was wrong—but not what.

Now? He ran through it in his head. There was nothing wrong. Cassie was safe and her stalker, whoever he was, wasn't going to find her here. His team was on the job and so was he. Nobody could get to her right now.

He wrestled with the feeling for a long while before he gave up and went to fix coffee. It was after four anyway, and he had to get to BDI for a meeting that morning. The feeling remained as he spooned coffee into the filter, as he poured water, as he turned on the pot.

It took him until the second cup of coffee before he realized what it was. His feelings for her were getting in the way. He loved her, and it was new to him. The fear of losing her was high, but he needed to stop worrying. She was with him and she was safe.

This wasn't the desert, and he wasn't a Marine obeying orders anymore. He had control of the situation, and he was going to find the man harassing his woman and take him down like a rabid animal.

He would end the threat and Cassie would have her life back. A life with him in it, but one where she could drive her car and run errands without being afraid. One where she didn't fear opening her mail or her front door.

He would give those things to her. And then he would give her so much more.

Chapter Thirty-Seven

CASSIE WOKE TO THE SMELL OF COFFEE. IT WAS RICH and delicious, and she let it pull her from bed. Her body was sore, in a good way, and she yawned as she reached for her robe and slid into the soft satin. A quick check of her phone told her it was only six a.m.

Good lord. She considered going back to sleep, but she knew Ty had an early meeting, and she wanted to see him. She thought about everything that'd happened last night, and it made her shiver with delight.

She'd loved every damned moment of telling him what she wanted, and then letting him make it happen. It had taken all her courage to say she wanted to use the big dildo with the suction cup, but she was glad she had. She still couldn't believe she'd tossed the thing into her suitcase. It'd been an impulsive decision, but a good one. She preferred Ty's dick over that thing, but it'd been exciting to suck him off while getting fucked by a realistic feeling fake dick at the same time.

A way to have a pseudo-ménage experience, like

he'd said when she'd been going through the box of toys. She definitely wanted to do it again sometime.

She went to brush her teeth and splash water on her face. She usually applied a little bit of concealer and lipgloss, maybe a light dusting of powder, before greeting Ty for the morning. But as she looked at her reflection in the mirror, she decided she wasn't doing it. Her skin was clear and moisturized, her lash extensions still looked great, and she felt rested and pretty.

She ran her fingers through her hair to rough it up and add volume, then smiled at herself. Straight, white teeth—because she'd been lucky enough to inherit good teeth, though she'd spent some time in plastic aligners and then gotten them whitened—and lips still plumped from kissing stared back at her. It was a good look. A natural look. Hell, she might film this look sometime.

That decided, she went into the kitchen to grab coffee. Ty was on the couch, the television turned on low. He looked over at the kitchen when he heard her, and her heart flipped at what she saw there. He was up in a flash and at her side, pressing her against the counter and taking her mouth in a hot kiss that made her wet and tingly.

"Morning, beautiful," he whispered, one hand sliding down to her ass and squeezing a handful.

"Morning, handsome," she whispered back, running her fingers over his naked abdomen. He hissed in a breath. "Do you ever wear a shirt?" she asked.

"Not when I want to turn my woman on," he said, kissing her cheek then her forehead. "Is it working?"

She splayed her fingers over his ribcage, tracing them down the center of his tight, tight belly. "It always works, Tyler."

He nibbled her neck. "Oh, Red, I want to bend you over the table and fuck you hello, but I think you might be a bit sore after last night." He straightened. "So let me get your coffee instead."

She melted against the counter with a sigh. "You're right, I am sore. Just a little. We went at it kind of hard last night."

He reached for a cup, then opened the refrigerator to get the cream. "We did. I'd be lying if I said I wasn't a little sore myself." He added a splash and emptied a Stevia packet into the cup before pouring hot coffee and handing it to her. His eyes twinkled. "My thighs got a workout with all that doggy style."

"You loved it and you know it." Who was this flirty woman? She lifted her lashes as she blew on her coffee with an exaggerated pucker of her lips.

"Tease," he said, kissing her cheek again, lingering as he breathed her in. "Still love me this morning?"

"I'm pretty sure I do," she said, her voice feeling tight with emotion and the newness of it all.

He grinned. "Same here. I hate that I have to go in. I'd rather stay in bed with you." He tucked a lock of her hair behind her ear. "Want to come hang out in The Cove?"

She shook her head. "I can't. Zoom meeting with Queen Amelia this morning. I don't know how long it'll last, and I can't do it from a bar."

He was still grinning. "They make backgrounds, you know. You could even turn yourself into a cat."

She snorted. "Uh, no. Amelia isn't an idiot, and she knows the background trick. If I have anything but a nice, staid background she's used to seeing, she'll think I'm not taking my suspension seriously."

"It's ridiculous she sent you home in the first place."

"She swears that was her compromise with Debra Kelly. But honestly, Debra isn't in the office every day to check on her convention plans. She calls or has one of her lackeys do it. Even Odin can't be there that often."

"Ah, good old Odin. I wonder if he's read the history of the Norse god, or if he just thought it was a good name? Odin sacrificed an eye. He also threw himself on a spear, hanged himself, and regularly left his body in a trance so he could shape shift."

"Sounds delightful. I imagine that our Odin watched a bit too many Thor movies though. And since Thor was kind of obvious, and Loki a little bit silly for a grown man, he thought Odin would be the best one to adopt."

"And here I'm hoping he's at least partially responsible for sending you crap at work so I can punch him in the eye."

Cassie shook her head. "Dear God, Ty, you'd kill him. He probably weighs a tenth of what you do. He's tall and thin and not very stout looking. Meanwhile, you used to be a linebacker."

"And a Marine," Ty said, sipping his own coffee. "It's more than a tenth. More than half, but still a lot less than me."

"I was exaggerating for effect. Don't punch him, no matter how much you want to."

He kissed the tip of her nose. "For you, anything. Now, what do you want for breakfast?"

"I haven't looked at what we have. I can fix eggs again. Toast. Bacon."

He shook his head. "No, I'm fixing it. You sit."

"So we're having toast?"

He gave her a look of mock offense. "I can scramble eggs. But we also have bagels."

"With cream cheese?"

"Of course." He ushered her to the table and pulled out a chair, settling her in it. "Sit here, darling, and let me whip up a bagel and cream cheese for you."

She watched him move around the kitchen, bare torso exposed, muscles flexing and popping as he moved, and she sighed. "One of these days, I think I might want to spread cream cheese on you and eat that instead."

He whipped around to look at her. "Naughty. I like it."

Her phone dinged. "It's Kari, asking how it's going. Should I give her the news?"

"If you don't, I will." He pulled the cream cheese from the fridge, then pointed the knife at her. "Don't forget to tell her I'm the best you ever had. Oh, and that big dick thing too."

Cassie snorted as she started to tap out a reply. "Riii-ight. Typing it right now. B-I-G-D-I-C-K. Sending."

He gaped. "You didn't really?"

She let him stew in it for a moment. "Of course not, Ty. That's between us."

He set the bagel in front of her and captured her mouth in a searing kiss. "Tease."

"Big Dick."

"Damn," he said, gazing at her with heat in his eyes. "Living with you is going to be fucking fun."

She winked, feeling happier than she ever had. "Count on it, sexy."

THEY HAD A GOOD MORNING TOGETHER, and then Ty had to leave. Cassie kissed him at the door, then locked it behind her like he said. She leaned back on it for a long minute after he'd gone. She finally couldn't contain the happiness that burst from her in a laugh.

Tyler Scott. Cassie Dixon. It was a *thing*. A hot, sexy, wonderful thing.

Kari had been ecstatic. *What?!?!*, she'd texted back. *Are you fucking kidding me? You and Ty? You're a couple?*

Yes, Cassie had said. *We're a couple.*

Kari: You aren't joking with me, right? You're being serious?

Cassie had known her friend wasn't disparaging her. She legit didn't know if Cassie was being a smart ass. It'd been known to happen, and Kari hadn't been taking any chances.

Cassie: No, I'm not joking. We're doing the bowchicka and all that, just like you wanted. She'd nibbled her lip and then typed another line. *Are you happy, K?*

Kari: JFC!! Hell yes! This is the best thing ever! OMG, I want to tell everyone. I know I can't, but YEAH!

Cassie: Thank you. This is all still pretty new, and it happened fast. It could fizzle out in a month.

Not that she thought it would, but she was still reeling from everything. The last thing she wanted was to start telling the world and jinx it, which was at least part of the reason why she hadn't told Kari that she and Ty had said the L-word. It was still too new, maybe too fragile, and she couldn't bring herself to tell a soul.

Kari: Well, I'm happy, and I hope it doesn't fizzle because I think you two are perfect for each other.

Cassie had snorted. *What makes you say that? Your cousin, Mr. Popular. And me, who never said boo to anyone. That doesn't even make sense, K.*

Kari: It does to me. You're both serious and driven, and you have me in common. What else is there? <Laughing emoji>

They'd texted a while longer, and then Cassie had gone to take a shower and get ready for the Zoom meeting with Amelia and her colleagues. The meeting lasted over an hour, and then Cassie had projects to work on for Elite before she could turn her attention to her channel for the day. She was thinking of filming a confessional where she told her subscribers what had been happening in her life and how she was dealing with the situation.

At first, she hadn't wanted to talk about any of it. She'd wanted to pretend like everything was normal and nothing was wrong, but what if it helped someone else? If someone was being harassed or stalked, maybe they didn't know how to deal with it either. Maybe they were feeling alone and scared, or maybe they just needed to know how to handle someone saying ugly things to them in their life.

Because the emails, though threatening, contained some elements that were common for fat people to hear. *Lose weight. Get surgery. Go on a diet. How can you stand yourself? Just stop eating.*

Why complete strangers cared so much about what someone else did with their body, Cassie would never understand. Not only that, but how they felt *entitled* to make comments about someone else's body—someone they didn't even know in real life—was doubly shocking to her.

It used to affect her more than it did these days. Maybe she was finally learning to stop giving people who didn't matter any of her thought, or maybe she was growing immune because of the channel and the constant wave of positive attention and camaraderie from most of her followers. The negative ones were still there, but they were being drowned by a wave of positivity.

There was a knock on the door that made her start. Her heart hammered as if someone had jumped out and said Boo! She got up and went to the door, peering through the peephole.

It was Brian Woodruff. He wasn't in uniform , but he had a folder in his hand.

Cassie nibbled her lip. She didn't want to open the door, but if she took the fact that it was Brian out of the equation, then a police officer was at Ty's door. A police officer she'd given a report to a week ago. She didn't remember Ty giving his address, but he must have. She'd been so nervous that there was a lot of detail she didn't recall about that afternoon in the station.

"Cassie," Brian called out, as if sensing her thought process. "If you're in there, we've had some information about the person harassing you. I just need to get some more details from you, and I'll be on the way. Officer Jones would have come, but he had a personal emergency. He asked me to take care of it for him since I was out this way for an appointment today. I realize it might be awkward for you, but I only need about ten minutes of your time."

Cassie sighed. She wished that Ty were there, but he wasn't. She undid the locks and opened the door. Brian gave her a tentative smile. "Hi. Sorry to disturb you, but it couldn't be helped." He held out the folder. "I have some photos to show you, or I'd have called instead."

"Please come in," she said, stepping back so he could enter. She closed the door and turned. He was standing with the folder at his side, taking in the apartment. "Can I offer you some coffee?"

"That'd be great. Thanks."

"Have a seat at the table and I'll pour you a cup. I just made a fresh pot."

She heard a chair scrape as she opened the cabinet and got a cup. "Black? Or sugar and cream?"

"You've forgotten. Wow."

She threw a look at him over her shoulder. "I'm so sorry. I don't have a great memory for these kinds of things."

In truth, she remembered one coffee date, and she'd been nervous so she hadn't paid attention to the order.

"Black."

She poured coffee and joined him at the table. He was staring at her, and it made her uncomfortable. She cleared her throat and looked at the folder he'd placed on the table. "So, um, what have you learned? Do you know who's been sending me those things?"

He still hadn't looked away from her, and his expression was intense. A chill slid up her spine and sent goosebumps over her skin.

"We have an idea," he said finally. "Why did you break up with me, Cassie? I thought we were getting along so well."

There was a knot in her stomach. "I, um, it wasn't you. I just—" She dragged in a breath. "Is this really relevant to the inquiry?"

"It is to me." He tapped his fingers on top of the folder. He hadn't touched the coffee. "You should have been grateful, but you weren't. And now you're fucking this guy like a bitch in heat. I don't get it. I really don't."

Cassie's heart lodged in her throat. Her phone was

beside her computer, and both were at the end of the table. She had to act as normal as possible. Had to get him out of here. Then she could call Ty and break down.

She got to her feet, her pulse fluttering, her stomach churning. "I think you need to leave. This is completely inappropriate, and you know it."

He made no move to stand. No move of any kind. He just regarded her with contempt. "I'm not going anywhere. And neither are you."

Chapter Thirty-Eight

THE MEETING WITH THE DEA CONTINGENT WAS OVER IN a couple of hours, but the discussion lasted all morning as the BDI operatives planned how to penetrate and neutralize the threat in Venezuela. The agencies were stretched thin right now, and the particular drug dealer in question was one that BDI had dealt with in the past. Venezuela didn't have a nuclear program, but there were plenty of bad actors willing to make deals on the black market.

That was where BDI came in. Determine who the drug lord was attempting to make a deal with and follow the trail to the potential nuke. If there was one, seize it. If not, there were still actions to be taken, but at least there wouldn't be a random nuclear weapon out there in the wrong hands. Made breathing a little bit easier for the time being if that was the case.

After the planning ended, Ty checked his phone to see if he had any messages from Cassie. Nothing. There was one from Kari, though, congratulating him on his great taste in women. He laughed and sent back a thumbs up with a message he'd talk to her later.

The heavy feeling in the pit of his stomach hadn't abated, despite the hours since he'd awakened in a cold sweat with that feeling of dread saturating him. It wasn't a deep dread anymore, so much as a sense of impending trouble.

"Bingo," Dax said, and Ty looked over at him. He was still at his computer. The other guys had gotten up to take a bathroom break or grab a coffee, but they were filtering back into the room.

"What is it?" Ian asked as he pulled out his chair and sat.

"Odin, aka Toby Belen. His expense account is backed by a company credit card, and we've just gotten the charges."

Ty sat up. Maybe this was the source of his bad feeling. "And?"

"Let's see…" Dax scrolled. "Yep, he bought a shit-ton of sex toys from Adam & Eve and had them shipped to… Elite Events."

Ty's gut was boiling. The fucking prick. "What else? The wreath?"

"I don't see it yet, but he does take cash advances sometimes."

"Any of the stuff sent to her home address?"

"I don't see anything. He could have paid cash, though. All I've got is the box of sex toys on here. The single dildo she got at home doesn't appear."

Ty growled. "Which means he's very likely behind the magazines and email subscriptions that came to her work, too. He wanted to humiliate her at her job. The prick was there the day we got the box. He must have known it was being delivered and wanted to witness the reactions at her office for himself. He could have gotten in on the gossip and helped fuel outrage, but we took the box away so he didn't get to do any of that."

"It's so juvenile in a way," Rascal said, returning with a sugary donut. "Like something a group of pubescent boys would do for giggles."

Ty was busy thinking. "So Odin is behind the work harassment, probably for the purpose of humiliating her in front of her boss and colleagues and maybe even other clients. Maybe he thought she'd lose her job or quit. Debra Kelly could be involved. Or not." He steepled his fingers and leaned on them. "We don't know he wasn't behind the crap at her house, too. But she'd been getting pizzas for two weeks when I first went to her house, and she'd only been sent home from her job that day because Debra Kelly had objected to her presence. Which seems to mean that Odin and his boss didn't know the woman from *Cassandra's Closet* and Cassie were the same person until then."

"Yeah, I'm thinking we might have a different asshole sending the pizzas and the other stuff," Ian said. "One is definitely work related, but the other seems more personal. Not that sex toys aren't personal, but that was more about the public shame than the toys."

"Do we have anything on Dylan Webb's location yet?" Ty asked.

"Nothing concrete. He's still in the area, but no definitive location. He's not exactly gainfully employed at the moment, so there's no credit card to follow."

"Might be crashing with someone. I'll ask Cassie later if she knows of any friends he might have in the area."

"That might help narrow it down," Dax said.

Ian's phone rang and he picked it up. "Phoenix. To what do I owe the honor?" His brows slanted together. "Okay, thanks. I really appreciate it. As always, I owe you one."

Ian put the phone down and pointed at Dax. "The file on Brian Woodruff. There's another incoming."

"Refreshing… refreshing…" Dax said, waiting for the email to sync. "And there it is."

"On the overhead," Ian commanded.

A file opened on the screen for all to see. There was a photo of Woodruff, an official department stamp, and a summary that had nothing at all to do with using too much force in an arrest. This one was about a complaint from a fellow officer who said she'd been systematically harassed by Officer Woodruff when she'd rejected his advances. She claimed that he'd sent her harassing emails under a pseudonym, and that when she'd asked him to stop, she'd started getting mysterious deliveries of food and flowers at her home. Nothing could be tied to him, though, and the complaint had ultimately died on the vine.

The female officer quit and moved out of state. Woodruff asked for and received a transfer. End of story.

"Shit," Ian said. "We need to get a team on Woodruff. Follow him, see where he goes and what he does. Dig into his phone and credit card records."

Ty's gut was churning. He felt hot and cold at the same time. Anger flared and he worked to press it down again. This new information was too much of a smoking gun for it not to be Woodruff. The MO fit, and Woodruff had a history with Cassie.

"How *the fuck* did that get put into a hidden file?" Ty exploded, slamming his hand on the table.

Ian looked as furious as he felt. "Old boys' network."

Ty knew exactly what his boss meant. It was one complaint, from one woman, and though someone had clearly taken it seriously enough to document, it was likely that Woodruff's chain of command had decided to bury it. The original report they'd gotten about the arrest was real, but this one was too. It'd just been hidden deeper.

"I need to call Cassie."

Ty hit Cassie's number and walked into the hall for some privacy. He had an urge to check on her, to hear her voice. He wouldn't tell her about any of this yet, but he needed to know she was there and she was going about her day like normal. She answered on the fourth ring. "Hello?"

He frowned at her greeting, but figured she was immersed in work and hadn't looked at the phone before answering. Maybe she'd been expecting a business call instead of him, or maybe she'd been filming and had to stop everything. "Hey, Red. How's it going?"

"Good," she said brightly. "I'm getting work done."

"That's good. I wanted to tell you I'm going to be tied up here for a while. I'll explain about it when I get home later."

"Okay. Fine. Yes. When do you think that'll be?"

He glanced at the clock on the wall. It was almost one now. "I don't know. Four o'clock or so. Want me to pick up something on the way home?"

"Yes! Tampons. I'm out."

Ty frowned. Not that he minded picking up personal items for his woman, because he didn't, but it surprised him she could even bring herself to ask considering her usual shyness about personal matters. Must be urgent. Or maybe last night changed things between them and she was comfortable asking for whatever she needed now.

"I can do that. How about food?"

"Oh, sure, whatever you want is fine with me."

"Korean?"

"Definitely. Don't forget the chopsticks. I love those."

"I won't."

"Okay, well, I have to get going. Stuff to do. See you later."

The line went dead and Ty frowned at his phone. The low-level hum of dread in his belly sharpened. He walked back into the conference room and gazed at his teammates, thinking.

"Everything okay?" Ian asked.

"Yeah," he finally said. "She's a little preoccupied with work at the moment. I didn't tell her about any of this. I'd rather do it when I get home."

"Probably a good idea."

Jared strode into the room. "Woodruff is in a continuing education seminar today. He checked in at nine this morning. It goes until three. I sent someone to tail him when he gets out."

"Excellent," Ian replied. "Let's get busy tying him to those deliveries. This time, we're burying *him* instead of the report."

Ty thought of all the evil things Glockman123 had said in his emails. The names he'd called Cassie. The stuff he'd said about not fucking her with a stolen dick, and then about making her suck his cock. He'd been brutal and specific. And threatening. Very threatening. He'd even threatened Ty.

The bigger they are, the harder they fall.

"Are there any copies of the emails he sent to the other officer?" Ty asked.

Dax shook his head. "No. They weren't included, probably because they couldn't prove it was him. You get me his computer, however, and I'll find those bitches."

"What's going on, Ty?" Ian asked, his voice deadly calm. Every man in the room stopped what they were doing to look at Ty.

His gut churned. That feeling of wrongness was strong. Just like the day he'd been ordered to lead his Force Recon team into what turned out to be an ambush. He'd wanted to refuse, but that's not what Marines did. They didn't refuse orders, and they didn't refuse to fight.

He wasn't a damned psychic. He didn't *know* that anything was wrong. It wasn't magic or mysticism or any bullshit like that. It was just… a feeling. But feelings were based on *something.* His feeling about the mission that day had everything to do with the intel. It hadn't seemed right. It'd been rushed. It had definitely been incomplete, but it'd been presented like it was written in stone.

It hadn't been. His concerns had been brushed aside, and he'd been told to go anyway. The enemy troops weren't where they'd been supposed to be. They were waiting for Ty and his men, and it'd been a helluva firefight.

Today didn't feel right either. He didn't know why

he'd awakened with a heavy feeling on his heart, but he knew what the problem was right now.

"Cassie. She didn't sound quite right. She sounded... distracted. And she asked me to get tampons on the way home."

Jace groaned. Brett laughed. Jared blew out a breath. They were all familiar with picking up ladies' sanitary products.

"It's not *like* her," Ty said. "She's an introvert, and she's shy about things. Hell, she won't even walk around naked in front of me yet"—*TMI, dude*—"but she can ask me to buy tampons for her? I'd expect Cassie to ask me to take her to the store later, not ask me to buy them for her."

"Maybe she needs them right away."

"Then she'd need them now, wouldn't she?"

"What else?" Ian asked, because the boss was sharp like that. He'd told Ty a long time ago to trust his instincts. Listen to them and don't question. Just do what they tell you.

"She asked for chopsticks with the meal tonight. Told me she loves them. She doesn't know how to use them."

Jesus, now that he said it aloud, everything about that conversation had been a red flag. Alarm bells were sounding in his brain. He shot to his feet. "Woodruff isn't at that seminar. He's with Cassie."

He didn't know how, but he knew that Woodruff was with her. He'd found her, and he'd talked her into letting him inside. Whether or not they were still at his apartment, he didn't know. It hadn't sounded like she was in a car, but that didn't mean she hadn't been. Or at another location.

Except, why would Woodruff let her answer the phone, if so?

Every man was on his feet except Dax, who was still typing. "Putting out an alert on his plates, though he might not have his own car."

Ty unlocked his phone and handed it to Dax. "Here's her number. Can you see where she was just now?"

He cursed himself for not having her turn on the *Find My Friends* feature so he could track her. But he hadn't expected her to be vulnerable at his apartment. *Fuck!*

"She's at your place," Dax said, what seemed like a day later. "Or was when you spoke to her."

Ty's blood ran cold. "I have to get back there before he takes her somewhere."

"We're all going," Ian said. "We'll make a plan on the way. Saddle up, kids! We're riding out."

Chapter Thirty-Nine

BRIAN TOOK HER PHONE WHEN SHE FINISHED TALKING TO Ty. She was surprised he'd let her answer it. He'd told her to be natural. Told her things would not go well for her if she warned Ty he was there. She'd been too scared to even attempt it.

She'd done what he'd said, though she'd tried to tell Ty in her own way. Tampons. Chopsticks. Stupid shit, though she'd at least partly blurted the word *tampons* so Brian wouldn't try to rape her. She chastised herself for not being smarter about the things she'd said. For not telling Ty in a more obvious—obvious *to him*—way. She'd asked for tampons and chopsticks.

For fuck's sake!

Ty would show up later this evening with tampons and chopsticks and Korean food, and he wouldn't have one damned clue that Brian Woodruff was waiting for him. Because Brian intended to wait. She wasn't sure why, but she didn't think it was good. She thought of the last email she'd gotten from him—because she had no doubt it'd been him now.

The bigger they are, the harder they fall.

Brian zip-tied her hands to the chair, jerking the plastic tight, and now he paced around the apartment, looking at Ty's things. His shadow box with his Marine Corp medals. The only photo he had in the room—him and his mother when he'd graduated from Basic Training. Brian tipped the photo over and studied the shadow box, blowing air out of his nostrils in a sound of disgust or disbelief.

"Fucking Marines," he muttered.

She watched Brian, her heart pounding, her mind reeling at the knowledge that *he* was the one stalking her. A man she'd dated.

A police officer.

It made no sense. He was supposed to uphold the law, not break it. How did he expect to get away with tying her up and waiting for Ty to return? What was he planning?

"Why?" she finally asked when she couldn't take it any longer. Her eyes stung with unshed tears and her heart hammered, but she had to know.

He spun to look at her. "Why? You disrespected me, Cassie. You, a fat fucking bitch. So fucking thick in the thighs and ass, but you've got a pretty face so you think you're hot shit. I took you out. Paid attention to you." His face scrunched up as he turned it sideways. Like he was smelling dog shit or something. "And for what? For you to tell me you weren't interested in me? You? Not interested in *me?* Jesus, I'm fucking Mr. Universe compared to you, and you told me to get lost."

He shook his head as he closed the distance between them. Leaned his twisted face down into hers and curled his fingers into her shoulders so hard she whimpered.

"You don't get to do that. You don't get to tell *me* to get lost. I would have pampered you, taken care of you. Worshipped you. But, no, you told me to go away—and then you started fucking this guy."

He straightened, shoving her away, and paced across the room again. She could see the outline of his weapon holstered beneath his shirt.

She started to say she was sorry but thought better of it. He wouldn't believe her anyway.

"I heard you," he said, swinging his hand toward the door. "Sitting out there in the parking lot with my parabolic mic. The two of you, moaning and grunting, your flesh slapping together like dogs in heat. You're a dirty bitch, Cassie. I should have known. I could have given it to you like that. I *should* have given it to you like that. Should have taken you inside and fucked you senseless instead of dropping you off that night when you said we shouldn't see each other anymore."

She didn't know what a parabolic mic was, but she didn't doubt he had listened in on her and Ty. He was turning something she considered beautiful into something dirty, and it angered her. Not that she could do anything about it. She bit her lip and kept her anger to herself.

She had to wait, but she didn't know for what. A chance, maybe. But what kind of chance? What could she do that would stop this man? He was *not* right. He was a narcissistic asshole—and he was dangerous.

Brian slammed his hand against the wall, and she jumped. "Christ, I was so patient! I took you out to coffee, to dinner, to that fucking idiotic lecture at the Smithsonian—and you told me to get lost. All you fucking bitches are the same. A man pays attention to you, and you bat your eyes and act all shy, but then you throw him away and start fucking the next guy who comes along."

He came over to her again and bent until his face was level with hers. His eyes glittered. "Your boyfriend the Marine thinks he's smart. He's not. I watched him install those cameras at your house. It was so easy to disable one. So easy to get inside and plant *my* cameras. But he found them, and you weren't there anyway, were you? I stopped sending things so you'd come back— though I sent a pizza to those assholes when they were combing through your house as a fuck you to all of them. You were supposed to come to *me* for help, you know. But you didn't. You went to him, and then you left with him and didn't come back. I knew you wouldn't after they found the cameras, so I came to you."

"H-how did you find me here?" The words he said —the way he gleefully admitted sending her all those things so she'd need help—terrified her. But she'd realized something about him, and it made her brave enough to speak. He wanted to be smart. He wanted to be the mastermind, the one who knew everything. The smartest man in the room. If she stroked his ego, he'd keep talking.

But then what? He was waiting for Ty to return, but for what? That's what worried her the most. She should have used her self-defense moves on him, but she hadn't even tried. Stupid.

"I'm a cop, Cassie. I traced your boyfriend's plates, then I drove over here and watched for a few days."

"That was smart."

He looked smug as he went over and put his eye to the peephole. "Yeah, it was."

"What happens now, Brian?"

"We wait. I told you he was going down, and he will." He stalked toward her again, stopping in front of her chair. His hand went to his zipper. "I told you that you were going to suck my cock. Remember? You do a good job, and I'll consider letting you live."

Her eyes filled with tears. "Brian, please. Please don't do this."

He caressed her cheek and it was all she could do not to shiver.

"You should have thought of that before you started thinking so highly of yourself. I saw you when you were just starting out. Your videos were sweet, vulnerable. I watched you for a long time, supported you as you grew. And then I found where you worked. I applied to be security for Elite Events, knowing I'd meet you." He reached out and took a lock of her hair between his fingers and rubbed it. "You were so pretty and sweet. I thought you'd be grateful. I didn't realize you were a bitch like the rest of them. I gave you a chance, Cassie —and you threw it back in my face."

He unzipped his pants and pulled his dick out. Then he thrust it toward her mouth. "Suck it, bitch. Suck it like your life depends on it. Because it does."

———

"SHE'S STILL IN THE APARTMENT," Dax said as they drove toward Ty's complex. They'd piled into one of BDI's vans for this mission because it was filled with comm equipment and assault gear. They pulled on bulletproof vests, holstered weapons on their bodies, and prepared for battle.

Ty's heart throbbed as he considered what that might mean. Cassie could already be dead. Woodruff might have killed her after the call and left her body for Ty to find. Hell, maybe he planned to frame Ty for her death. He clearly had no idea who Ty worked for, or he would have thought twice about that one.

Ty couldn't focus on the idea that Cassie was dead or he'd lose his mind. But if Woodruff had killed her, there wasn't a force on earth that could stop Ty from the things he would do to the man in response. There wouldn't be anything left of Woodruff to bury when he was done.

It was also possible Woodruff was there to rape her, that he didn't intend to kill her at all. He might intend to humiliate her and damage her by forcing her to have sex. Woodruff must think he could get away with whatever he'd planned, but Ty wasn't about to let it happen.

He acknowledged deep in his soul that Cassie might be irreparably damaged if Woodruff raped her, but he wasn't going to abandon her to deal with it alone. He'd be there for her, no matter what.

They'd gotten copies of Woodruff's psych evals from the police department, and they'd gone over them on the way. At least one had said he showed traits of narcissism, but it wasn't enough to prevent him from doing the job. Woodruff had never tripped any alarm bells on self-harm either, but they all knew it didn't mean he wasn't capable of a murder-suicide. Especially if he felt trapped.

Jared reached over and squeezed Ty's shoulder. "I know, man. I know. Keep faith. We'll get there in time."

Ty nodded. He knew that Jared had been through something similar when Libby had been abducted by helicopter and flown to a remote location. They hadn't known for a long time if she was okay, or if she'd been killed. When they got to her, she'd been tortured. But she'd recovered. Libby was strong, and she'd fought for her survival.

Cassie was strong too. He knew that. Deep down, whether she believed it or not, his girl was hard as steel. She'd survived her childhood, survived a relationship with a man who took her for granted and treated her like shit, and she'd channeled all her fears and her belief in a better life into *Cassandra's Closet*. She was a fucking dynamo, and he loved her fiercely. He wanted her to know how amazing she was, and he wanted to tell her every day until she believed it, too.

"Jace will cut power to the building," Ian said, running over the plan again. "Ty and Jared will breach the front door with me. Rascal, Brett, and Finn will come through the rear windows. Dax will monitor the comm from the van. Any questions?"

Nobody spoke.

"Good. Then let's get in there and get Cassie."

They all knew they were facing a foe who would be armed and knew how to use a weapon, if he was still inside. Ty raked a hand over his head. There were so many possibilities. Woodruff could have killed her. Raped her. Raped and killed her and killed himself. He could be preparing for a siege, or he could already be gone. Ty hadn't tried to call Cassie again because to do so might tip Woodruff off that they were coming.

There was nothing Ty could say to her on the phone, no way he could prepare her. If Woodruff let her answer, he'd be listening. Ty couldn't ask her outright, and, fuck, if he heard fear in her voice, he'd lose his damned mind. And if she didn't answer at all?

He didn't even want to think about it.

They reached his complex in record time, circling through the parking lot. "That's his SUV," Dax said, jerking his head toward a white Chevy Blazer as they passed it.

Ty shut off the wave of emotion that threatened to overwhelm him. He didn't have time to wallow in feelings right now. Woodruff was there, which meant he was still upstairs with Cassie. But was she alive? That's what he didn't know, and what he couldn't spend time thinking about.

Do the job. Get in, get Cassie, get out alive.

"Fucking hell," Ty muttered as tears stung his eyes. He wasn't going to cry, but Jesus, he was teetering on the verge of a meltdown.

"We're going to get her," Ian said firmly. "Cassie is resourceful. She's going to be alive, Ty. And while I can't guarantee she won't be hurt in some way, she's got you to help her through it. Now call her again. If she answers, ask her what brand of tampon she wants."

Ty blinked. He hadn't thought of that. He dialed Cassie's number. It rang six times, and his stomach fell deeper into the pit every time. But then she answered, her voice soft and a little shaky.

"Hello?"

Relief flooded him. It was so strong he had to lean back against the wall of the van for support while he recovered. He fought tears again, swallowing them down before they could fall.

"Hey, Red," he said, trying to sound normal even

though his throat ached and his heart pounded. "What brand of tampon do you need? I forgot to ask earlier."

"Um, Playtex is fine. Regular, please."

"Great. How's your day?"

"Okay. Busy. I'm working on some editing."

"Oh, sorry. You in the kitchen or the bedroom this time?"

"I'm at the table."

He made eye contact with the guys. They all nodded, smiling triumphantly. *Yeah, this was good. So good.* "I'll let you go," he said. "Hey, bulgogi good with you or did you want something else?"

"It's fine. Thanks."

Ty's breath hitched at the thought he was going to have to hang up. But he knew she was alive, and he knew she was at the table in the kitchen. That was huge. "I love you, Cassie."

He had to say it. You never ended a call before a mission without telling your family you loved them. Never.

"Me too," she whispered.

"See you later, babe. Gotta run now. Ian just called another meeting."

He ended the call and kept leaning against the side of the van for support as Brett found a spot where they weren't visible from his apartment and parked.

"Good work," Ian said. "I know that was rough."

"Yeah."

"All right, kids." Ian rubbed his hands together gleefully. "Let's get into position. I'll give the go signal when everyone's set. You know what to do."

Chapter Forty

CASSIE WAS TREMBLING WHEN BRIAN TOOK HER PHONE away and pocketed it again. His dick had been in her face only moments ago, but then her phone rang. He'd swore, and she knew he'd considered ignoring it, but for some reason it was important to him that Ty thought everything was fine at home.

So he'd taken the phone out, told her she'd better act like everything was normal, and slid the bar to answer as he'd held it near her face. Of course he'd put it on speaker, like the last time. She'd had to endure listening to the man she loved talk to her like everything was completely normal, knowing that he was going to hang up soon and she might never talk to him again.

She didn't know what Brian's plan was, but he clearly planned on hurting Ty. And her. She didn't doubt that he was lying about letting her live if she did what he wanted and sucked his dick. He might kill her before Ty arrived, or he might force her to watch him kill Ty before he killed her.

It had taken her a while to wrap her head around

that, but when she remembered everything he'd said to her as Glockman123, she had no doubt he was planning violence.

"What are you going to do to us?" she asked as he strode over to the door and looked out the peephole.

He turned and strolled back to her like he had all the time in the world. "It's not what I'm going to do to you, Cassie. It's what you're going to do to each other."

Her heart thumped. "You said you'd let me live if I…" She couldn't finish the sentence.

He caressed her cheek. She resisted the urge to shrink from his touch, but only barely. "I did say that, didn't I? And I still might. But I'm afraid you're going to have to take a bullet regardless. If it doesn't kill you— and it might not—you'll still be alive, right? You might be messed up as hell, though. Can't promise anything there."

"I-I don't understand."

He tugged a chair out and sat facing her. He took his gun from the holster and studied it. It was black, and she could see a big *G* etched on the barrel. *Glockman123*

"I got the idea from a case a few years ago. A man killed his wife, and then he killed himself. It was all very tragic, as they left behind a fifteen year-old son who was in his bedroom playing *Halo* when it happened. He called the police, he sobbed, he screamed. Everything you'd expect. But you know what?"

She shook her head.

"He's the one who pulled the trigger. He killed them both, and then he told a story about how they'd been fighting over someone his dad worked with. He said that his mother accused his father of having an affair. It was all very messy—and damned if the kid wasn't right. The dad *was* fucking this bitch at work." He shook his head. "Took a year to figure it out, but it was the kid. He was pissed because his parents planned to take his game console away due to bad grades. He shot his dad with the pistol the man kept for home defense, then shot his mom in her bed. Left the gun there, wrapped her fingers around it, everything. She wouldn't have had the powder residue on her skin, or not enough of it, but sometimes the evidence seems so strong that things get missed. You'd be fucking surprised how often things get missed or shoved onto the back burner. Obviously, they figured it out eventually. The kid confessed when he was confronted."

Cassie's belly twisted. "You plan to kill us and make it look like a murder-suicide? Don't you think someone's going to figure it out, just like they did with the kid?"

"Why would they? I'm currently attending a seminar, and though we dated briefly, I've moved on. Got a date later, in fact. And I'm a lot smarter than a fifteen-year-old."

She looked at the gun. He held it up and laughed. "I'm not using my gun. Your boy has a gun safe in his room, and I'm sure he's got one on him. But even if he doesn't"—he pulled another weapon from his waistband—"there are so many ghost guns out there on the streets. You just can't believe how these things change hands. The serial numbers get filed off, the slides get changed, the grips change, the triggers change. But the barrel? The part that the bullet travels through? That doesn't change. It's the same no matter how many criminals have used it, and it can be traced back to the original owner. Usually, that person has reported it stolen, but not always."

Horror and fear rolled through her.

"Either way, you're shooting him and turning the gun on yourself. Be easier with his, but it'll work with this one. Some poor asshole will get a visit about it, maybe. But the police will eliminate the original gun owner eventually."

He put the guns away and got to his feet. His fingers went to his zipper. "We've got unfinished business, Cassie. I suggest you get busy."

It was almost as if he had to talk himself up, glory in his brilliance, before he could think about sex. Maybe he needed it to get hard. She didn't know, but she tossed her hair, feeling suddenly defiant. "Why should I? You're going to kill me anyway. And you're going to kill Ty. So why should I bother?"

His eyes flashed. "Maybe because you don't want to die now instead of later."

She snorted, though fear simmered just beneath the surface. Her default setting was to cooperate, to make herself blend, to buy time. To hide in plain sight, like she'd always done. But, dammit, she didn't want to do that this time. Because it wasn't going to make a difference anyway, and she was done with letting people steamroll her.

"Right. But then my time of death won't match Ty's. The police will know it's not a murder-suicide, won't they?"

His expression blackened. Before she knew what he intended, he slapped her so hard her head rocked sideways and pain burst across the side of her face. She cried out—and then the lights shuttered and the room went black. She thought maybe she'd passed out at first, but glass shattered and wood splintered, the sudden violence of it thumping inside her like a bomb going off. She could see Brian silhouetted in the bright lights that shined from three points in the doorway. He'd turned away from her and dropped to his haunches, but now he was reaching for his weapon.

What Ty had taught her flashed through her mind. *Use what you have. Fight dirty. Go for his balls.*

Brian was still close, and though her hands were tied, her legs were not. She kicked with all her might, aiming for the sweet spot between his legs.

———

TY RUSHED OVER TO CASSIE, dropping his flashlight as he did so. Brian Woodruff was on the ground, groaning as Jared and Ian disarmed and cuffed him.

"Cassie. Baby," Ty said, kneeling beside her, pulling out his knife so he could cut the zip-ties. "Are you okay, honey? Did he hurt you? Jesus, baby, I'm so sorry."

He got the zip-ties sliced and then her arms went around his neck and she put her head on his shoulder and sobbed. He held her like that for a long while as the lights came back on and the guys cleared the apartment, making sure Woodruff hadn't set any devices or had any accomplices. Not that they actually thought he had an accomplice, but being thorough required they consider it.

Police sirens screamed in the distance, getting closer. Ty rubbed a hand up and down Cassie's back. "Honey, are you going to be able to tell the police what happened?"

"Yes," she whispered. And then she pushed back and looked into his eyes.

His gut twisted at the red mark across her face. Her skin was split over her eyebrow, and murderous rage filled him again. "I'll kill him," he growled, trying to stand, but she held him tight.

"No, Ty. Please. Don't leave me right now."

He closed his eyes and swore as guilt sliced into him. He hadn't been here to protect her, and she'd suffered. "I won't. Tell me what happened, Red."

"She's a liar," Woodruff rasped. "She invited me over. She wanted to play rough and—"

Finn slapped a piece of duct tape over the asshole's mouth, which was a good thing since Ty was reconsidering killing him. He looked at Cassie again, ready to soothe her and tell her none of them believed anything Woodruff said, but her eyes were flashing fire. She looked good and pissed, and he found that encouraging.

"You shut the fuck up," Cassie yelled, "Or the next time I kick you in the balls, I'll get a running start, you lying piece of shit!"

Ty was shocked at the vehemence coming out of Cassie's mouth—but in a good way. She'd cried, and now she was pissed. Maybe that boded well for her recovery from the trauma. Whatever she needed, he would give it to her. Space, time, love, tenderness, a gun and lessons so she could unload into a target at the range—whatever.

"He isn't going to say another word, Red. Now, tell me everything."

She did. She told him every single thing that had happened from the moment Brian Woodruff had appeared at the door until they'd burst in and she'd kicked him in the balls. The guys listened too, none of them saying a word, though Jared handed her a cold pack to put on her brow and Ian got her a bottle of water.

By the time she was done, the police had arrived and Ian went to talk with them. Jared examined Cassie's face, which was still swelling a bit, and gave her painkillers for her headache.

Ian was still with the police. After a hushed conversation, he took out his phone, made a call, and handed it to one of the officers. Things happened fast then. Brian Woodruff was hauled away in handcuffs, mouth still taped, screaming things no one could understand. A senior officer arrived on scene and took a statement from Cassie. He was gentle and thorough, and he asked her repeatedly if she was all right or if she needed a break.

She didn't waver in her conviction to tell the whole story, and she didn't shrink away from any detail. She was brave and determined, and Ty was so proud of her. He held her hand, gripping it firmly, letting her know he wasn't going anywhere. She assured them all that Woodruff had not sexually assaulted her, though he'd intended to. Ty gritted his teeth as he listened to her recite again how Woodruff had tried to make her give him oral sex. Listened again as she detailed his plans for them—staging a murder-suicide—and how he thought he'd get away with it.

When everything was over nearly two hours later and the police were gone, the BDI operatives helped board up the windows they'd crashed through, swept up the glass they could find, and rigged the door so they could close it.

The complex manager had stopped by, taken a look at the damage, and gone pale. Ian had stepped in and smoothed everything over. Ty knew his boss would send a team tomorrow to fix what they'd broken, but for now the apartment was uninhabitable.

"We can't stay here tonight," Ty told Cassie. "We need to get a hotel room. Ian will send a team in tomorrow to clean and replace the windows and doors, and we can return then—unless you'd rather not come back."

She blinked at him. "Why wouldn't I want to be here with you?"

Ty's heart ached with equal measures of love and guilt. He'd feared what the passing hours might do to her when she thought about her captivity and Woodruff's plans.

He caressed her cheek on the side that hadn't been hit. She turned into his palm, closing her eyes, and for a moment he was sorry he hadn't shot Woodruff between the eyes. "I'm glad you want to come back, because I want you with me. But if it was too hard on you to stay here, I'd go where you wanted."

She gazed at him. "I want to be with you, Ty. I don't care where we go so long as we're together."

His throat was tight. "I'm so fucking sorry, Red. I should have protected you better—"

She pressed her hand to his mouth, stopping the flow of words. Her eyes flashed as her brows drew down. "No, Tyler Scott. No, sir. You did *not* cause this. You didn't fail, and it isn't your fault. Brian was clever. He waited and he watched and he made his move. That isn't *your* fault." Her eyes glittered with sudden tears. "If anything, I failed. I let him in, and then I couldn't figure out how to send you a signal when he let me answer the phone. Good God, I told you I needed tampons! My brain was mush and that was all I could think of, though I admit I also said it so he would think he couldn't have sex with me. Then that stupid chopsticks comment. Why didn't I say that I loved to use them? You would have known instantly."

He gently pulled her hand from his mouth, kissing her palm and then kissing her lips. "You were perfect, Cassie. You gave me the clues I needed. My Cassie wouldn't ask me to buy tampons. She'd ask me to take her to the store because she's still too shy with me to say what she needs. And she wouldn't remind me to get chopsticks, because she doesn't use them and doesn't know how."

She looked at him wonderingly. "You mean my clues helped?"

"Yes. And then when you said you were at the table? Perfect. We knew where you'd be and that helped when we breached."

She let out a shaky sigh. "Oh, thank God. I really thought I'd been such an idiot."

"You aren't an idiot, Red. You're fucking amazing."

She giggled, and his heart soared at the fact she could do so after her ordeal.

"So are you, you know. You figured out my silly clues, and you and your posse rode out to save me."

Jared appeared out of the blue, leaning in, hand to one side of his mouth as he said in a stage whisper, "We thought Woodruff was in a seminar. Ty's the one who insisted he was with you." He slapped Ty on the back. "I'd say your instincts are just fine, my friend. And you, Miss Cassie Dixon, are not only a pretty face, you're also pretty damned smart. So cut the crap, you two, and stop feeling guilty for being human in a crisis. Thanks for coming to my TED Talk."

Jared strolled away again, and Ty shook his head as a laugh burst from him. "Shit. He's right. You're alive, Woodruff's going to pay for what he did this time, and I've got the rest of my life to love you the way you deserve."

"Starting tonight?" Cassie asked with a waggle of her eyebrows.

Ty snorted. "Starting the minute I get you alone."

Chapter Forty-One

THREE WEEKS LATER...

"HOW DID Snooty Amelia take it when you quit?" Kari asked.

Cassie had just left Elite Events after clearing out her cubicle, and she was talking to her friend on speaker. She was on the way to the post office to pick up packages, then back to her townhome where Ty would join her. After the incident at Ty's apartment complex, it'd been *suggested* by management that he find somewhere else to live. He was crashing with her while they looked for a house to move into together.

"She offered me a raise to stick around and handle the Alexandria Spring Festival."

"Please tell me you said no."

"I said no. I gave her what I had so far, recommended Pamela for the work, and collected my things. Oh, and I stopped by Janet's desk to thank her."

"You didn't!"

Cassie snorted. "Yes, I did! If she hadn't sent Odin my video, Kelly Cosmetics might have never given it a second look. It might not have gone viral, either."

Odin had apparently sent the link to someone he'd thought was a friend. That person had sent it to a vlogger friend who'd shared it to another vlogger friend —and so on. The video went viral, and Cassie's stats had soared. Meanwhile, Odin had panicked and thought that putting pressure on Cassie at work would get her to take it down. If her job was in danger, and all that she had to do was remove one little video, then surely she would do it, right?

That was what he'd told the police when questioned, anyway. He'd also said that his boss had told him to "take her down," but hadn't specified how to go about it. Though Debra Kelly was notoriously thin-skinned and reactionary to criticism, she was smart enough to maintain her deniability about specifics. She'd even dared to suggest that her employee had mistaken her meaning.

In the end, the stock went public, and it did what it was supposed to do. Ms. Kelly was even richer than she had been, and Odin had probably paid down his mortgage with his proceeds. So far as Cassie knew, he was still employed there. And if he wasn't, then it wasn't her problem.

Cassie made a video about the whole thing and put it on her channel. She'd told her viewers about the systematic harassment she'd gotten from an employee at Kelly Cosmetics. She hadn't named him, and she wouldn't because the internet could be notoriously dangerous when names were exposed, but she hadn't left anything out about the things he'd sent to her in an effort to silence her or that he'd done it on the company dime.

She'd considered not making a video, but when she'd thought about how Odin had been a part of making her life miserable—and how he'd treated her personally—she'd decided she had to. If a big company like Kelly Cosmetics could harass an individual over a product review and get away with it, what else would they do? What else *had* they done that no one knew about?

A lot, it turned out. Other beauty vloggers had left comments that they'd also been harassed over negative reviews, though not to the extent that Cassie had. Kelly Cosmetics was known to send their fangirls after negative reviews, and sometimes they succeeded in harassing people enough that they took their reviews down.

Cassie was considering suing the company, and Ian Black had put her in touch with an attorney who could help with that. It wasn't about getting money so much as holding them to account for trying to intimidate her. If she put them on notice, then maybe they wouldn't do it to anyone else.

"How many subscribers are you up to now?" Kari asked.

"It's crazy, but almost a million."

"Whoa. That's just freaking cool, Cass! I'm so proud of you! Is my cousin treating you like the queen you are?"

Cassie's skin heated as she thought of what Ty had done to her last night. It had involved vibrators and blindfolds, and she'd been so turned on she'd thought she would die of too much pleasure before he finished making her come.

"He is. When I hit a million, we're going to Paris."

"Paris! Whoa."

"One of his friends is a French American, and he's apparently got this amazing hotel suite in Paris where we can stay."

She still couldn't believe that Colt Duchaine was French nobility. He was so ordinary. Well, not ordinary in the sense you wouldn't notice him, because he was big and blond and gorgeous, but ordinary in the sense he was just another guy who worked with Ty. His fiancée, Angie, was pretty awesome too. In fact, everyone at BDI was pretty great. She'd been there a few times now, hanging out in The Cove, and she always felt like she belonged. They treated her like family, and she was finding it easier to talk to them instead of hiding in her shell.

And Dax, Hollywood handsome Dax, had told her if she ever got tired of Ty she should give him a call, because he'd love to take her out. Ty had growled at his friend, but Cassie had loved the compliment and told him to hush.

She'd also started taking a few more self-defense lessons with Natasha. It was hard not to feel her self-confidence expanding when hanging out with the other woman—especially when they'd discussed makeup techniques. Natasha had explained how she'd spent so much of her life disguising herself for work, and how much she loved wearing her own face and body instead of having to be someone else. That really struck a chord with Cassie, and she'd been thinking about it since.

She'd always thought life would be so much better if only she was thin—but would it? She was in love with an amazing man, who made her feel good every day and loved her the way she was, she had a successful brand and it was growing exponentially, and companies were sending her sponsorship offers all the time. Her life could not be any better. She'd finally realized that problems couldn't be solved by changing the skin you were in. It was the inside that had to change first, and she was working on it.

"Paris. I love it. Who knew Tyler could be so romantic?" Kari said.

"He's pretty incredible, really. I'm a lucky girl."

"He's lucky, too. I feel like the smartest woman on the planet for suggesting you two get together."

Cassie laughed. "You talked me into getting over myself and letting things happen, so you definitely get credit for that."

They talked a little bit longer and then Cassie reached the post office and got the packages that she had to sign for. She wasn't afraid to pick up the mail anymore. She knew it was possible she could get something shitty from time to time, but with Brian still in custody, she wasn't worried that every delivery could be something terrible.

One day, she would share with her subscribers that story too, because too many women dealt with violent stalkers, and it was important to know you weren't alone and you weren't crazy. Brian had tried to manipulate her and terrify her, and he'd used email and various social media accounts to do it. He was Glockman123 and Big Guns, and probably several more names too.

It was still too raw for her to talk about to her subscribers, plus she'd been advised not to do it until the case went to trial and Brian was sentenced. That worked for her.

Ty was home when she got there. He'd been watching for her, and he came outside to help her get the packages in.

"Damn, Red, what did you order?"

She gave him a look. "Lingerie."

He almost tripped on his feet, but he managed to right himself before he did anything more than miss a step. "Really?"

"Yes, really. I'm filming a try-on haul for lingerie. Big girls need to feel sexy, too."

He held the door for her, then followed her inside. "Do I get to watch?" he asked, setting the packages down, taking hers and dropping them on top, and backing her into the door as his hands ran down her thighs and up to her ass. He put his mouth on her throat, nibbling her skin, and a shiver rolled down her spine and right between her legs.

All he had to do was look at her and she was horny. And when he touched her? Oh lord, look out.

She put her hands on his shoulders, looped them around his neck, and arched into him.

"I missed you, Red," he whispered against her skin.

"It's only been about eight hours," she said with a laugh.

"An eternity." He dragged her V-neck top aside to expose a breast, pushed the cup down, and sucked her nipple into his mouth.

"Ty. Oh my God, I can't think when you do that."

"Good," he growled.

It was about an hour later when they lay in Cassie's pink bedroom, clothes strewn all over the floor, that Ty seemed to remember he'd asked a question.

"How about it, Red? Do I get to watch the lingerie try-on?"

They were beneath the sheets, but the lamp was on. They'd started making love with a light on sometimes, and she'd discovered that she really liked being able to see detail. She could turn her head and look into the mirror when they were in her bed. It was naughty to watch what he did to her, but she loved it. Made her orgasms even stronger and more intense.

"Can you watch and not touch?" she asked, pushing the sheet down to run her fingers along the planes of his abdomen.

"Maybe," he said. "Or maybe I can help out."

She snorted. "I think YouTube frowns on pornography, honey. That's a whole different platform."

"As if I want *anyone* seeing my baby naked besides me."

"You realize some of that lingerie will be a little sexy, and I'll be putting it out there for nearly a million people to watch, right?"

"Yeah, but that's not naked." He pushed the sheet off her, too, and ran a hand over her curves. "Mmm, you make me hard, Cassie. I think I can go again in about five minutes."

She reached for his cock. "That long?"

Naturally, he was ready soon after she started stroking him. It was slower this time, sweeter, with whispered words of love and devotion. They showered together a little while later, and then went down to the kitchen to fix dinner.

"Can you get the butter?" Cassie asked.

Ty opened the refrigerator. "Wait a minute—is that banana pudding?"

"I got the recipe from Kari. She said you specifically requested it for helping me."

He blinked at her with wide eyes. "You made banana pudding?"

She shrugged. "It's your favorite. Of course I made it."

"When?"

"This morning when you left for work. Didn't you wonder why I bought bananas and vanilla wafers?"

"Never occurred to me." He grabbed the butter, slapped it on the counter, and tugged her into his arms. "You're perfect, Cassandra Mae Dixon. I hope you realize that."

She loved it when he held her. "It's just banana pudding, Tyler."

He shook his head. "No, Red. It's love. You love me."

"I've been telling you that, haven't I?"

He swayed them back and forth gently, tucking her head against his chest and sighing. "I know. But cooking my favorite dessert for me? Without telling me? That's epic, honey."

Cassie giggled. "You're a food whore. Natasha said if I made mac and cheese for you, you'd never leave."

He made a sound of derision. "She's only partially right. I'm never leaving, but not because of food. That's just a bonus." He tilted her head back and kissed her. "It's you, Cass. The best I ever had."

Epilogue

Two months later...

"YOU READY FOR THIS?" Ty asked as he turned into the driveway of his parents' home.

Cassie smiled and squeezed his hand. "Ready."

"My dad's a dick, but Mom is an angel."

"I know, sweetie. You told me." She reached over and caressed his cheek. "Don't you worry about me. I'm not afraid of your dad."

"I know."

The door to his childhood home—a two story brick colonial set among big shade trees on five acres of land—opened, and his mom came running down the steps and toward the car. Ty opened his door and caught her a few steps later.

"Baby," his mom said, wrapping him in a cinnamon-scented hug that told him she'd been baking. "I'm so happy you're here."

"I'm happy too, Mom." He turned to look at Cassie

climbing from the truck. She looked amazing in a bright pink floral top with jeans and sandals, her reddish-brown hair flowing in a mass of curls over her shoulders. Her makeup was perfect, and she was the prettiest thing he'd ever seen. "You know Cassie Dixon, Mom."

He'd told her about him and Cassie over the phone a few times, but he'd never made Cassie talk. She wasn't an extrovert and she wouldn't have liked that. But she'd assured him she was fine with coming for a visit.

His mom hurried over and wrapped Cassie in one of her hugs. "Oh, honey, welcome to our home. I'm *so* happy you're here."

Cassie hugged his mom back, shooting him a look as she did so. "Thank you, Mrs. Scott. I'm happy to be here, too."

"Oh please, call me Leta. Or Mom. I'm fine with whatever makes you comfortable." His mom hesitated, and he could see her thinking. "Maybe you're most comfortable with Mrs. Scott. It's up to you, dear. Really."

She squeezed Cassie's arm and smiled nervously. Cassie—his beautiful, brave girl—didn't falter for a moment. She knew exactly what to do. She was getting so much better at realizing that she *was* Cassandra. The woman on YouTube was her, not a projection of what she wanted to be. She was shy Cassie sometimes, and bold Cassandra at others. And she was the one in charge of who she wanted to be at any given moment.

"Thank you, Leta. I think I'd like to call you that."

His mom's smile was genuine. "Yes, I'd love it."

One day, he wanted Cassie to be able to call her mom, but that would come later when they were married. Because they would get married, he had no doubt. He hadn't asked her yet, but he was going to. She was it for him. The only woman in the world he could imagine spending all his time with. Having kids with. Loving for the rest of his life.

He shuddered to think what would have happened if he'd refused Kari's request to help her friend.

The door opened again, and his dad came out on the porch. Tom Scott was a big man, like his son, and he wore a perpetually displeased expression on his face. Ty sucked in a breath and told himself he was doing this for his mom. At least he'd refused to stay here for the visit. He and Cassie had booked a bed and breakfast in the center of Bear Creek. His old English teacher, Mrs. Stone, had turned her home into an inn, and it was gorgeous.

His mom looped her arm in Cassie's and walked toward the house. Ty followed.

"Tom, this is Cassie," his mom said when they walked onto the porch. "Tyler's girlfriend."

Cassie smiled and held out her hand, looking so pretty and sweet that it made him ache. And then, as if his dad had been struck by lightning, he smiled and accepted her hand in his. "Hello, Cassie. You're Kari's friend, right?"

"Yes, sir," she said brightly.

"My goodness, you sure are a pretty thing." He tucked her arm into his. "Come on in. I hope you're ready for lunch. My wife made all of Tyler's favorite things."

Ty couldn't move. He stood on the porch and watched as Cassie disappeared inside with his dad, who was smiling and fawning over her like she was the

Queen of England. His mom put her arm in his and jiggled him.

"Your daddy's been looking forward to this," she said. "So much."

Ty blinked down at her. "Really?"

"Yes, honey, really." She sighed. "We do stupid things in life sometimes. And sometimes our pride gets in the way of acknowledging those things."

She didn't say anything else, and he didn't either. It wasn't simply a matter of saying his dad had done stupid things and then all was forgiven. There would be a long road to travel for that, but maybe this was a start. He didn't know. Truthfully, his dad could just be bowled over by Cassie. That was equally likely.

They spent the afternoon visiting, eating good food, and going for a walk on the property. When it was time to go, his dad put a quick arm around him and squeezed, then turned around and went back inside.

"Well, *that* was weird," Ty said when he and Cassie were in the truck and reversing out of the drive. His dad hadn't been critical at all. He hadn't been apologetic either. He'd just been kind of ordinary.

"You okay?" Cassie asked, running her hand over his arm.

Just that simple touch was enough to fill him with love and contentment. He took her hand and kissed it, keeping his eyes on the road. "Yeah, I'm fine. I guess I expected more tension. But Dad saw you, and that was that. It's like that story about pulling a thorn from a lion's paw. Him being the lion and you pulling the thorn, of course."

She shook her head. "He was nice, but I know that

doesn't mean he *is* nice. I'm on your side, Ty. No matter what."

He loved that she was fierce for him. "I know, Red." He shrugged. "You know what, I'm not going to think he's turned over a new leaf or anything, but maybe he's figuring out how not to be a bastard. So if he wants to be nice, I'll be nice. If he wants to be a bastard, I don't have to put up with it anymore. I'm a grown man, and he can't control me."

"People change. Except Lottie, of course," Cassie added.

"I'm sorry, honey."

She laughed. "It's okay. She's still partying and having fun. I heard she mooned the sheriff last week for the hell of it."

Ty snorted.

"I thought she would have asked me for money by now, but she hasn't," Cassie continued. "All I can figure is she has no idea how YouTube works."

"Probably not. At least Dylan hasn't asked again."

They'd found Dylan Webb crashing at a—quote, unquote—friend's house in Arlington while he tried to score off Cassie. He'd been promising the friend he had a windfall coming. Once the friend—a lonely woman he'd met online and conned into taking him in with promises of being her sugar daddy after he came into his money—learned the truth, she'd kicked him to the curb and he'd high-tailed it back to Bear Creek, licking his wounds. If he was in town now, they hadn't seen him yet. But he wasn't going to ask Cassie for money again. Ty had made sure of that.

"You kind of scared the shit out of him, Ty."

"Good."

They reached the bed and breakfast and went inside, visiting with Mrs. Stone and her husband for a while before going up to their room. They lay in bed, naked bodies twined together, and Ty grumbled, "The bed's too squeaky. If we do it, they're going to know."

Cassie laughed. "True. Also, this was your idea."

"It was. Crap."

Her laughter grew until she was laughing so hard the bed shook. And squeaked. "Sorry," she giggled. "I can't help it."

Ty tried not to laugh, but he couldn't help it. Soon, they were both laughing and the bed was squeaking like they were going at it. "This isn't working. Shit, we have to stop laughing."

"Yes," Cassie said solemnly. "We do."

And then she burst into giggles again. He did too.

Finally, he pulled her to him and buried his face in her hair. "If we're going to squeak anyway, I want to make it worth my while."

And then he rolled her under him and scandalized the whole inn by squeaking the bed harder than it had ever been squeaked before…

Bonus Epilogue

One year later...

CASSIE STARED at the test stick on the counter. *Pregnant.*

Oh my God, she was pregnant. She hadn't been trying to get pregnant, not at all, but they'd been a little lax lately with the condoms. She'd taken a break from the birth control because she'd been having some issues with side effects. Ty was like most men and didn't enjoy condoms—neither did she—but he would do whatever he had to do for her health.

It was just supposed to be a six month break, and then she'd try something else. Except, no.

Not now.

Part of her was terrified—and part was jumping for joy. Ty had asked her to marry him last summer, and they'd been planning the wedding since. They were planning it for June—just a couple of months away—in Bear Creek, with a big reception up here for their friends at BDI. Kari was looking forward to being the maid of honor and everything. Even Lottie was planning to attend, and she'd even promised to behave.

Cassie nibbled her lip as she stared at herself in the mirror. Would she be showing by then? Was she going to have to get a different dress? Or let hers out a little?

Ty was at BDI today, and she was home filming makeup and try-on hauls. She'd hired an assistant to help her with the filming and editing, which made things easier. Her assistant was waiting in the studio room that she and Ty had set up for her. She started walking that way so they could get started.

In the end, they'd bought a house near BDI, and Cassie'd had fun decorating and getting everything just right. It hit her that she was going to have to decorate a nursery now. They'd bought a four bedroom house, so they had the space, but—

Her breath caught.

OMG, she was having a baby!

"You okay, Cassie?"

Cassie looked at her assistant, a cute college girl named Erika, and nodded. "Yes, fine. Just pre-occupied."

"These swimsuits and cover-ups are so glam," Erika said, looking at the rack where they'd hung up her changes of clothes. "Your subscribers are going to love them."

"Yes, I think so too."

Somehow, she got through the clothing changes, filmed the video, and managed not to spill the news to Erika. Ty had to be first. Then Kari. Then his parents. Their friends at BDI. Lottie would probably have a shit fit when she found out she was going to be a grandmother.

By the time Erika was gone and Ty came home, Cassie had fixed one of his favorite dinners. Mashed potatoes and gravy, steak from the grill—medium rare—and buttered green beans. And, of course, banana pudding for dessert.

Ty backed her into the kitchen island and kissed her senseless, then lifted his head and said, "What's the occasion, Red?"

"Nothing special. Just wanted to show you how much I love you."

Her heart hammered with the news she wanted to share, but first she wanted him to eat. She knew what kind of work he did at BDI, and she was so proud of him. And more than a little in awe of everyone over there, truth be told. He'd had to go on a few missions since they'd been together, and she was always fearful, but he came back to her. She prayed he always would.

They ate dinner and he told her about things at work. Jared and Libby were expecting. Jared had just announced it, and they'd all been thrilled for him. He'd been a little shell-shocked, but he'd be fine.

It turned out that Ian had eaten all his words about how easy it would be to raise children, apparently, and had no advice to offer other than, "Sleep when you can. Seriously. If the kid's asleep, you sleep."

Cassie fiddled with her steak until Ty frowned. "What's up, Cass? You feeling okay?"

"I'm fine, Ty. Are you ready for banana pudding?"

He gave her a puzzled look. "When you're done."

"I'm done." She jumped up and went to get the pudding, then returned with two bowls. "Here you go."

He caught her to him before she could sink into her chair and pulled her down on his lap. Then he tucked her hair behind her ears and ran his fingers down her cleavage. "Something's up, beautiful. I know when you aren't telling me everything."

Cassie sighed and pressed a kiss to his cheek. "Come with me."

She took his hand and led him to the bathroom, then reached beneath the counter and took out the foil packet where she'd carefully replaced the test. She thought it would still show the result, but if it didn't he'd get the idea.

He was still as she pulled it from the package and placed it on the counter. Ty's eyes were big as he stood beside her. He turned to her, then back to the test.

"You're pregnant?"

She nodded. "Seems like I am."

He raked a hand through his hair. "Whoa." Then he sank onto the edge of the tub and stared at her. She clasped her hands together and waited. He just blinked at her.

"Are you mad?"

"Mad?" He seemed to shake himself, and then a big grin spread over his handsome face. He jumped up and grabbed her, spinning her in his arms. "Mad? Fuck no! Stunned, yes. Oh my God. I'm going to be a dad."

He held her tight and kissed her hard, and she sighed into his mouth. When he finally broke the kiss, she knew her happiness showed in her eyes as she gazed up at him. "You're going to be the best dad, Ty."

"I'm damned sure going to try," he said with conviction. "But I know you'll be an amazing mom. Wow, Cassie Mae. How in the hell did I get so lucky?"

She shrugged. "Same as I did, I guess. We listened to your cousin."

He snorted. "Yep, that's right. I let her badger me into showing up at your house. You shut the door on me, but she badgered you into letting me in. That was all it took."

"Well, not quite all. She had to tell me to get over myself and believe that you really wanted me, but once I did that—well, I'm not stupid. No way was I letting you and your big dick get away."

He sighed dramatically. "Always with the potty mouth. We're going to have to work on that, you know."

"What do you propose?"

He rubbed his nose against hers. "I've got something you can suck on while you consider your words carefully."

Cassie laughed. "You're on, big boy."

He stopped her before she could unzip his jeans though. "I love you so much, Cassie. I can't wait to be your husband and I can't wait to meet our kid."

"I can't wait either," she whispered.

He took her hand and led her to the bedroom. "I think I need to show my appreciation properly."

"What happened to giving me something to suck on?"

He waved a hand. "Later, honey. First I'm going to take care of you. Because that's what I'm always going to do. Take. Care. Of. You. Always."

And that's what he did.

Books by Lynn Raye Harris

HOT Heroes for Hire: Mercenaries
Black's Bandits

Book 1: BLACK LIST - Jace & Maddy

Book 2: BLACK TIE - Brett & Tallie

Book 3: BLACK OUT - Colt & Angie

Book 4: BLACK KNIGHT - Jared & Libby

Book 5: BLACK HEART - Ian Black

Book 6: BLACK MAIL - Tyler Scott

Book 7: BLACK VELVET - Dax Freed

———

The Hostile Operations Team ® Books
Strike Team 2

Book 1: HOT ANGEL - Cade & Brooke

Book 2: HOT SECRETS - Sky & Bliss

Book 3: HOT JUSTICE - Wolf & Haylee

Book 4: HOT STORM - Mal & Scarlett

Book 5: HOT COURAGE - Noah & Jenna

———

The Hostile Operations Team ® Books
Strike Team 1

Book 0: RECKLESS HEAT

Book 1: HOT PURSUIT - Matt & Evie

Book 2: HOT MESS - Sam & Georgie

Book 3: DANGEROUSLY HOT - Kev & Lucky

Book 4: HOT PACKAGE - Billy & Olivia

Book 5: HOT SHOT - Jack & Gina

Book 6: HOT REBEL - Nick & Victoria

Book 7: HOT ICE - Garrett & Grace

Book 8: HOT & BOTHERED - Ryan & Emily

Book 9: HOT PROTECTOR - Chase & Sophie

Book 10: HOT ADDICTION - Dex & Annabelle

Book 11: HOT VALOR - Mendez & Kat

Book 12: A HOT CHRISTMAS MIRACLE - Mendez &

Kat

———

The HOT SEAL Team Books

Book 1: HOT SEAL - Dane & Ivy

Book 2: HOT SEAL Lover - Remy & Christina

Book 3: HOT SEAL Rescue - Cody & Miranda

Book 4: HOT SEAL BRIDE - Cash & Ella

Book 5: HOT SEAL REDEMPTION - Alex & Bailey

Book 6: HOT SEAL TARGET - Blade & Quinn

Book 7: HOT SEAL HERO - Ryan & Chloe

Book 8: HOT SEAL DEVOTION - Zach & Kayla

———

The HOT Novella in Liliana Hart's MacKenzie Family Series

HOT WITNESS - Jake & Eva

———

7 Brides for 7 Brothers

MAX (Book 5) - Max & Ellie

7 Brides for 7 Soldiers

WYATT (Book 4) - Max & Ellie

7 Brides for 7 Blackthornes

ROSS (Book 3) - Ross & Holly

Filthy Rich Billionaires

Book 1: FILTHY RICH REVENGE

Book 2: FILTHY RICH PRINCE

———

Who's HOT?

Strike Team 1

Matt "Richie Rich" Girard (Book 0 & 1)
Sam "Knight Rider" McKnight (Book 2)
Kev "Big Mac" MacDonald (Book 3)
Billy "the Kid" Blake (Book 4)
Jack "Hawk" Hunter (Book 5)
Nick "Brandy" Brandon (Book 6)
Garrett "Iceman" Spencer (Book 7)
Ryan "Flash" Gordon (Book 8)
Chase "Fiddler" Daniels (Book 9)
Dex "Double Dee" Davidson (Book 10)

Commander
John "Viper" Mendez (Book 11 & 12)

Deputy Commander
Alex "Ghost" Bishop

Strike Team 2

Cade "Saint" Rodgers (Book 1)
Sky "Hacker" Kelley (Book 2)
Dean "Wolf" Garner (Book 3)
Malcom "Mal" McCoy (Book 4)
Noah "Easy" Cross (Book 5)
Ryder "Muffin" Hanson
Jax "Gem" Stone
Zane "Zany" Scott
Jake "Harley" Ryan (HOT WITNESS)

SEAL Team 1

Dane "Viking" Erikson (Book 1)
Remy "Cage" Marchand (Book 2)
Cody "Cowboy" McCormick (Book 3)
Cash "Money" McQuaid (Book 4)
Alexei "Camel" Kamarov (Book 5)
Adam "Blade" Garrison (Book 6)
Ryan "Dirty Harry" Callahan (Book 7)
Zach "Neo" Anderson (Book 8)
Corey "Shade" Vance

Black's Bandits

Jace Kaiser (Book 1)
Brett Wheeler (Book 2)
Colton Duchaine (Book 3)
Jared Fraser (Book 4)
Ian Black (Book 5)
Tyler Scott (Book 6)
Thomas "Rascal" Bradley
Dax Freed
Jamie Hayes

Finn McDermott
Mandy Parker (Airborne Ops)
Melanie (Reception)

Freelance Contractors

Lucinda "Lucky" San Ramos, now MacDonald (Book 3)
Victoria "Vee" Royal, now Brandon (Book 6)
Emily Royal, now Gordon (Book 8)
Miranda Lockwood, now McCormick (SEAL Team Book 3)
Bliss Bennett, (Strike Team 2, Book 2)
Angelica "Angie" Turner (Black's Bandits, Book 3)
Natasha "Calypso" "Athena" Oliver, aka Natasha Orlova, aka Natasha Black (Black's Bandits, Book 5)

About the Author

Lynn Raye Harris is a Southern girl, military wife, wannabe cat lady, and horse lover. She's also the New York Times and USA Today bestselling author of the **HOSTILE OPERATIONS TEAM ® SERIES** of military romances, and 20 books about sexy billionaires for Harlequin.

A former finalist for the Romance Writers of America's Golden Heart Award and the National Readers Choice Award, Lynn lives in Alabama with her handsome former-military husband, one fluffy princess of a cat, and a very spoiled American Saddlebred horse who enjoys bucking at random in order to keep Lynn on her toes.

Lynn's books have been called "exceptional and emotional," "intense," and "sizzling" -- and have sold in excess of 4.5 million copies worldwide.

To connect with Lynn online:
www.LynnRayeHarris.com
Lynn@LynnRayeHarris.com

Made in United States
Orlando, FL
25 March 2022

16159837R00207